"All of Ms. Baumbach's books are unique and this one is no exception. As this story unfolded, I was stunned and quickly drawn into the story. I couldn't stop reading … Maymon and Talos were from completely different times and worlds, but they struck a cord within each other which quickly built to a love that was consuming and captivating. … *Details of the Hunt* was one of the most delightful books I have ever read. This book rightfully deserves a recommended read."

Teresa, reviewer for Fallen Angels Reviews

shade of white as warm blood welled between the fingers of the hand he had pressed to his neck, but he refused to plead for his life or beg for mercy. Maymon admired that in a man. He clapped the captain on the shoulder and casually shoved him toward his own men, out of Perkins' reach.

"The Captain's been right generous in giving us all that he has. Only fair we leave him alive to tell others the benefits of doing the same." Maymon pointedly pushed Perkins' blade to one side and stared the pirate in the eye until the other man surrendered in the silent battle of wills.

Not bothering to hide his displeasure, Perkins backed down, a vicious scowl as large as the entrance to Port-Royale's bay on his florid, pitted face. Sheathing the deadly weapon, Perkins gave Maymon a murderous glare then spat on the deck, hitting the bleeding captain's boots with his spittle. With a final grunt, Perkins walked away and boarded the *Jamaican Maid*.

A rumbling of discord rippled through the pirate crew, some disturbed by Perkins' disrespectful behavior to their captain, but most irritated by Maymon's decision to allow the Spanish captain to live. Maymon hastened his men back on board his own schooner before it could grow into more.

Back on familiar ground again, Maymon called for the crew to break out a few barrels of rum and opened a bottle of fine brandy for himself, newly procured from the merchant's captain's quarters, and he loudly toasted his crew.

After chugging a full quarter of the sharp burning liquor, Maymon bellowed, "Set the sails, me stumble and pause in his task as the sea grew rougher with each passing white-crested wave.

In a hurry to set sail against the changing weather, Maymon jumped up onto the top of the railing, hand entwined in the rough rope of the ship's rigging. Cupping one hand at the corner of his mouth, he called out to the men below, "Look lively, you lazy dogs! The winds be aturning on us."

The men scrabbled to finish, shoving aside the less fortunate of the merchant vessel's officers, several of whom defiantly eyed the pirates, despite their disadvantage of being out numbered, injured and disarmed.

An older pirate, swarthy and scarred to ugliness, stood guard over the small group of bound men. Drawing a long, thin blade from his boot top, the pirate unexpectedly lashed out, grabbing the portly Spanish captain by the front of his ruffled shirt and finely-tailored, velvet waistcoat. The dagger had already drawn blood from the helpless captain by the time Maymon noticed the pirate's actions. The captain's crisp white collar was now smeared with a growing slash of bright crimson.

Jumping down from the railing onto the deck below, Maymon stayed the pirate's murderous hand with his own tar-stained fingers.

"Hold up there, Perkins! There'll be none of that." Maymon's voice was low and throaty, raw from years of salty sea breezes and too much cheap rum. He yanked Perkins' arm back, mindless of Perkins' snarling frown and muttered curses.

The injured captain wheezed, turning a paler

flag, Maymon's talents were many and varied, most of them larcenous, underhanded and self-benefiting. He possessed a keen mind with a flare for navigating and charting the remote and sometimes hidden islands and lagoons dotting the waters in this part of the seafaring world. Lithe and quick-witted, the young pirate ruled his small domain aboard the *Jamaican Maid* with a casual hand and a sharp tongue. He was quick with his sword if his word was challenged, but even quicker with a biting retort or an amusing anecdote to diffuse a situation and restore the balance among his crew. Even still, there were always those on board who chafed under the command of anyone, especially a charismatic, younger man.

The *Jamaican Maid* had just chased down and captured a fine Spanish merchant ship. Her entire swag-hungry crew and their scallywag of a captain were busy plundering the ship's packed hold, transferring their ill-gotten fortune aboard their own vessel.

Maymon stood on the captain's deck of the Spanish vessel, surveying the activity below him, waist-length black hair stirring in the breeze, as restless and wild as its owner. A scarf of deep burgundy fabric held the mass of hair out of his coal black eyes and kept the blazing sun from scalding the top of his head.

Leaning into the rising wind, Maymon cast a calculating glance at the darkening horizon, then turned to watch men scuttle across the thin boarding planks precariously positioned over the gap of open sea between the two ships. Their arms were laden with bolts of fine silks, sacks of sugar, barrels of rum and precious medical supplies. Occasionally a man would

Chapter One

Caribbean Ocean – 1769

The *Jamaican Maid* was one of the fastest schooners in the Caribbean. With her sleek lines, narrow hull and shallow draft, her captain and crew were an envied lot among their brethren. The ship's two tall masts and billowing, full sails cut an impressive silhouette on the blue, Caribbean horizon. She was a coveted prize among the unscrupulous lot of cutthroats sailing this part of the sea, a prize that presently belonged to a rather clever and devious soul by the name of Captain Aidan Maymon and his deadly, but jovial dancing winged-skeleton flag.

Maymon was something of an enigma among his fellow pirates. At twenty-four, he was younger than most men who held the position of elected captain, but he made up for his lack of grizzled age with experience and clever wiles that usually kept him one step ahead of his peers and enemies alike. These characteristics served him well over his seventeen adventurous years at sea. Having served on every type of ship that hoisted sails since he was seven years old, and with all kinds of shipmates and captains running under the Red Jack

Details of the Hunt

Copyright 2007 by Laura Baumbach
Published by MLR Press, LLC
3052 Gaines Waterport Rd.
Albion, NY 14411

Cover Art by Lorraine Brevig
Editing by Sue H.

Printed in the United States of America.

ISBN# 0-9793110-2-0
ISBN# 978-0-9793110-2-4

Second Edition
2007

Laura Baumbach

Details of the Hunt

hearties. A mother of a gale from the east appears to be brewing to cross our bow afore the sun sets. The *Maid*'ll need to be aport by then and our own fine selves have need of the pleasures of the *Charred Horse* and the charms of its lovely ladies. Step to it, mates!"

There were yells of agreement and crows of excited anticipation as the pirates hastened to release the Spanish vessel from the moorings that bound the two ships together.

As the crew made ready to set sail, Maymon rooted through a small pile of personal belongings taken from the Spanish ship's few passengers, tossing gold watches and strands of semi-precious jewels into a small heap at his side. Once he amassed a small fortune in glittering treasure, he carried the heaping handful of swag to the railing, all under the watchful, spite-filled eyes of Perkins and two of his more disreputable cohorts, Williams and Tate.

Maymon peered over the edge of the schooner's aft and studied the swirling waters twenty feet below. The rising wind tossed his long hair in the air until it danced around his head like a wreath of sea serpents hell-bent on taking flight. His body curved over the railing, the thin, worn fabric of his black breeches and stained white tunic clinging to the lean lines of his back and firmly muscled buttocks. The twisted length of burgundy and white-striped cloth he wore wrapped snugly around his waist defined the curve of his slim hips and the flatness of his abdomen. More than one man below turned to eye the inviting stretch of fabric over the rounded flesh of the young pirate's ass. Maymon knew it and ignored it, confident his position

5

as captain and the sharp edge of his blade would be enough to keep even the boldest of black-hearted jacks from making a move on him he didn't consent to first.

Straightening, Maymon wormed a small statue from within the maze of folds in his waist sash, and lovingly rubbed a tar-stained thumb over the face of the worn stone. The four-inch carving was a deep jade in color, the primitive markings and curves fashioning a brawny, human-like figure topped with the head of sea creature the likes of which no God-fearing, seafaring man would fancy running into. The head and bare chest of the statue sported rows of stubby horns similar to a turtle's bumpy shell with fin-like appendages on its thick arms and legs.

The carving symbolized the Cemi gods of the afterlife that his Arawak Indian mother had raised him to believe in. His absent, Spanish sailor of a father had only given Maymon his first name, his fine-boned good looks and his devil-may-care attitude toward life.

Idol clutched tightly in one hand, Maymon murmured a short prayer in a soft, wistful voice before reaching down and throwing his small horde of treasure and gold overboard into the swelling waves of the green ocean waters. Behind him, several crewmembers grumbled and cursed, outraged, the cutthroat Perkins among them.

"What goes on here? That be our swag, Captain!" Perkins' alcohol-roughened voice had a threatening edge to it this time. His bloodshot eyes were narrowed down to slits, making him look more snake-like and villainous than usual to Maymon.

"Offerings to the gods, man!" A rakish smile on

6

his lips and a dark gleam in his eye, Maymon showed his tobacco-stained, but even teeth. He defiantly tossed a small gold ring that had slipped from the pile over the side, then watched it swirl out of sight, swallowed by white foam and grasping black tendrils of floating seaweed. Once it was gone he turned back to face Perkins and his small band of disgruntled cronies. "Want them to be kind to you when your time to leave this world comes, don't you, man?"

"Sea Gods!" Perkins stepped forward and spit on the deck, gesturing at the Cemi statue still gripped in Maymon's slender, stained hand. "Heathen creatures only the likes of you believe in, whelp!"

Maymon moved up to meet Perkins' challenge, quickly drawing his long knife from its sheath at his side. He fingered its thin, sharp edge, letting the bright sunlight glitter menacingly off the fine Spanish steel as he talked.

"I can only hope you meet your maker first, Perkins." Smaller in build, but an equal to the other man in height, Maymon met his challenger eye-to-eye.

"Then your tortured," he lightly poked Perkins in the chest with the tip of his blade, letting the sharp steel slice through the first layer of the man's ragged clothing, "homeless, cursed, malingering spirit can come back from its watery grave and tell me which one of us was right." Dropping his voice to a less forgiving tone, Maymon shoved a little harder, forcing the blade to touch skin. "Until then, this is still my ship." One more push and the blade pierced skin. "Savvy?"

Flinching slightly, Perkins managed a small sneer, but relented. "Aye, *Captain*." He jerked his head in a parody of a nod, his lips twisting to reveal numerous gaps where his teeth used to be. With a backward glance at Maymon, the gnarled cutthroat rubbed at the small stain of fresh blood on his chest and muttered ominously, "For now."

Wiping the droplet of red marring the gleaming knife's tip, Maymon's grin widened. Perkins' dissatisfaction with Maymon's style wasn't a new element in their relationship and Maymon had learned long ago not to turn his back on the man. It was the way of a pirate's life and he had come to accept it. It was part of the challenge of living free.

An older man moved past Perkins and stood close to Maymon's side in a silent show of support and protection. First mate Nathan Sterns had been on board the *Jamaican Maid* for the last eight years, two years under Maymon's dancing winged skeleton flag and six under the rule of its previous captain, Jonathan Street. An older, tired version of Street, Sterns was a loyal and fiercely protective friend. The tide was threatening to turn against him soon, but Maymon knew Sterns would stand by him at least until it did turn. Self-preservation was the only way to insure revenge on another day.

Bearded, dirty, but with a kindly, grizzled face twisted into a frown of fear and disgust, Sterns shoved his young captain back to the railing. "Put that heathen statue away, boy! Didn't Street learn you nothing in all the years he trained your sorry, lash-scarred hide!" He grabbed the statue and tucked it forcibly into Maymon's tight waist sash, blocking his actions from the rest of the gawking crewman with his own stocky frame. Slipping his hand out of the sash, he wadded the worn silk into

8

his fist and gave Maymon a harsh shake, hissing, "And you gotta stop throwing away the men's hard-earned swag! It ain't right, boy!"

"Have to pay a proper tribute to the gods, Nate." Maymon deftly plucked his statue back out of the sash and waved the carved creature in Sterns' wrinkled, grimacing face. Sterns grappled with Maymon a moment before tearing the figure away and stuffing it deep into Maymon's pants pocket.

Playfully slapping the man's heavy hand away from his thigh, Maymon patted his pocket. "The Cemi spirits guide me way, man. Watch over me. A man can't forget who it is he needs to pay tribute to." Maymon tapped his lips with a dirt-creased finger and whispered, "Mark my words, Nate, it's the proper thing to do."

Sterns glanced back over his shoulder at the pirates milling around close by, trying to eavesdrop. "Those heathen gods aren't going to help you none if the men take a mind to toss you overboard in place of their swag." His voice was rough with concern, made harsh with a genuine fear.

"That's where you're wrong, mate. The gods'll be waiting when it's me time to join them down under the ocean's swell." Maymon winked at Sterns and clapped him on the shoulder, making the man sway on his feet. "I always say a prayer for you as well, mate. You'll see." Maymon smiled and shrugged, turning away to sort through the remaining treasure, seemingly oblivious to the pack of disgruntled men led by Perkins, who gathered to whisper behind his back.

***

The *Jamaican Maid* sailed into Tortuga just as nightfall settled its inky veil around the stench-filled town, softening the edges of the garbage-strewn streets and mold-stained, crumbling buildings. Comfortably ensconced in the bawdy, noise-filled Charred Horse, the Captain and crew were deep into their cups in no time at all. The smell of rotting fish and sea brine that usually permeated the air around them was replaced by the odor of alcohol, sweat and human waste.

The rum at the *Charred Horse* was only moderately watered-down and the rough-hewn, stout tables and chairs weren't prone to break easily, making it a favorite of many a ship's crew.

Seated at a table with his lean back to a wall, a disheveled, drunken serving wench on each side and third snuggled on his appreciative lap, Maymon gulped down the remains of his current tankard.

Bestowing a quick kiss on her lips and a sharp pinch to her backside, he pushed the giggling young lass off his lap, and tucked a gold coin between her partially exposed, tiny breasts. "Sally, my sweet, be a luv and fetch us another round of the innkeeper's best. Enough for all." He swung his arm in a wide circle, taking in the women at his side and the unconscious Sterns. "Everyone looks like they could use a few sips more, darlin'."

Sally blushed and giggled then hurried off to do his bidding, doing her best to avoid grasping hands and catcalls as she made her way toward the bar.

Sterns was sprawled on the table beside Maymon and his flock of whores. His fitful snores and swine-inspired grunts lent a certain rhythm to the jeers and catcalls punctuating the rowdy conversations and frequent outbursts of fighting going on in every corner of the dingy, lively room. Maymon playfully let the last few drops of drink trickle out of his tankard and onto Sterns' face, smiling affectionately when the older man turned in his sleep to capture the small rivulet of beer with an open mouth before it could disappear from his lips.

Maymon's attention was caught by three men standing apart from the more active carousing by one end of the bar, an unwashed trio of stubble-covered, pox-marked faces, all twisted in various dark and foreboding sneers, kept a watchful eye on Maymon and Sterns. In the center stood Perkins, blatantly staring at Maymon, his half-hooded eyes doing nothing to hide the hatred in them.

It was no secret among the crew that a few of the newer men felt the Spanish/Indian half-breed was too young and too undeserving of the command. But none could dispute that Maymon had earned the title of Captain fair and square through a majority vote after their prior leader, Captain Jonathan Street, had met his fate at the end of the hangman's noose two years gone.

Perkins had signed on six months ago, accepting Maymon's station and the plundering and swag under his carefree and clever command. Maymon was calculating, inventive and tricky. He outmaneuvered and outwitted many a seasoned sea captain, robbing them of their luscious cargoes with few major human losses on either side of the battle. Until such time as death or the majority rule changed things, Aidan Maymon would remain captain of the *Jamaican Maid*, no matter how much Perkins envied and despised him for it.

Leaning against the bar, Perkins hunched over the counter, one hand down the barmaid's blouse. When she grinned and saucily slapped his hand away, he frowned, but pulled a red leather purse from his shirt and threw a coin down in front of her.

The barmaid quickly grabbed up the silver piece, tested its authenticity with her few remaining teeth and moved around from behind the bar. Joining Perkins, one hand grabbing at his groin as she plastered her elf to his side, she pushed a fresh tankard into his hand and murmured something in his ear.

Thrusting his crotch into her grip, Perkins' grabbed the tankard with one hand, and her chest with the other, dragging a sagging breast out of the top of her soiled and ragged-edged blouse.

Sally finally arrived at the bar and tried to worm her way past the groping couple. In her haste, she accidentally bumped Perkins' drinking arm as she wiggled past. Sally smiled at the ugly lout she had jostled and murmured, "Sorry, sir, bit crowded, what?" She managed to get one step away before Perkins reacted.

Shoving the scowling barmaid to one side, Perkins jumped back with an indignant roar. His complexion turned a deeper shade of crimson and one corner of his mouth curled up, revealing an ugly gap of broken teeth. Snarling, he bellowed in the young girl's face, "Stupid, gutter-sniping whore!"

Not a single drop of Perkins' drink had spilt, but he instantly swung at the startled Sally, slapping her viciously across the side of her face, his rough knuckles abrading the skin off her cheek with the force of the blow.

Caught off guard, Sally shrieked and crumpled to the floor. Perkins raised a slop-covered boot in the air. Sally scrabbled backwards across the filthy flooring, navigating an erratic, panicked path through a sea of boots and heedless legs to put herself as far away from Perkins as possible. Once she reached the relative safety at the other end of the bar, she pulled herself up off the floor. Dabbing at the blood gathering in the corner of her mouth with the hem of her skirt, her lips quivered as she appeared to try to stop the flow of tears.

Maymon watched the exchange from his seat across the room, dark eyes narrowed and lips pinched tight at the sight of blood on the young girl's sallow, pale face. Perkins' harsh manner and blatant bullying of anyone smaller than he was had been a sore point for Maymon since the man had signed on to the crew. It was bad enough when the sod turned his abusive and sadistic attention on another able-bodied man, but to bully and abuse a small slip of a girl didn't set right with him.

Rising from his chair, Maymon grabbed each of his trollops and pulled them close. He wove an unsteady path through the crowd of drunken pirates, buccaneers and sailors, his own weight supported largely by the women.

Heading toward the stairs that led to the tiny barren bedroom on the second floor the ladies used to pleasure whatever customer could afford them for the night, Maymon swayed his way to the bar and passed

Perkins and his men.

Tripping over his own feet, Maymon lurched drunkenly into Perkins. Hands fumbling over Perkins' body, Maymon finally latched onto the man's shirt and worn vest to right himself, then smiled a cheeky grin and mumbled a slurred, "Sorry, mate. The floor keeps moving out from under me boots."

Jerking out of Maymon's grip, Perkins gave him a small shove backward into the waiting arms of his two whores. "Useless whelp. Can't even hold your liquor like a man."

Smiling, Maymon pursed his lips and tilted his head in an agreeable shrug, before moving off, pulled along by his eager entertainment for the night. As he moved past Sally huddled by the bottom of the staircase, Maymon surprised her with a quick kiss and leering grope. He used the lecherous advance to covertly empty the coin from Perkins' red leather purse down the front of her dress, unseen save by the two of them. He leaned in close and murmured a soft, low whisper of slim comfort to the girl, knowing Sally couldn't be more than fourteen. "Makes up for the damages, Sally, me dear. A man should pay when he blemishes the face of a pretty young woman."

Tears welled again in Sally's eyes and Maymon chased them away with a playful pinch to her bottom that made her jump and yelp, her feathery, young laughter still light and high-pitched like the child she was beneath the harsh make-up and grown-up petticoats. The sound made Maymon sad for a moment. He touched her cheek and whispered, "Go home for the night, missy, there be enough coin in there to make up for a quiet night or two."

She gave him a hesitant smile, but shook her head no and slipped out into the crowd of men, eyes nervously glancing at the watchful innkeeper. Maymon sighed and refocused his attention on his companions as they began to drag him up the stairs, undressing him along the way.

The whole time he moved Maymon was aware of Perkins' unrelenting gaze boring into his back, following him up the creaking, rickety staircase. With a last glance over his shoulder as he turned to enter a shabby little closet of a room, Maymon caught a glimpse of Perkins as the man nudged Tate and pulled Williams closer. The three of them hunched together in conversation, like squalling rats locked in a ship's empty hold.

***

Three days later, ship's stores replenished and a few minor repairs accomplished, the *Jamaican Maid* set sail for open water. On the fourth morning, Maymon woke to the sound of fighting and a knife tightly held to his throat. Tate, the bigger of Perkins' lackeys, overpowered him by the grace of his sheer size and physical strength. The scoundrel pulled him from his berth, already manacled and still half-drunk, the unusually heavy after effects from several fine bottles of stolen brandy he had consumed the night before. By the time Tate dragged him out of his cabin and onto the main deck, the fighting was all but over. Only the most loyal or the most rebellious pirate resisted during a mutinous overthrow of a sea captain.

The first body Maymon stumbled across,

literally, was Sterns, face down on the deck outside his cabin door, his sword at his side where it had fallen in an obvious attempt to defend the cabin. Sterns had been a good, loyal friend to the end.

Shackled in irons, Maymon was pushed through the crowd of mutinous sailors, but he held his head up high. Until the moment he died today, he was still Captain. Yells and curses filled the air and more than a few threats and jeers were spit in his face. Dead crewmen lay scattered around the deck, a full dozen by his count, his only true mates gone.

"The best of the morning is yet to come, lads!" Perkins stepped forward and grabbed Maymon's arm, wrenching him over to the side of the ship's railings. He leaned in close to Maymon and whispered, "Sleep well, Captain? Amazing what a little laudanum in a bottle of brandy will do to a man, ain't it, boy?" With a harsh, biting laugh of triumph, Perkins addressed the crew again. "We'll be free of this heathen whelp and all his 'offerings' of our hard earned swag to the cold bowels of the ocean."

A cheer went up from the men, knives and swords brandished in the air like triumphant flags of glory.

Maymon stared at his attackers, a sudden, surreal feeling invading his mind and body. Sterns had been like a second father to him. Losing the older man was a blow to his heart, but he was glad Sterns had died like a true pirate, at sea, a sword in his hand, and probably a curse on his weather-chapped lips, fighting for something he believed in and cared for. Leaving this world for the next wouldn't be so bad, knowing that his friend would be there, too.

Maymon tilted his chin in the air, defying Perkins, refusing to cower or beg. "The deepest, darkest bowels of the ocean have a place for a murderous bastard like you, Perkins. Mark my words, you'll be seeing it for yourself soon enough. The gods'll see to it."

Perkins grabbed the hairless, jutting chin and clamped his hand hard enough to leave marks on Maymon's smooth skin. "Maybe, but you'll be there first to greet me, boy!"

Releasing his hold, Perkins shoved Maymon closer to the edge, face turned to the dark water below. Caught up in the bloodthirsty wave of excitement the mutiny had inspired, the crew began to slice open the dead and throw the bodies overboard to attract the few hungry sharks always trailing the schooner.

Sharp, rancorous laughter carried on the rising wind and several pirates began to shout and point as more and more sharks circled the ship, feasting on the mutilated bodies, drawn by the scent of fresh blood. The ocean churned and rippled with swirls of dark crimson that grew and ebbed, marring its jade-colored waves, as the sharks grew increasingly frenzied with each new offering.

Perkins transferred his brutal grip to Maymon's thick hair and forced him to watch, calling out to the feasting sharks. "I'm saving the sweetest meat for dessert, you bloodthirsty bastards." Laughing, Perkins pulled Maymon back from the railings and gave him a hard shake with the hand fisted in his hair.

"You'll make a lean meal, to be sure, but I know you'll be right pleasing to them, lad." Perkins sneered in

Laura Baumbach

Maymon's face, a menacing, lustful gleam in his eyes. "Unless you'd like to live a few hours more and be pleasing to me and the boys. Might even decide to let you live, if the pleasing is good enough."

Maymon smiled, then spit in Perkins' face. Perkins backhanded him, but he couldn't stop the feisty young captain from proclaiming, "Rather take my chances with the sharks than play with barracudas like you, Perkins." Casting an accusing glare at the men surrounding him, Maymon added, "You lot make the cold-blooded creatures down under look infinitely more inviting."

Snarling, Perkins shoved his face to within an inch of Maymon's, his fetid breath releasing the stench of tobacco and beer-laced fumes into the young man's face. "Let's see how you feel when their teeth start tearing out your innards, boy."

Maymon wrinkled his nose, lips twisting in disgust. "That'll still be better than the thoughts of your reeking mouth anywhere near me, you triple damned, scurvy swine."

Outraged, Perkins fisted Maymon's shirt then ripped it open down the front. "Arawak bastard whelp. Think you're better than most." He pulled Maymon away from the railing, wrapping a stout arm around Maymon's waist, pinning the young man's back to his own chest, groping at Maymon's ass with his free hand.

At the sudden, intimate contact, Maymon began to struggle, twisting and trying to butt his head, but Perkins' greater height and strength gave the older man the advantage. "Get the wine barrel and some rope, boys. We got us some entertainment."

18

Details of the Hunt

The remaining crew scrambled to comply. Maymon tensed, prepared for a fight to the death, refusing to surrender to gang rape.

He was surprised when Perkins threw him into the men's arms and commanded, "It'll be more satisfying to watch him eaten alive. I've waited a long time for this and I'm not going to wait any longer. Tie him down good boys. I want to see him struggle long and hard."

After tying Maymon, hands still shackled, face-up around an empty wine barrel, several men heaved the barrel up onto the railing. Perkins grinned and leered once more, grabbing the ties to Maymon's breeches with one hand. "Last chance, lad, me or the fishes."

Maymon spit his answer, hitting Perkins directly in the eye. "A curse on you and your bitch mother's black heart for ever giving birth to the likes of you, you son of a cunt-slurping whore."

Perkins slowly withdrew his hand to wipe the spittle from his face, his glare hard and eyes narrowed.

"Drop him. Leave him to Davy and the sharks."

The men obeyed, shoving the barrel off the railing and into the water.

Helpless, Maymon tumbled down into a circle of fins. He lay bent and spread across the wooden surface, torso bound tightly to the curved barrel. Suspended in time for a brief moment, Maymon looked up into the clear Jamaican sky, getting what he knew would be his last glimpse of sunshine in his life before his weight offset the balance and the barrel rotated, plunging him under the foam-capped waves.

Underwater, air slowly escaping from his nose in a thin stream of bubbles, Maymon struggled against the ropes binding his torso to the barrel. Eyes wide open, he kicked out, legs heavy against the force of the churning water, and the wake of the swimming predators. He kicked one particularly aggressive shark that came too near, raking his boot against razor sharp teeth and solid muscle.

Just as the last of his breath leaked from his lungs, a huge shape rose up out of the depths directly beneath him. It was unlike any sea creature he had ever laid eyes on. Twice his physical size, with rough nubs of bone on its head and chest, it had scores of fin-like growths protruding out of its massive arms and broad back. Even as it cut the ropes that bound him to his fate, Maymon realized this was the Cemi god come to save his miserable soul and take him to the afterlife, just as his mother had said it would. The tribute paid over the years had been worth the sacrifice after all.

Letting the hazy cloud of darkness that pushed insistently at his mind have its way with him, Maymon smiled a greeting and passed out just as he felt his limp body enfolded in a pair of strong, cold arms.

Chapter Two

2587 Planet Oracan

Inside the two foot by three foot, transparent box the small, fragile Ahlee lay suspended in midair, eyes closed and motionless, frozen in stasis. She was beautiful, with vibrant, jewel-colored body segments and gossamer wings that, even now, shimmered with an inner light all their own.

On either side of the floating box, an Oracan warrior towered over the tiny receptacle as they escorted the creature to its new home deep beneath the High Council Chambers. Miles of impenetrable rock surrounded them, the substance's natural luminous properties lending a ghostly glow to the hidden underground keep.

Each warrior focused on the task at hand, scanning the bare surroundings for unusual signs of discord, their sensitive nostrils flaring as they scented the air, checking for changes from what they knew to be acceptable within the familiar chamber.

Unlike the Ahlee they accompanied, the Oracans were a humanoid race. Over six and a half feet tall on average, broad shouldered and heavily muscled, they resembled a cross between a man and a reptile. They were hairless, with bone and cartilage ridges and nubs along their scalps and chests. A thick, gray hide covered their massive bodies and 4-inch long bone spikes protruded from their forearms and shoulders at will. Violet eyes sported two sets of eyelids, the transparent, inner skin fold used for seeing underwater at great depths and for long time periods. The warriors were an impressive-looking race.

Coupled with their tendency to shun most forms of conventional clothing and a fondness for wearing numerous weapons, the intimidation factor was very high for most other species that interacted with them, a fact the Oracans had used to their advantage over the centuries. With a finely developed system of order and a high sense of personal and racial honor, the Oracans had firmly establishing themselves as peacekeepers in their segment of the galaxy for the last several centuries. Their society was deeply entrenched in ritual and ceremony, some of it brutal and deadly, and few outsiders visited the Oracan home planet for anything less than necessary business.

Arriving at the center of the hidden chamber, the threesome were scanned and their identities verified by an unseen source. A twelve-inch thick section of the rock wall blocking their path silently slid aside and the three were admitted into a large, bright room filled with cylindrical holding bays. A variety of alien species were held locked in stasis within six of the transparent bays, none of them human.

In front of a flat, broad monitor panel stood the chamber technician, Reblan. Physically, he was a near duplicate of the warriors who entered the chamber, but his brawny form was draped in a thin, green robe signifying his rank and position as a lower Council member and no weapons adorned his body. Reblan strode forward to intercept the new arrival, his footsteps lost in the low hum of the energy used to maintain the stasis fields.

Stopping, both warriors bowed slightly, each pressing a fisted hand over his left abdomen then moving it up and over his heart in the traditional greeting of their people.

Reblan mirrored the gesture as the taller of the two warriors, Nican, spoke. "You have a new dweller, Reblan. An Ahlee. Her buyer died before she could be turned over during the finalization of their Details. Council has terminated his contract and marked the bounty for relocation." He handed Reblan a small information chip.

Glancing into the hovering box, Reblan slipped the chip into his panel and verified the transport and identified the being. "Pity. She's quite beautiful." He walked to an empty bay and opened the tube with a press of his hand on a clear screen on the side of the bay. "Her kind are too valuable to waste."

The warriors followed him, carefully guiding the small creature's transport. The second warrior, Malic, opened the box and gently lifted the delicate creature out.

Malic handled the creature with a gentleness and appreciation that befitted her sensitive race. "She doesn't match the DNA structure of anyone else on the medical needs list. The buyer should have come to us earlier, before his illness had progressed so far. She

23

could have cured him."

Inserting her into the tube, Reblan activate the controls on the chamber and the small creature was once again suspended in midair, this time in the center of the much roomier chamber. The more powerful energy within the bay aligned itself with her body chemistry. Her eyelids flickered and her wings shimmered brightly as permanent stasis was achieved.

"Waste of a good healer. She won't last long in stasis. Her race is too fragile. Almost as bad as humans." Reblan gently sealed the chamber. A flicker of what could have been regret crossed his face, and then quickly disappeared, replaced by his usual stoic expression.

A flashing light accompanied by a quiet beeping interrupted them. Although subdued, the alarm had a note of urgency to it. Reblan responded immediately, moving to the control panel in front of one of the other stasis tubes.

"A problem?" Nican asked.

Reblan shook his head and altered a few of the settings on the panel. "Not really. This one has been here for a very long time." He stared at the four foot round, spider-like being inside of the chamber. "The stasis field just eroded. The creature's neural pathways have disintegrated."

Both warriors came to stand beside Reblan. Malic pointed his sharp chin at the creature and asked, "Dead?"

Reblan slowly nodded and shut down the chamber's energy field. The bay changed from transparent to darkly opaque, hiding the deceased creature from prying eyes. "It took him three hundred and sixty-seven of his time periods to do it in, too. That's nearly a record. Most of his species don't last nearly that long."

The two warriors gave a small, respectful bow in the direction of the dark chamber then gathered up the now empty transport receptacle. Wordlessly, they strode from the main chamber, leaving Reblan to do his job.

Once the thick slab of entry wall was back in place, Reblan returned to the main console and began keying in data. After several moments, he stepped back to the dark chamber and rested a hand on the glass. Closing his eyes, his deep guttural voice filled the cavernous chamber, a tuneless Oracan ritual chant for the dead echoing off the high stone walls and ceiling. Once the small ritual was over he stepped back from the stasis tube. He activated a handheld remote and two bright searing bolts of energy illuminated the creature's chamber. The first flash clearly showed the being's round, eight-legged form suspended in stasis. The second flash divulged an empty space, the creature's lifeless body disintegrated in a single moment of time.

Looking into the now empty bay, Reblan sighed, snapped on a recorder in the control panel on the tube and announced, "Dogles Key from the planet Povos. Relocation complete."

***

The Main Council Chamber was huge and dimly lit, but the rough-carved great room walls shone with the same hazy glow as the stasis chamber hidden deep below it. Dim spotlights highlighted several wide, deep

---

alcoves that had been carved at regular intervals down one stretch of the great hall. The low droning hum of deep-throated chanting filled the air and blazing torches flickered in their holders ten feet above the polished rock floor.

The eerie atmosphere in the official meeting place was dark and heavy with unease, making the first time, non-Oracan attendees squirm restlessly in their seats. Spectators and official visitors waited on cold rock benches placed at irregular intervals to one side of the chamber, facing the Council table.

In the center of the room, the twelve Oracan Council members formed a semi-circle around a polished stone table. Their reptilian bodies were loosely draped with a thin layer of dark fabric that cloaked their large bodies in floor length robes. The light ceremonial fabric was held in place by a single clip center-chest that could be instantly removed if the wearer needed to be free to move for battle.

All of the Council members wore a weapon of some type, but they were concealed on their bodies during the meetings. To an Oracan, getting dressed without putting on a weapon was an unnatural act. Each one at the table had answered a calling to give service to their people as a Council member, but they were all still warriors by birth.

In front of the Council table stood a human male named Agustus Barlow. Swarthy, and sharp-featured, Barlow was an antiquities dealer who specialized in rare and one-of-a-kind treasures from all over the known galaxies. He had a reputation for harsh business methods that produced results.

Details of the Hunt

Hawkish in appearance, Barlow's choice of dress was flamboyant, giving him an old-time earth look to his obviously expensive clothing. Dark pants, a white shirt and a black velvet cloak cut a lean silhouette on his tall frame. A brightly patterned red and yellow sash adorned his waist, and an antique swashbuckling sword hung from a wide, leather belt. Cuffed, knee-high, black leather boots added another inch to his height.

Stepping forward into a beam of light that spotlighted the area directly in from of the Council table, Barlow respectfully addressed the twelve Oracans. As he talked, one jeweled hand constantly caressed the curved handle of the ancient sword at his side.

"Honorable and revered Council members of Oracan, I have come to you today on behalf of the people of my planet Earth, seeking help only you are capable of giving." Gracious and solicitous, Barlow bowed slightly to the Council.

The Oracans silently appraised Barlow, their sensitive nostrils flared, many wrinkling in distaste as they gathered his distinctive scent.

An imposing Oracan, with numerous, old battle scars on his arms and face, was seated in the middle of the Council members. High Principal Belith had been on the Council longer than any other and he had done battle on more planets than he could remember during his youth. Now he was committed to spending the last hundred years of his life helping to maintain order in the world he and his family inhabited.

Belith stared at the smiling human and slowly

rumbled, "The Council will hear your request, Mr. Barlow. But keep in mind, no Hunt will be authorized and undertaken for mere personal gain."

"Of course, High Principal, but of course." Barlow presented both of his hands, open and palm up. He extended an arm and gestured to the attendees behind him, several of who were humans, all members of his own entourage. "This request benefits all of my fellow earthlings, not only by the return of priceless artifacts, but by enriching our knowledge of our ancient, poorly explored past. An archaeological find of unimaginable, *scientific* significance."

A thin, bookish-looking man rushed forward and shoved a document into Barlow's outstretched hand. Barlow barely glanced at his aide, Sherman, before addressing the Council again.

"Distinguished Councilors, you see before you an official affidavit declaring an eighteenth century Earth map that has come into my possession recently as authentic and legally mine." He extended the document back to Sherman, who delivered it to the table for examination. "The map shows the location of the last undiscovered pirate treasure known to exist on my planet." With a dramatic sweep of his arm, Barlow brought his hands down in a gesture of worship, pressing his palms together. "The very last."

Belith accepted the document and Sherman hurried back to Barlow's side, one step behind him. "How does finding this *pirate treasure* benefit the knowledge of your planet's history?"

"The treasure was the cargo of a Spanish merchant vessel that was carrying Aztec and Mayan relics from their Central American colonies." Barlow took several small steps closer to the table, an imploring, sincere expression on his face. "Reclaiming these treasures would be of priceless archaeological value, as well as tremendous historical significance to us, High Principal. Imagine the secrets these items could reveal about those long lost cultures."

Belith looked thoughtful for a moment as he eyed Barlow. "Why has this not been done before?"

"It can't be found." Barlow took a pace back and grimaced as if he had just eaten something unpleasant. "The map, although authentic, has proven to be… indecipherable."

Several of the Council members snorted and Belith held out the document Sherman had given him and slowly stated, "Oracans are not archaeologists, Mr. Barlow. They are bounty Hunters."

Brightening, Barlow gave a small grin of triumph and took the offered paper. "Oh, I don't want you to find the pirate treasure, Principal Belith." He absently handed off the second document as Sherman automatically scurried forward to retrieve it. Barlow paused to let his gaze wander over each of the twelve Council members in turn to be certain he had their undivided attention. "I want you to find the pirate that made the map."

A wave of interest rippled through the Council.

"The pirate?" Belith arched the rigid of cartilage that defined the thick ridge of bone over his left eye.

The corners of Barlow's mouth twitched and he appeared to relax marginally. "The pirate, one Aidan Maymon, was an underhanded criminal and a vicious raider, as well as quite clever. I regret to say that the best and brightest our cultures have to offer have been unable to find anything at the location pinpointed on his map. I need this pirate, *in person*, to solve the mystery and return the artifacts to the cultural communities where they rightfully belong."

Belith exchanged a skeptical glance with the Council member sitting on his right. "And the responsibility of bringing a vicious criminal back into your culture? Once this pirate has been claimed, he can not be returned to his own time."

Taking another hastily produced document from his aide, Barlow allowed a sly smile to grace his thin lips as he held it up to show the Council the large, easily recognized, green seal from an Earth court. "The pirate has already been legally declared a criminal, forfeiting all of his rights and freedoms. He will be incarcerated at the end of his, ah, usefulness. He will not be a threat."

The Councilor to Belith's right, Zeban, leaned forward and examined the seal. "A living bounty is well protected under Oracan law, Mr. Barlow."

Zeban's deeper, more penetrating voice made Barlow flinch and narrow his eyes as the Oracan's words resounded off the high walls and ceiling. "Yes, yes," Barlow placated, "But he is a pirate, Principal Zeban. A criminal of the most disreputable type, a *murderer*."

Barlow put an emphasis of heavy disdain on the final word, but his eyes sparkled with anticipation and his scent carried the smell of lust. Belith leaned in close to Zeban as quiet conversations erupted around the table and among the audience.

Tilting his head closer, Zeban murmured to his old friend and confidant. "Can he be trusted?"

Belith extended the talons on the backs of his arms just a tiny fraction of the way in a reflexive, aggressive response to Barlow's scent change, then retracted them.

"With his reputation it would be unwise." Both Oracans subtly scented the air again, keeping their disgust hidden. "His normal scent is putrid. It doesn't change enough to read his intent beyond his sexual interest in the pirate. I suspect he has other motives, but..." He shrugged, unwilling to speculate.

"Even his body chemistry deceives." Zeban's nostrils flared and clamped shut, blocking out the majority of the smells in the chamber. "Antiquities dealer or not, this man is no better than this pirate he is seeking."

Nodding vaguely, Belith eyed Barlow, taking in the human's restrained swagger and the offensively harsh color of the brightly patterned sash around his waist. "Agreed, but the map is real, and the artifacts have significant value to Earth's history." He took a deep breath and proclaimed, "The Hunt itself has merit."

"Agreed." Zeban flashed a glance at one of the dimly lit alcoves across the great hall. A small, sly smile tugged at the corner of his mouth. "Offer this Hunt to Talos. My brother is making himself too much of a loner of late. Our little brother's death has affected him deeply. Too deeply. Guilt is a powerful emotion a Hunter can not afford to wallow in for long. He is becoming distant from his family, exiling himself on that human-filled space station, refusing to live among his own." He glanced at the alcove again. "He needs something to occupy his mind. He has a fondness for Earthlings. He won't be able to resist the idea of obtaining one, even as a bounty."

A self-satisfied light sparkled in the elder Oracan's eyes. "*Barlow* is human."

Zeban nodded and glanced at the man in question. He felt his hands twitch and he stilled them by spreading their palms flat on the smooth, cool surface of the table. "He is. Talos will enjoy the Hunt all the more because of it. Buyer and bounty, both his favorite species to study."

Belith made a soft hissing sound in the back of his throat. He and Zeban shared a look of agreement between them then glanced at each Council member in turn. All the Council members faced the waiting human, turning twelve sets of luminous, violet eyes on Barlow.

The soft, guttural chanting grew louder and the air in the room seemed to change, growing warmer and heavy. The audience behind Barlow squirmed and shifted, while Barlow himself stood silent and tall, a half smile plastered on his sweat-beaded face.

In front of each Council member lay a trio of deep jewel-colored stones, one blue, one yellow and one red, all positioned around a small stone pedestal. Each Oracan deliberated a moment, and then picked one stone and placed it on top of the pedestal in front of them. Several lingered over the choice, but all eventually picked red. When the final stone was in place, Belith stood and addressed the entire room.

Details of the Hunt

"The Council of Oracan is united. The request for a Bounty Hunt has been granted. Details of the Hunt proclaim bounty on one Aidan Maymon, pirate and legally declared criminal of the planet Earth, to be brought back to this place and time for the sole purpose of rendering aid in retrieving stolen artifacts significant to Earth's history and peoples." He gestured with one arm toward the shadowed alcoves. "The Hunters shall step forth."

The alcove spotlights instantly blazed brighter, revealing six Oracan Hunters standing in wait. Moving as if they were one entity, the Hunters strode forward into the circle of light outside each of their niches. They were all massive, brawny warriors, covered with a startling array of deadly weapons and little else, all oiled, gray skin and gleaming metal, glistening in the flickering firelight.

Looking down the row of candidates, Belith's gaze stopped on the third warrior in line. "Because of his unique understanding of human ways, Council asks Talos, Son of Menalon, to accept this Hunt."

Staring straight ahead, emotionless and cold, the third warrior stepped forward one pace. Talos of Menalon was an especially fierce-looking warrior with a chiseled, attractive face. He was the largest of the Hunters in line. His huge, heavy body was a mass of curves and lean dips with every muscle defined and highlighted by the oil and the dancing light from the primitive torches. Each bulging, sinewy strip of flesh weaving around his limbs and torso led to another, forming an impressive tapestry of immense strength and power. His thick, protective skin was oiled to a soft gleam, embellishing its harsh gray color and making charcoal shadows in the shallow dips of his body's contours.

The dull, gray ridges and nubs of bone on his chest were spread out in a regular pattern, dotting the valleys of his broad chest wall and breasts then tapering down to disappear under the small scrap of green cloth he wore over his groin. Their sharp, ragged edges belied their sensual nature and the part they played in Oracan biochemistry.

Belith rang a small bell by his chair. As the last crystal sharp note faded, he demanded, "Proclaim."

Never taking his eyes off Barlow, Talos hissed his answer out through sharp, bared teeth. "I accept the honor of this Hunt, High Principal."

The rest of the Hunters immediately stepped back into the shadows. Talos gave Barlow another hard, appraising once over and added, "Principal Belith, in light of this buyer's *impatient* reputation, I ask for extended rights as Hunter in this Detail, from now until such time as Council declares the bounty the property of the bidder. The bounty is mine until I deliver it to Council for allotment. I will tolerate no interference in the Hunt."

A pink flush spotted the crest of Barlow's cheeks and his gray eyes flashed a piercing glare at Talos, but only for a moment. Then his swarthy expression slipped back into place as he clamped his lips together and remained silent.

Belith scented the air and smiled. Amusement touched his eyes, even though his words didn't reflect it. "Granted. Said bounty is yours in all things, until

34

such as Council declares otherwise, Hunter." He turned to Barlow and gave the human a long, meaningful stare. "Agreed, Mr. Barlow?"

"Agreed." Barlow bowed slightly and leisurely tilted his head to one side, looking up at Talos under half-hooded eyes. "Whatever the esteemed Hunter wants."

"Request has been granted. Proclamation declared and accepted." Belith addressed the assembled audience, as well as the Council members. His voice carried on the thick air, echoing faintly. His R's trilled slightly and there was a soft hissing at the end of each of his sentences as he fell into the ritualistic, ancient phrases of his forefathers. "Council is ended. Let the Hunt begin."

Talos bowed to the assembled Council, right fist placed over his mid abdomen then he slid it up his body until it covered his heart in the millennia-old tradition of his race. "Honor and compassion, Council."

Standing, Council returned the gesture as one. "Honor and compassion."

These were more than mere words to the Oracans. They were a declaration of what their race held in the highest of regard – their personal and racial honor, and their responsibility to regard each situation or being with compassion. Unfortunately for the people that became involved with Oracans, compassion was sometimes a very harsh gift.

Once the Council members began to leave, Talos strode intently over to Barlow, purposefully invading his personal space.

The antiquities dealer rocked back on his heels to

gain distance without appearing intimidated by the warrior. He stared Talos in the eye, seemingly undaunted. Only the scent of his fear on the thick, warm air gave his true feelings away to the Hunter.

"We will not meet or talk again until I have captured the bounty. Be ready to accept the pirate when I contact you." Talos tapped Barlow on the chest, causing the human to flinch at the impact. "And have payment ready. I like my credits in large denominations."

Arrogantly raising an eyebrow, Barlow drolled, "I'm ready now, as is your payment." A pleasant, but false smile decorated his thin lips. "Universally negotiable credits, as agreed." Barlow eyes turned hard and he lowered his tone until it was flat and cold. "Don't underestimate me, Hunter, I'm more than able to handle this prize."

"You just think you are," Talos scoffed. "Any pirate is scum. If this Aidan Maymon is everything you say he is, he's going to be tough to hold onto." He clenched a powerful fist in Barlow's face, extending its two-inch long, razor-sharp talons for effect. "Have a set of your own bracelets ready. Mine stay with me."

Subtly backing up a pace, Barlow sniffed and rested a hand on the ornate handle of his sword, striking a confident pose. "I've spent my life studying Earth's pirates and buccaneers from Maymon's time period. It was a glorious time in history. I'm well aware of how devious they can be." He lifted his chin and managed to appear to swagger while standing in place. "After all, I *am* descended from one."

Talos pondered Barlow's claim. "I believe it. Like

I said, pirates are all scum." Talos sauntered off, leaving the silently fuming human behind him.

Sherman broke away from the small crowd of spectators and Barlow's personal aide scurried to his side. He rubbed the palm of one hand on his pant leg and whispered, "Do you think he knows about the Arugalain scepter?"

Eyeing his aid contemptuously, Barlow snorted. "I doubt it. And only three people alive know about the scepter's existence." Barlow gave Sherman a cold smile then stared at Talos' back as the Hunter exited the great hall. His voice was cold and threatening as he turned back to Sherman. "That can easily become two."

Adam's apple bobbing with each convulsive swallow, Sherman paled and asked, "What if the pirate tells him about it?"

Barlow raised one eyebrow imperiously and tossed an aggrieved glare at his aide. "I suppose it could be a problem -- if I'd actually intended to wait for Council to turn the pirate over to me."

Sherman frowned and studied his employer's face. "How else will you get him? You need an Oracan Hunter for the time travel."

"Yes, I do." Barlow turned to run a contemptuous glance over the few Council members still mingling in the chamber. "Compassionate creatures that they are, Hunters always sedate their prey until delivery. The pirate won't have a chance to talk to anyone."

He walked away, following Talos' earlier path out of the hall. Sherman scrambled to keep up with him.

Drawing himself up to his full height, Barlow

stiffened his spine and pulled back his shoulders in a regal pose. "I've already made alternate arrangements. I'll have my pirate almost as soon as the Hunter re-enters our space. And no one will ever know suspect a thing." He threw Sherman an arrogant sneer. "You know my motto, Sherman. Why pay full price when you can get it at a discount?" Barlow walked off leaving the flustered, open-mouthed aide behind.

Sherman hesitated, shifting his gaze warily to the remaining warriors in the hall. His glance met a pair of deep violet eyes as Zeban stood nearby, intently studying him. It only took a moment before Sherman was running after Barlow, having apparently chosen the devil he already knew.

***

Inside the complex maze of the common information keep, Talos sat reviewing disc after disc of information on Earth's pirates on a small view screen. The monitor currently showed a supposed sketch of the infamous Maymon. He was portrayed as a haggard man with darkly tanned skin, masses of black hair that danced like serpents under his hat and a villainous air about him. He was pictured onboard a crippled merchant vessel, sword swung high and dead bodies all around him, a true cutthroat and traitorous dog of his time. Numerous tales of his plundering and ransacking of small seaport towns along the Caribbean coastline were mentioned in private journals and even a few public records, though the accounts were sketchy and open to interpretation. By the time he was done researching the man, Talos felt Maymon deserved whatever Barlow had in store for him.

Details of the Hunt

After spending another hour reading tales and vague tidbits about the pirate, Talos decided he had all the facts he needed for a smooth capture that would not affect the timeline of Earth's history. He knew when the pirate was supposed to have died and where. Now all he needed was a way to keep the "how" from happening before he got to the man.

Chapter Three

The sleek, black Oracan fighter sat alone and motionless in space just outside the Oracan gravitational pull. Inside it, Talos efficiently ran through a myriad of systems rechecks. Speaking out loud, Talos addressed the ship's computer. "Central computer, verify current settings."

A soft, clinical, feminine voice answered him in clipped, distinct Oracan. "Destination - planet Earth. Date - August nineteenth, seventeen seventy. Location - two degrees, seventeen point eight minutes north by ninety-six degrees, twenty-one point one minutes west. Gulf of Mexico off the coast of the Isle of Tortuga. Open water."

After setting the ship's recorder to capture the coming events, Talos studied the control panel. On the main view screen, he adjusted the viewer so he could see the outside of his ship. It sat in space, silent and alone, the vague outline of his home planet in the distance, cloaked in a haze of murky, red and beige swirls of atmosphere. A sudden, small twinge of loneliness twisted his stomach. He tried to force it to unwind, but the annoying, jabbing pain stuck in his gut and refused to budge.

Every time he returned home during the last

year it was the same. The concerned faces of his brothers and friends only intensified the guilt and loneliness he had been wallowing in since his younger brother's death. No amount of carefully worded messages of reassurance and forgiveness would wipe away the fact he had failed in his responsibility to teach and protect Bakus as the younger Oracan learned nuances of the Hunt.

Forget that Bakus was old enough to decide his own fate and that he wanted to follow in Talos' footsteps. Bakus had turned out to be too naïve and trusting to succeed as a Hunter. Deep down Talos had known that, but he had still allowed the young warrior to join him. He had been responsible for bringing the youngster into a world he wasn't prepared to handle. He was responsible for Bakus' death just as much as the two Kenraks were who had actually ambushed and killed the young Hunter his first time out on his own. Nothing could wash away that guilt. He couldn't understand how his own family cache could bear the sight of him now. He was better off alone. The Hunt was his only purpose in life now, the Hunt and restoring his honor.

Shaking off the cloud of self-indulgent depression, Talos settled back in the massive pilot's chair and ran a critical eye over the ship's settings again. "Engage stealth shielding."

Responding instantly, the computer echoed his command. "Stealth shielding engaged." On the viewer the Oracan fighter flickered and disappeared.

Once shielded from sight, Talos leaned back in the seat. He rolled his neck to relax the muscles of his shoulders and closed his eyes. The distortion rift during time travel was always easier to tolerate when he was completely relaxed and his mind was unburdened. Today, he'd have to settle for just relaxed.

Taking a deep breath, he gripped the arms of his seat to ensure good contact with the ship and exhaled, long and slow. Talos and the interior of the ship wavered, then blinked out, only to reappear in a shimmer of air, much like a heat wave distortion. As the distortion faded, Talos opened his eyes and released the tight grip he had on the chair.

On the view screen where his fighter had been, the endless, inky darkness of space was now replaced with a beautiful, clear blue sky. Hidden from view of the human world below, Talos and his fighter now hovered over an 18th century sailing ship anchored in the blue-green water beneath him.

His research had been accurate. Talos recognized the winged, dancing skeleton on the black flag flying proudly from the ship's mast. The design on the flag symbolized that time was running out for all and this pirate captain had no cares about his fate or that of his victims. It marked this ship as his prey's schooner, the *Jamaican Maid*.

The trim, wooden vessel had her sails down, and she had thrown down her anchor. Two tall masts pierced the cloudless sky like a skeleton's long, bony fingers reaching up from the depths of the croppy, blue-green waters. The sturdy ship rocked against the waves, pitching and swaying in time to nature's insistent, commanding rhythm. On board the schooner, Talos could make out a flurry of action as the pirates fought among themselves.

    Narrowing the focus on his view screen, and enhancing his sensors to pick up the verbal exchanges, Talos watched closely for his anticipated opening. Two men in particular drew his attention first. Shackled in irons, a young man was pushed through a crowd of cursing, jeering, filthy men, dragged along by his long black hair by a husky, unkempt bear of a man. Both were sweat-covered and sun-baked, the young pirate tanned to a golden brown while the older, grizzled pirate was a livid rose color that spoke of too much sun and too much alcohol.

    Talos caught a glimpse of the young pirate's features, even though his lean face was dirt-streaked and hidden by strands of disheveled dark hair. Eyes as dark as a starless horizon blazed from a smooth, tanned face defined by high cheekbones and a gracefully angled chin. Talos would have considered the man delicate if it weren't for the fire in his snapping dark eyes and the stream of livid, lively and very creative curses coming from his full, wind-chapped lips.

    Intrigued, Talos regretted having to tear his attention away from the struggling young man to look for some sign of the pirate he was searching for. No one he had seen so far came close to resembling the sketches of the vile creature in his research. He continued to meticulously scan the crowd for his prize, his Hunter's instincts on high alert, the desire to engage his prey rising to the top of his ingrained priorities.

    In the aftermath of what Talos knew was a mutiny, growled yells and foul curses filled the air, each pirate having his own bit of spite-filled bilge to sling at their fallen compatriots. Everywhere the Hunter looked, dead crewmen lay scattered on the red-stained deck. Suddenly the large, hefty pirate dragging the dark-haired young man came back into Talos' view, as the man pushed his shackled prize to the quarterdeck. There he forced the young pirate to watch as the mutinous crew sliced open the lifeless bodies and threw them overboard into the churning waves. The sea turned darkly foreboding. The sharks that had been trailing the schooner, eating the garbage and chum thrown overboard, gathered in greater numbers, enticed by the scent.

Studying the growing onboard interest in the shackled young pirate, Talos suddenly realized where his prey was located. Standing, Talos stripped his broad body of all of his weapons save a knife, and discarded the thin fabric of his trousers on the floor of the fighter.

Below him, Talos watched as the young pirate was tied to a wooden barrel, and then raised in the air and thrown overboard into the bloody circle of the sharks' feeding frenzy. Quickly closing his eyes, Talos took a deep breath, and then vanished from the cockpit.

Re-materializing twenty feet under the surface of the churning ocean, Talos easily located Maymon with his enhanced underwater vision. Swimming skillfully between the writhing gray bodies as they fought each other over the fresh kill, the Hunter approached his newfound bounty, coming up from beneath him. He watched as the pirate struggled against the ropes binding him to the half-empty wine barrel. A bold, open-mouthed shark dove at the man, driven into a mindless frenzy by the scent of fresh blood. Still holding his breath, Maymon lashed out with his feet, kicking the overbold predator in the nose with his square-heeled boots. He twisted and turned in an attempt to roll the barrel over long enough to draw in a new lung full of sweet sea air, but the barrel's buoyancy fought him to the last of his strength. Bubbles escaped out from his flared nostrils and the cold of the deep ocean waters rapidly weakened his efforts.

Like an apparition from a pirate's rum-soaked dreams, Talos rose up out of the depths in front of Maymon, cutting the startled pirate free just as the young man's surprised face melted into a knowing grin as he passed out.

Pinching off the human's nose and covering his mouth so the reflex to breathe didn't drown the man, Talos grabbed Maymon's unconscious and still-manacled body and protectively pulled the slight frame close to his own hulking build. Punching a passing shark square in the eye, he gutted the next one that passed by, then closed his eyes, and vanished.

***

Water dripping off every ridge and crest of his naked body, Talos reappeared in the cockpit with Maymon grasped tightly in his arms. He checked that the feisty pirate was breathing, then lowered him onto a bunk, and strapped him down. Taking a syringe from a medical kit under the cot, he carefully pushed back the tangles of waterlogged, black strands of filthy hair and injected Maymon in the neck. He lingered a moment, his nostrils flaring. He leaned in close to the young man's exposed neck and chest, and inhaled deeply, drawing the human's scent into every corner of his

45

lungs.

His groin responded immediately to the odd scent and Talos was startled to feel a rush of possessive desire flood his entire body. He felt hot and short of breath. A flash of light-headedness washed over him, instantly replaced by a primal burst of white-hot energy that made him feel very, very powerful. Pushing away the instinctive urge to claim his prey in a very intimate physical manner, Talos forced himself to rock back on his heels and gain some distance from the unconscious man. He closed down his nostrils and let Maymon's scent fade until he had regained control.

Satisfied his bounty was contained and safe, Talos closed the lid on the trunk-like bunk, dressed and resumed his seat at the helm of his fighter. Closing his eyes and gripping the arms of his chair firmly again, the fighter, the Hunter and his bounty disappeared from the peaceful blue, Jamaican sky.

Chapter Four

Winking through the seven hundred-year differences between Maymon's time and his own, Talos' fighter, the *Dango*, reappeared in space. The surrounding brilliant star clusters were sparsely patterned across the open, desolate blackness. Talos checked his ship's settings, a frown marring his face, making his eyes narrow and his inner eyelids blink several times over his deep violet eyes.

Suddenly the ship rocked, an explosion hitting it just off the port side. Another blast hit the ship from behind followed by two more. Talos hurriedly maneuvered the ship out of its present position. All around him equipment sizzled and snapped, and the scent of smoke filled the air. A small fire broke out on a side panel, which he quickly extinguished with his open hand.

"What the hell?" Talos pushed the sleek fighter into evasive action. A laser blast cut across the bow, just missing the front viewer as a two-seater, vicious-looking fighter streaked past the nose of Talos' ship. Recognizing the compact design and the menacing laser guns protruding from the ship's undercarriage, the Hunter snorted and hissed. "Mercs. Always out to steal someone else's hard-earned cargo."

47

Talos tracked the opposing ship, firing his own weapons in a rapid barrage of devastating hits. On screen, the mercenaries' ship wavered and veered off, showing heavy damage on one side.

Talos gave a mirthless smile that showed the straight, even rows of his sharp, white teeth. "Didn't know your kind had wandered this far out again."

Swinging the ship around for another pass, he re-targeted the enemy and fired, scoring another hit. "I wonder who rattled your dung-filled cages this time."

Rallying, the injured enemy ship limped into view and returned fire, making a direct hit on Talos' tail end.

Possessed by a sudden protective surge to safeguard the human in his care, Talos growled, "Shit! I'd love to stay and play, but I have more important things to do right now."

Talos maneuvered the ships face-to-face. They both fired their weapons at the same time, hitting each other head on. The Merc vessel took the worst of the force. Its outer hull peeled away and drifted off into the cold void of space. It only took a few nanoseconds for the rest of the vessel to crumble as the ship depressurized and collapsed.

The *Dango* rocked with the force of the explosion and the resulting ripple of energy sent it spinning out of control, forcing the ship thousands of miles from the attack site. On board, Talos fought to regain control of his spiraling ship as an outpost space station suddenly loomed dead ahead on his forward monitor screen.

Talos slammed the thrusters back in a desperate bid to avoid a collision. Despite all his efforts, the space station grew closer and closer. Just as the nose of his four-man fighter seemed destined to slap into the force field protecting the station's docking wing, the *Dango* came to an abrupt halt in mid-downward spin. Everything not tied down, including the pilot, scattered within the ship's interior.

Regaining his command seat, the Oracan bounty Hunter realized his ship was locked in the grip of the station's shipping tractor beam. He jabbed at the intercom link and signaled the station.

"About time, *Pathos Six*. You just saved us both a hell of a fine for littering. I've already lost enough pieces off this bird without having her nose kiss your station's ugly butt, too."

A tinny, strained voice buzzed over a smoking speaker near Talos' head. "We strive to please. Welcome back, *Dango X69*. Docking in twenty croms. Please refrain from touching your ship's controls."

"No shit. Did it look like they were working right anyhow, asshole?" The Hunter's voice thundered, dark and ominous.

"Ten croms to docking. Secure for retrieval, Dango X69." The buzz from the speaker managed to be both professional and biting.

"Yeah, yeah, I know. Keep your hands and feet inside the ride at all times. Just put a rush on it."

The *Dango* lurched, doing a slow spin into an upright position. A dull thud shook the hull and Talos knew he was inside the docking bay. He began shutting down the few remaining active systems, mentally cataloging the damage.

"Docking secured, *Dango X69*. You may

49

disembark your vessel. A security team awaits your arrival. Please have all necessary ID and documents in hand. Commander--."

The rest of the droning transmission was lost in the sizzle of burning circuits. Talos grunted and slapped out a small eruption of flames with his bare palm. The white-hot burn never even penetrated the outer layers of his thick, gray hide.

Damage to his beloved ship ranged from light to extensive, but it was the repair time that was the real annoyance for him, considering the bounty on board. Bidders always wanted their shiny baubles delivered in good condition. Talos hated it when the prize had to be watered and fed. The last thing he wanted was to have to spend time with it awake. Despite his body's instinctive, undeniable, and overwhelming reaction to the man, bounty was bounty, nothing more.

He snapped off the power to everything but the faint interior lights before heaving his massive bulk out of the com seat. He shouldered a heavy pack covered in bulging pockets, strapped another on top of it and checked to be sure that his sidearm was secured to his hip. Opening the compartment's doors, he jumped the four feet down to the bay's surface.

His face assumed a vague, reptilian smile, which he aimed at the contingent of waiting security officers. One tall, distinguished-looking man in a Commander's uniform stepped forward.

"Talos, I'm glad to see you, like always, but I'm surprised. I thought you were going after a new bounty."

Talos glared at the man, but exchanged a

familiar nod of welcome with him.

"Hello, Marius. Good to see you're keeping this sorry excuse for a space station in one piece. I needed a rock to crawl under."

"We aim to please." Marius Webb stepped closer and ran an appraising gaze over the damaged ship, then turned a questioning eye on the Hunter. "A lot of fresh damage. Run into a little trouble this time?"

"Got jumped by some Mercs when I came out of the time flux."

"Mercs? This close to the station? How many? Why?"

Talos waved a cargo manifest microchip in front of Marius. "I'm guessing they were after my new bounty." He grunted in disgust and narrowed his eyes, letting their thick, gray hoods and inner, reptilian-like lids flash closed for a moment in anger. "No other sane reason to jump a Hunter."

Talos slapped the microchip into Webb's outstretched hand. "And don't worry. There aren't any of them left to torment your little station."

"Terrific! More paper work to file with corporate headquarters." Relieved but exasperated, Webb slipped the chip into a small handheld viewer and began to read the contents. "You should try to remember that you live here more often than on Oracan, too, you know."

"And I depend on you and your fine highly-paid security forces to keep my cache safe and sound while I'm on a Hunt." Playful sarcasm dripped off of each word.

"Right." Marius managed to echo Talos' tone even if he couldn't match the deep bass of the Hunter's rich, guttural tones.

Webb glanced up at the open door to the ship to peer inside, then over at the damaged panel on her underside.

"And to think, we used to be known as the 'Quiet Quadrant' around these parts." Tilting his head to one side, Marius gave Talos an accusing stare. "That is, until you started docking here, my friend."

Talos stepped closer and towered imposingly over Marius' tall form.

Marius matched him glare for silent glare, then blinked and muttered, "Asshole." The Commander stared up into Talos' violet eyes, waiting for an outburst.

A low rumble of laughter bubbled up from the Oracan's massive chest. Webb flinched slightly when a spiked arm grazed his shoulder, nearly knocking him into the man behind him.

Although they were fierce, aggressive warriors by nature, Oracans were not known for having easily ignited tempers. Rough in manner and speech, overbearing and seemingly inconsiderate, they were, in fact, the peacekeepers throughout much of the galaxy.

One of the rare species that could tolerate the immense stresses of time travel, some Oracans became bounty Hunters -- adventurous retrievers of lost or stolen items for those fortunate enough to be able to pay handsomely for their expert services. Only the Oracan Council decided what bounty Hunt was acceptable and Hunters could not use their time traveling skills for personal gain without risking permanent exile from their people.

Talos regained control and shook a knobby finger in Webb's face. "Damn, Marius, I've missed you! It's good to be back."

He stepped back to the open hatch of his ship and hoisted himself up to sit in the doorway. Leaning to his right, he unlatched a large lid and tipped the attached bunk with a nudge of his hand. A slender, five-foot long object rolled out and into the shadows of the ship, leaving only a few links of rough, metal chain visible.

Talos grabbed hold of the chain and jumped down from the fighter, dragging the attached object with him. A soft, low moan accompanied the movement.

Talos gave a tug and Maymon slid into view, his wrists still manacled together with the ancient irons. The pirate was semi-conscious, weakly rolling his head from side to side in an effort to pick it up, a haphazard array of twisted, dirty braids falling loose about his fine-boned face. Some strands were beaded and tied with colorful bits of string. Even but discolored teeth showed between bow-shaped, dry lips.

"It's a man." It was a useless comment, but the only one Webb could think of. "A boy."

"Nope. Cargo." Talos ignored Marius' troubled stare and continued to pull Maymon into the open, fighting back his rising desire for the small human. Even dampening his ability to smell wasn't helping this time. Maymon's distinctive odor was branded onto his neuro receptors and entwined with his libido pathways. He hadn't had this pirate five minutes and he was already a major problem. Talos felt his sex organ ripple

Laura Baumbach

with desire deep inside his abdomen.

"But you don't like to take live bounty." Marius' face pinched and his lips formed a thin, unhappy line. "Not since… your brother."

"I made an exception. He's legal bounty. A pirate, a criminal, he has no rights. He doesn't even exist." Letting anger push aside lust, Talos raised the man's wrist to snap in place a snug, seamless, silver band around it, marking the pirate as the spoils of a legal Hunt, proclaiming him as belonging to Talos. That same, sudden sense of primal possessiveness surged through Talos again. "*Mine*. To transport and care for as I see fit."

Talos paused for a moment to carefully toss the young man over one shoulder, ignoring Maymon's faint groan of protest.

"And I see fit to chain his scrawny ass to a pallet in a locked room so I can get a drink, a meal and some decent shut-eye." Grimacing, Talos shifted the man more comfortably on his shoulder. "Damn, he's still damp."

Webb raised a questioning eyebrow, which Talos ignored.

Semi-conscious, Maymon wiggled and kicked out as he was jostled on Talos' hard, ridged shoulder. A fast swat from the Hunter's massive hand to the black-clad hindquarters produced a weak yelp, but the struggles faded.

Talos grinned at Marius and stooped down to retrieve his dropped bags.

One of the new, younger security officers rushed over to help grab the bags, accidentally brushing his hand over Talos' massive arm in the process. The young officer cried out and jumped away from the Hunter.

"What the--?" The officer cradled his hand to his chest, wide eyes examining the reddened flesh of his fingers and palm. He hurriedly backed away from Talos, fear clearly written on his shocked face.

Talos straightened up and shot the man an impatient glare. "First lesson on other species relations, kid, -- humans don't touch Oracans. Got it?"

The young man nodded convulsively, clutching his arm. His uncertain eyes darted to Marius.

The Commander patted him on the shoulder and sent him away with a gentle wave of his hand. "See Dr. Rice in the sickbay, Rodgers. Tell her what happened. She'll know what to do."

Rodgers scurried away. Marius turned back to Talos and sighed. "He's new. He didn't know. Hasn't seen many Oracans before. He'll learn. Forget about it."

Talos picked up his bags, balancing the restless load on his shoulder with ease. He voice was low and unusually quiet. He muttered in a pitch meant for only his friend's ears. "I know. I just don't like being reminded no one can get close to me."

Abruptly, Talos headed out of the docking bay. Fifty feet down the hallway, he realized he was alone. He turned and called out to Webb.

"Christ. Hurry up, Marius. Let's get moving. I need to take a piss."

Interrupted in his curious examination of the fighter's damages, Webb frowned, but hurried to catch up with his massive friend.

***

55

The main reason Talos allowed himself the indulgence of an entire suite on the luxurious third level of the station was the showers. The living areas were beautiful, the bed huge and the suite afforded his larger bulk the room he needed to feel comfortable in, but the custom arrangements in the bathroom were the real attraction for him.

His thick skin amply protected his body from minor injuries, extremes in temperature, and also prevented loss of precious moisture from his largely fluid-based body. It was supple and soft despite its coarse appearance and very silky to the touch. In contradiction to their startlingly fierce features, Oracan were very much a sensory motivated species. An experienced Oracan could read another being's emotions and mental state by the odor and level of heat radiating from its body.

Talos found the hormone levels particularly strong in most humans, but they were extraordinarily strong in the young pirate. Maymon's scent called to him on a primal, genetic level and challenged him, daring him to ignore the overwhelming, instinctive demand to claim the newly acquired male as his own mate, but claiming the pirate as his own would dishonor the Hunt, something he could never do.

Which was why he was now standing under the hissing spray of four huge shower heads, letting the fine stinging mist of hot water purify and cleanse his skin, washing away all traces of the pirate's scent, at least temporarily. Unfortunately, the fine spray wasn't capable of washing away the firm, insistent erection emerging from his groin.

Details of the Hunt

He leaned one outstretched arm on the shower wall for support and bowed his head under the waterfall positioned directly above him. Water streamed over his hairless scalp and trickled behind his ear ridges and around his neck to cascade over the soft cartilage nubs on his chest. The sensation was a delicate touch to his thick hide, but the sensitive nerves and astute heat sensors in his skin magnified the pleasant sensation tenfold.

His lower abdomen quivered and his snake-like cock poked out of its protective pouch, stretching and wavering in the warm, moist air like a flower emerging from the ground after winter. It grew to its full length of fifteen inches, long and slender. The satiny-smooth, triangular-shaped tip thickened to a two-inch diameter cap ringed with firm nubs of very soft cartilage. The cap was a smoky black compared to the dusky gray of the long shaft. The opening at the very apex of the triangle secreted a clear, yellow, oily substance in a continuous, lubricating stream. In place of pubic hair or a scrotum, Talos possessed a mass of six-inch long, spongy tubular appendages that surrounded his cock and masked the opening to his organ's protective pouch.

His cock swayed and squirmed, undulating in an exotic, questing dance performing for some unheard flute of an invisible snake charmer, looking for satisfaction and attention. Adjusting one of the side spray nozzles to hit his chest and gently stimulate the pleasure receptors under the chest ridges and nubs, Talos ran his free hand through the tubular appendages and then took a firm hold of his quivering shaft.

It immediately responded, curling around his

fingers and looping once around his wrist, then shimmied free. He stroked it with his fist, thumbing the nubs rimming the cap in a slow, leisurely rhythm that made him pant and sent small bursts of sizzling need to travel along his nervous system. Each long caress up the shaft brought a fresh stream of liquid from the tip. His cock grew shorter and thicker as his excitement mounted, until it was only a still impressive nine inches long, but a stout two and a half inches in diameter. The firm nubs under the leaking cap fanned out, creating an irregular collar of hard beads that extended past the width of the shaft and cap. Each upward stroke of Talos' snug fist along its hypersensitive surface brushed over the nubs and sent a shock of passionate need straight to the Hunter's complex sensory receptors.

Motivated by a primal calling, and against his conscious will, Talos threw back his head and inhaled deeply. Flaring his nostrils and parting his lips to let the olfactory sensors in the roof of his mouth taste the air, his mind reeled and his body spasmed as the heavy musk of unwashed pirate assaulted him. He grunted and nearly deserted his approaching climax, but the several dozen tubular rods that surrounded his straining cock captured his hand. Adhering to his skin with small suction pads on their tips, they clung to him, extending in length with each upward stroke of his arm, refusing to be dislodged.

Giving into his body's desires, Talos tightened his grip on his cock and flicked the cap with his thumb, inflaming the beaded rim. The sharp jolts sent ribbons of pure, white-hot pleasure up his spine. Grimacing, teetering on the edge of the biggest climax he had ever experienced, Talos abandoned any pretense of control and pulled in a deep breath, forcing Maymon's rich scent into every molecule of his body and mind. Salt, sweat, tar and exotic spices blanketed his senses and catapulted him to climax. It was akin to falling off a high cliff into a raging river of emotion.

At first he thought he would never stop spiraling out of control, consumed by the blood-curdling exhilaration of free-falling through the flames of white-hot passion, followed by the terror of hitting bottom with permanent scarring, forever linked to a mate he could not have. Sagging against the shower wall, Talos washed the residue of his orgasm off his skin and shoved his own desires back into the dark place in his soul where he normally keep them during a Hunt. He refused to listen to the little voice in his head that insisted this wasn't a normal Hunt anymore.

***

The soft chime of the commlink in the main living area summoned Talos out of the shower, the faint tones clear and biting to the Oracan's sensitive hearing. He stepped out of the tepid, fine water spray, muscles rippling with each movement, wet, silver-gray skin glistening in the subdued lighting.

He glanced at the sleeping body sprawled on the large bed, wrists chained to the metal frame of the bed, a modern unbreakable restraint looped through the ancient manacles the pirate still wore.

Talos sniffed the air, dampening his body's sexual response to the human's scent, then relaxed. "That's my boy, still asleep." He continued through to the outer suite, satisfied the human was drugged enough to miss overhearing the coming conversation.

Looking at the commlink, he immediately identified the caller's ID code as Agustus Barlow, his bounty's buyer. Talos muttered to the empty room, releasing a little of the growing irritation he felt each time that he had to deal with the man. "Sleazebag asshole."

Naked, Talos shook the water from his shallow ear canals and rubbed a rough hand over the sensitive nubs of cartilage on his sternum, releasing s short burst of hormones into his system, calming himself.

Massaging the oily moisture from his cleansing ritual into his pores with one hand, Talos activated the commlink with the other.

Another chime sounded and the crisp image of a rotund man filled the viewing screen. Even so many light-years away, Talos could still see the fine beads of sweat pop out of Barlow's pores and seep into the rich fabric he swathed his body in. Talos was sure the man's naturally unpleasant odor, combined with the scent of fear and loathing would assault him even now, if he inhaled deeply enough.

"Barlow." Talos settled for a low, rude growl, knowing his mere presence unnerved the human, even on a viewing screen. All Oracans did. Esteemed antiquities dealer and buyer or not, the man was a bigoted pig. "Didn't you understand that we weren't to have contact before I got the bounty?"

"Of course, I did." Barlow snorted and smiled confidently. "I received word you had returned from your Hunt. There was a rumor you had a run-in with some Mercenaries, too. I felt the need to check and see that my bounty wasn't in any jeopardy. I'm most anxious to get my hands on him."

Talos gave into a sudden, unnecessary urge to be non-committal. "I'll just bet you are." He gave Barlow a narrowed, hard glance. "Your sources of information are pretty quick."

"They should be, I pay them very well." Barlow returned the hard glare then his expression morphed into one of fanatic pleasure. "I can't believe I'm finally close to having him!" Barlow rubbed his hands in anticipation, but added in a neutral, business-like tone, "For the historic contribution his assistance will unearth, of course."

"Of course. For history's sake." Talos didn't try to keep the sarcasm out of his voice.

Sweat poured down the man's lean face and his eyes took on an odd light, looking for all the galaxy like a demented old earth actor in the gangster films Talos loved to watch when he was growing up.

A frequent visitor to his father's salvage freighter in deep space as a child, Talos gained most of his foreign language skills from rescued pilots and recovered knowledge discs found on damaged ships from all over the galaxy and beyond. His English was a bit unique. Tainted by repeated viewing of salvaged Earth's gangster-era films, 1920-1950's street slang colored his speech, and the rude, gangster attitude complemented his true Oracan nature.

A sudden movement behind Barlow drew Talos' attention. The viewer showed a young male sprawled on a rumpled and stained bed. Talos' sharp eyes picked out splatters of what appeared to be blood on the sheets and across the male's slender back and one exposed leg. Talos' dislike for Barlow took a huge leap toward a stronger emotion. Maymon looked much like the young male in Barlow's bed.

"I'll put you wise when I'm ready to turn over the goods." The Hunter growled out the command, letting every ounce of his disgust for the man seep through their connection. "Don't contact me again."

Barlow stiffened and pulled himself up to his full height, an arrogant, manic glint in his eyes. "I'm sure I don't have to remind you I'm the legal owner of the map and I claim sole rights to its treasure. Don't even think of trying to get this pirate to make you a new one to retrieve the artifacts on your own. I have enough wealth and power to buy second bounty just as easily as I bought this one. One on *your* head!"

Talos stepped back from the viewing screen, bringing his whole, impressive, muscle-bound, naked frame into Barlow's view. The spikes on his arms and shoulders sprung to their full six-inch height, razor sharp and bristling.

His sensitive hearing caught the reedy, strangled gasp from Barlow as the man automatically took in the length of Talos' naked, massive body. The look of amazement on Barlow's face when his gaze reached the Hunter's groin brought a burst of satisfaction to Talos' alpha male ego.

Barlow seemed to shrink back without really moving. Talos briefly considered holding negotiations in the nude all the time. The intimidation factor seemed to work wonders.

"All Oracans honor the letter of the Hunt,

lowlife. We are the Hunt. Threaten me and you threaten all Oracans' honor, Human." The Hunter let the natural growl and rumble of his language trilling deep in the back of his throat, engaging the short bones above his vocal cords, turning his voice into a weapon of power and deadly intent. "Try to make an Oracan the object of a Hunt anywhere in the known universe, and I promise you, you'll find yourself the *prey* in a Group Hunt, sleazebag."

Being the *bounty* for a single Oracan Hunter was a terrifying event for anyone, but one the bounty usually survived. Becoming the *prey* for a group of the legendary Hunters, ones who were once rumored to eat their offending prey, was beyond imagining. Bounty had a purpose. Prey had no profit attached to it outside of revenge.

Barlow paled, his breathing shallow and slightly irregular. "I didn't.... You've misunderstood.... I--."

"Go fuck yourself, Barlow." Talos gave the screen a classic, old-time Earth gesture of a one-fingered salute before terminating the link, delighting in the expression of panic wrinkling the man's severe face.

"Vermin." Talos hissed to the empty room. Touching the nubs on his chest again, he relaxed into the sense of calming release. He didn't usually indulge himself with personal attention like this during a Hunt, but the close quarters with a creature that made his nerves tingle and his cock dance at the mere scent of him was making his thoughts unfocused. Talos needed a clear head to help him refocus on his mission.

He hated to admit it, but he was developing a sense of responsibility toward the stolen young man in his bed and it made his teeth ache. This was the first time he had reacted physically to a bounty before. It was disconcerting. One of the first rules of the Hunt was to always regard living bounty as cargo or merchandise. Getting attached only meant conflict and pain for everyone involved.

Walking to the bedroom, Talos stared at the lithe, young body stretched out on his bed and sniffed the air. Human male hormones mixed with the smell of rum and the ocean Talos had pulled Maymon out of filled his head, but Maymon's own scent was even more unusual. Under the filth, grime and unkempt personal hygiene odors, the pirate was still different than other human males Talos had encountered.

The scent called to Talos and made his sex quiver, the large, snake-like appendage thickening and wiggling in an exotic serpent dance. It reached out from his groin, stretching toward the source of the Hunter's attraction. Talos ground his back teeth together until his jaw cracked and forced his arousal down. The young pirate was bounty, cargo, merchandise, nothing more. Talos just had to keep reminding himself of that and ignore the hollow yearning that was tearing at his insides.

Quickly dressing, Talos grabbed his sidearm, strapped on a few spare weapons and left the suite, locking the mechanism behind him. He applauded himself for not looking back once.

Chapter Five

A sleepy moan floated up from the rumpled bed. Maymon stretched, arching his back, testing each set of muscles down the length of his wiry frame. The pirate ended the exercise with an unsuccessful attempt to bring his outstretched arms down to his sides.

Maymon started and let his heavy-lidded, dark eyes slit part-way open to run their tired gaze up his extended arms to the manacles at his wrists, then follow the chain up to the restraint around the top of the bed frame half way up the wall. The pirate's only outward reaction was a lifting of one eyebrow before he curled his lithe frame into a ball and scrambled up to the head of the bed, bracing his back against the wall by the chain, eyes darting back and forth, surveying the unusual surroundings.

Masses of coarse, matted, black hair swirled around his body. A shake of his head and a measured shrug sent a fair portion of it over one shoulder. He began muttering in a long-standing conversation with himself.

"Me dreams are getting more bloody real all the time. Must have been the laudanum Perkins slipped me." Looking around the unfamiliar room, Maymon paused a moment to consider the vague events of the past day. Confusion gave way to a dark memory. "Have to remember not to tip me cup so often in the future. Puts a body at a definite disadvantage for fighting off a mutiny."

His gaze lingered over the sleek furnishings in the sparse bedroom, taking in the odd blinking lights and smooth glassy walls. "Or was that all a dream, too?" He shook his head and huffed out a deep breath. "Could've sworn on me Aunt Sadie's grave I drown'd."

Maymon inched up to the wall to let his fingers comb through his dark mass of hair. They emerged carrying a thin length of metal from inside of one braid, perfectly shaped for picking eighteenth century locks. He'd needed to do this a time or two before.

As many times as his body and clothing had been searched over the years, no one ever thought to look in his hair. The mass of braids and tangles held an assortment of useful items beyond the treasured glass beads his mother used to string in his hair to mark each passing year of his life. Lock picks were just a small offering.

After a few twists and turns of the pick, the heavy, ancient manacles suddenly clicked open and Maymon dropped them to his vacant pillow. Practicing all the grace and dexterity he had learned over his short, but adventurous lifetime, he took flight, pausing only long enough to grab his boots and to rifle through all of the drawers and belongings in the room. He pocketed a small cache of brightly colored baubles and several shiny discs from a box he found in a cabinet.

Perplexed by the absence of a doorway, Maymon began running his hands over the smooth walls, looking for hidden passages. Inadvertently triggering the main living area door lock during one pass, he jumped back from the silent, sliding door as it opened to reveal the outer corridor and a scattering of odd-looking people walking by. While standing at what he considered an inquisitive, but safe distance, Maymon flinched and blinked, frowning as the door slid shut again after a few seconds. He stared the door, then looked around the suite. Catching sight of the discarded manacles through the open bedroom doorway, he narrowed his eyes and frowned. Captivity had never set well with him, even if it was all just a dream.

Drawing in a deep, fortifying breath, he ran his hands over the release panel again, flinching only slightly this time as the door opened.

"Let's just see where that old horizon went to, shall we?" With one last look around the strange room, Maymon set off to explore his newest dream world head on.

***

Morell's Den was quietly busy with a middle class group of diners of all species and races imaginable. Located on the sixth level near the main observation lounge, it was popular with the business crowd and couples.

Delayed by Barlow's call and irritated by his body's continued arousal for Maymon, Talos arrived at the restaurant in a touchy mood. The bone spikes on his arms bristled erect to half-mast, and an almost palpable aura of menace radiated off the Hunter.

Marius was already seated, meticulously studying the touch screen menu. He glanced up as a small ripple of murmured voices drew his attention. Following the flow of diners and serving machines as they hurriedly backed away from his table to create a wide corridor that opened to the doorway, he caught sight of Talos stalking down the middle of the pathway.

"Hello, again." Staying seated, Marius nodded a greeting and gestured to the chair opposite him. "How's your cargo? Better yet, who's your cargo?"

"No idle chit-chat tonight. You really must be curious, Marius." Returning the nod, Talos eased onto the wide metal frame of the seat and adjusted his weapons to a more comfortable position. "My cargo is a eighteenth century Earth pirate named Aidan Maymon. 'Curse of the Caribbean' according to your history books." Talos scanned over the screen menu and made a choice, touching the pad with a large, but very deft finger.

Marius made his own dinner choice and within seconds a service droid appeared to deliver their meals. "Who in God's name would want a seven hundred year old pirate?"

Taking a bit, Talos savored the taste of a hot meal, chewing slowly before answering. "A pirate-obsessed jerk named Agustus Barlow who owns a seven hundred year old treasure map with Maymon's name on it."

Marius silently mouthed "wow" and began meticulously cutting his main dish into bite-size pieces. "Map must be worth a fortune."

"It is." Talos swallowed and tossed back a huge gulp of blue liquid from a tall, frosted glass. "Maymon and his men scuttled a ship with a hold full of priceless

Mayan artifacts on board and then Maymon hid it. The crafty little bastard somehow encrypted the map that leads to it so that he's the only one that can read it. This creep Barlow needs the guy to find it." Talos twisted his mouth in contempt and sneered, "For Earth's history's sake, of course."

"You don't sound too impressed with your client."

"I'm not." He tore off another piece of the meat on his plate and ate it with gusto. He pointed his fork at Marius and added, "I'm beginning to doubt Barlow just wants Maymon for the treasure's historic value."

"Oh?" Marius sipped his wine inbetween bites of his own meal.

"I did some research on my buyer, as well as my bounty. Barlow fancies himself a descendant of some famous Earth pirate. He's obsessed with them. Collects anything connected to them. He can't seem to wait to get his hands on this one." Talos' expression turned ugly and his tone had a tinge of regret in it. "And he likes his personal entertainment young and male. Like Maymon."

"Oh, well…that's not your problem though." Marius gave the brooding Hunter a thoughtful stare and slowly chewed a mouthful of food before pointedly adding, "unless you *want* to make it your problem."

Talos shot the Commander an angry glare and swallowed down a raw tentacle whole off his fork. "Not a lot I can do about it. The Details have to be honored. And Maymon doesn't have any rights. Legally he doesn't exist in this time. He's not a person any more, he's property."

"You can live with that?" Marius paused, holding his wineglass still halfway to his lips.

"I'm a Hunter, Marius. I live by the Details. Honoring the code is everything to a Hunter."

"When do you turn him over?" Taking a sip of wine, Marius placed the wine goblet back on the table and idly spun the stem between his fingers.

"Barlow went crazy and threatened me just before I came here. I haven't told anyone I've got the pirate yet." Talos dropped his gaze to his food then looked the Commander straight in the eye, daring the man to challenge him on the matter.

"Well." The unspoken accusation hung in the air.

"Well what?" Talos fought the urge to confess his growing feelings for the pirate to his friend. "Wipe that look off your ugly mug."

"What look?" Marius raised one eyebrow in an attempt to look innocent.

"The one that says I'm a sap. Look, Marius, I don't need any emotional attachments in my line of work." Despite his gruff words, Talos looked as if he still hadn't convinced himself of that fact.

"But...?"

Grimacing, but giving in to his friend's prying, Talos looked off into the distance, the memory of the first meeting with his new captive flooding his thoughts. His gaze flickered to Marius and then back to some undefined point across the room.

"You should have seen the runt's face when he first saw me. Part of the crew had mutinied. They'd handcuffed him, tied him to a barrel and then threw the gutted bodies of the dead crew overboard to attract sharks. Once they had a sea full of fins, they tossed him in to be eaten alive." Talos shifted his gaze to meet Webb's. "He never cried out or begged. Not once. I even watched him spit in the face of one of the baboons heaving him over the side."

Alarmed, Marius quietly said, "He's either very brave or very foolish."

Talos snorted. "You should have seen his expression when I swam up under him. He was barely conscious, but still kicking at sharks. He caught sight of me and just stared, like he couldn't believe his eyes. Then he gave me this great big grin, like he'd been expecting me. And then he passed out."

"What did he say when he woke up?"

"Hasn't yet. He's drugged." Talos avoided Marius' disapproving gaze. "Makes it easier. For both him and me."

Webb paused, a thoughtful expression on his face. "He doesn't know what's happened to him?"

"Nope." Talos busied himself with his dinner.

"Don't you think he has a right to know before Barlow gets him?" Marius quietly resumed eating his meal.

"He's a criminal." He tightened his grip on his fork and Talos felt the metal crimp under the pressure.

"Barlow isn't much better from the sound of it. He crossed the line when he threatened you. What if he violates the Details?"

"Then the Hunt is suspended and the bounty's relocated." The idea appealed to Talos.

"Relocated? Where?" Surprised by this piece of

information, Marius leaned forward and lowered his voice. "Another planet? Another time?"

"Something like that." Talos dug into one of his many side dishes. "Forget about that for now. Keeping Maymon here while my ship is repaired is problem enough for me to deal with."

***

Aidan Maymon didn't have the slightest idea of where he was or where he was going, so getting lost was impossible. The bar was easy to find. The colorful array of lights, smells and people called to him once he reached the lower levels of the station. He stood just inside the crowded room in the *Pink Tentacle Lounge* and watched the exchange of colored discs, like the ones he had liberated from Talos' suite, for drinks or trays of food. The variety of people, many more odd in appearance than even his sea monster from his dreams, gave him confidence he wouldn't be out of place.

Regaining his natural swagger, Aidan followed his instincts as he worked his way through the crowd, picking pockets and nicking bright baubles from any and all he passed. A fight broke out beside him and he relieved one of the combatants of a half-full cup as the man went down to the sticky floor in an ungainly heap.

The mug held a liquid in a shade of green Maymon had never seen before. Never one to shy away from new things, he took a huge swallow. The grog was spicy, thick like melted butter and the first gulp made the roof of his mouth numb. Undaunted, he chugged its contents and banged the counter top for more. A purple-tinted man appeared behind the bar.

"Blimey! 'Tis neither beer nor rum, but it'll do,

mate. Pour another. I seem to be a bit behind in me cups next to the rest of this scurvy lot."

His speech slurred with the numbing effects of the grog, but the bartender seemed to get the gist of his intent. Aidan tossed a pink colored disc on the countertop, motivating the man to move faster. A row of brimming mugs appeared before him.

Maymon beamed and muttered to himself, "A lovely dream, indeed. Must have been the spiced pork Cook served just afore Perkins waylaid me, the black-hearted, mutinous dog."

Aidan grinned his thanks at the barkeeper, then guzzled the drinks one by one. He paused at one point to ask bystanders if anyone would share a bit of tobacco with him. One thin, blue-tinged man with tentacles for hair and heavy lidded eyes of gold and gray offered him a smoldering pipe from a webbed appendage. Aidan hesitated then accepted, scooping up his drink in one hand and the pipe in the other, reveling in the substitutes for the familiar comforts of home.

Three puffs of the bitter weed later, Aidan was reminiscing about the Caribbean he'd been forced to leave behind. Luckily, his host was more intent on examining the glass beads in his hair, than in his drunken ramblings. His next gulp left him with an empty mug and he was startled to realize all of his mugs were now empty.

Aidan signaled for the bartender, his voice foreign, more slurred against the din of the boisterous crowd. "Innkeeper! If you'd be so kind, me bucko and me need another round of your fine grog."

He pulled a newly pilfered purse out of a fold in

his waist sash to find the right colored disc. The bartender seemed to prefer the pink ones. Suddenly, a hand clamped over his raw wrist and a very angry, suspicious face shoved itself into his blurred vision.

"That's my credits keep! Where did you get it?" The purse was yanked from Aidan's hand and the bag examined. "My mark is burnt into it." The man fumbled over his own pockets, coming up empty. "Why you little thief!"

Sighing, Aidan gave thanks that this one was human. No extra appendages or odd colors to distract him while he tried to wiggle out of being caught red-handed. The burn mark on the bag was going to make this one a challenge.

With an impish grin and an elegant shrug, Aidan decided to cut to the inevitable finish by throwing the first punch, artfully grabbing the purse back as the big man reeled from the unexpected attack. Like wildfire, fighting burst out in all directions and spread throughout the entire bar.

Aidan landed several punches, and took at least two solid, bruising hits to his left jaw before purposefully dropping to the floor. He wormed his way through the jungle of flailing legs to prop himself up in a quieter corner of the room. Along the way, he liberated his earlier companion's pipe, a handful of roasted meats, and a few more credits, pacifying his blatant tendency toward kleptomania. Despite his drunken state, he was still very good at picking pockets.

The pirate relaxed against the wall and marveled at the sight before him.

"Never knew I had such a bloody wonderful

imagination. I be a right clever bloke, if I says so meself." He patted at his aching left jaw. "Feels so bloody *real*."

Drunk on alien grog, smoking the remains of a hallucinogen, and heavy with the ill-gotten gains of his pickpocketing, the sated pirate watched the colorful brawl continue, happy for the first time since waking up in this dream.

***

The moment he entered his suite, Talos knew something was out of place. The air felt dead and the rich scent of the young human was barely present. Talos sniffed the air and strode directly to the empty bedroom.

Grabbing the discarded, open manacles off the bed, he yanked them forcefully between his hands, ripping the ancient iron chains apart.

"Why you devious, little SOB. Barlow doesn't deserve you." He tossed the cuffs into a corner and snorted, part frustration and part admiration. "You are goddamned amazing. *Stupid*, but amazing." His personal feeling for the pirate grew, adding admiration and amusement to his lust and desire.

Moving to the living area, Talos activated the comlink. Webb appeared on his screen.

The Commander arched his eyebrows and put down the handheld display he was reading. "Talos. I'm surprised. I thought you'd be asleep by now." He frowned and hunched closer to the viewer. "Is there a problem?"

"Yes, there's a problem, Marius. My *cargo's* done a clean sneak." The Oracan scowled at the screen, his words escaping past clenched jaws. His tone could be considered civilized only because he wasn't using the raw, small bones in the back of his throat that turned his voice into a grating roar. "I'm betting he'll head for the nearest dive."

"Wouldn't he try to make it to one of the flight bays? Steal a ship?"

"Hell, no. He can't pilot a ship unless it's in water." Talos huffed and rolled his eyes. Humans could be so dense.

Marius looked like he was resisting the urge to do the same. "He doesn't have any ID or credits. How much trouble can he get into?"

"He's a pirate, for Christ's sake. He's a dip, a pickpocket, a thief." Talos' voice threatened to convert back to a roar, his r's trilling and his pitch dropping three registers again. "He doesn't need any of his own. By now he probably has half the credits on the station in his pockets."

"All right, all right." Webb hesitated, looking away as a light flashed off to his right on a security panel. "There's a disturbance call coming in from a bar in the lower end of the entertainment sector. Ten credits says it's your missing pirate."

Talos blew out a deep breath and rubbed a hand over his chest to calm down and focus. "I don't take sucker bets."

"Good policy. Let's hope your precious pirate is still in one piece."

"You should be more worried about your station. He'll be fine. At least until I get my mitts on him."

Details of the Hunt

Removing his weapon from the desk drawer and attaching it to his belt, Marius pressed a button on his desktop. "I don't want to know about it, now *or* later. And if he's going to be running around the station, he'll have to be run through the sickbay. I know you decontaminated him, but this is for his sake." Tapping a communications band strapped to his wrist, Marius added, "I'll alert a team to meet us. See you in three."

After punching off the link with more enthusiasm than necessary, Talos opened a recessed panel in the wall and removed another sidearm and holster. He'd be damned if he was going to lose his mangy little nance to a drunken brawl on some fucking, dreary outpost named Pathos.

Chapter Six

Outside the *Pink Tentacle,* Marius and Talos were greeted by breaking glass and shouts of profanity in a number of different languages. The security men accompanying Marius waded into the free-for-all. Marius followed his men, but Talos hung back, sniffing the air.

Pinpointing his quarry, the Hunter skirted the perimeter of the shattered room. Scenting the air every few paces, he fended off assaults as easily as if they were pestering flies instead of deadly attacks. When he reached one far corner of the room, he bent down and peered under one of the few tables left standing. Reaching under the table, he snagged a familiar boot and dragged the attached body clear of its hiding place.

A drunken smile beamed up at him from a sea of black hair that was dotted with pinpoints of color as light reflected off the glass beads woven on the underside of Maymon's braids.

Talos allowed the human to scan his immediate surroundings for a moment before stepping into the light. The same startled expression he had seen underwater returned to the young man's dark eyes. Maymon tilted his head back and gave Talos a thoughtful, speculative look. He smiled, pipe in one hand, and a drink in the other. His speech was heavily slurred, but he managed to croak out a greeting of sorts.

"Eh? There you be. Me own fine God of a sea creature. Was wondering where you were. I ask you, guv, what good's a dream if you can't bloody well make it do what you bloody want?"

Sighing, Talos pulled the pirate upright and Maymon leaned heavily against him. Stroking a hand down Talos' broad chest, the pirate inadvertently rubbed over the Oracan's cartilage nubs. A small burst of warmth blossomed behind Talos' sternum, dampening his anger and making him gasp at the unexpected contact. The pirate didn't know what his touch was doing, but the soothing gesture impacted the Hunter. "What the hell do you think you're doing, you conniving little shit?"

"Just slipped out for a wee bit of a nip. Drowning is harsh on a man."

Talos growled.

"You'll be giving no quarter on this, then?"

Glaring, Talos growled, "If that means am I going to go easy on your runaway ass for all this," he gestured at the fighting and destruction all around them, "the answer's no."

The smoldering ash from the pipe still clutched in Maymon's hand made Talos' nose burn as the pirate drunkenly waved it in front of his face. He pried it from the pirate's nerveless fingers and dropped it into a nearby plant.

Maymon reached for it as it sailed by, but his depth perception was off and he missed it by a mile. Turning sad, repentant eyes on his new companion,

Laura Baumbach

Maymon murmured persuasively, "Didn't mean any harm, guv. It's me dream, after all. I should enjoy it."

Pulling Maymon along, Talos maneuvered them toward the exit, shoving combatants out of the way as they walked.

"This isn't a dream, Runt. It's real."

"You're wrong, guv." Maymon slurred and stumbled, but his words held the strength of supreme confidence. "You gotta be wrong."

Talos propelled them through the crowd. Even this drunk, Maymon was able to fight, and at one point his quick actions prevented Talos from being stabbed from behind. The Hunter gave Maymon a surprised look that Maymon casually shrugged off.

"For a pirate, you're a goddamn lunatic, you know that?"

"Ah. And to you, kind sir, the same." Aidan gave him a two-fingered salute and a suggestive wink that made Talos pause until a flying chair forced both of them to duck. When they straightened, the Oracan tossed the swaying pirate over one shoulder and barreled through the throng of battling bodies. Once they reached the outer corridor, Talos ignored the indignant cursing from his struggling companion and began to search for a quieter place to talk.

***

The observation lounge was huge. Two-thirds of the front wall was constructed with thick, transparent shield that allowed the wonders of being suspended in a star-studded galaxy to be admired and appreciated by all. The center of the shield faced the distant sun of Mexis and the brilliant collection of fifteen superstars

80

making up the constellation of Annubane.

Once through the doors into the deserted area, Talos gently tossed the befuddled, endearing, completely infuriating human onto a couch. If one looked around, stars met the eye at every turn. There could be no question where they were, but Maymon took no notice of his surroundings as he continued to struggle and curse.

The scent of the human's pheromones was heavy in the air. Talos' body was already reacting to them, his groin growing heavy and his cock squirming to be let out of the confining cloth of his pants.

Settling awkwardly beside a suddenly quiet Maymon, Talos flinched, surprised by a sharp burning sensation in his left shoulder. He looked down to find a small, tar-stained hand pressed against his flesh, a thin trickle of his own pale blood welling between the slender fingers.

Talos stared at the pirate in amazement and jerked away. "Doesn't that burn?"

"What?" As the Hunter scooted away, the pirate stubbornly followed, seemingly determined to stop the flow of blood from the shallow wound.

"Touching me." Talos frowned, but inside he yearned for the contact to continue. He rarely felt another's touch and he couldn't think of anyone else that his body wanted to be touched by more than this wild creature from another time and planet. "Humans usually complain that an Oracan touch burns their flesh."

"Don't know 'bout that, guv. You feel just fine to me." Putting action to his words, Aidan soothed over

Laura Baumbach

the shallow cut, then surprised the massive Oracan by leaning in and swiping his tongue over the wound, licking all traces of blood from the alien's shoulder.

"What the hell are you doing?" Talos was too stunned to move.

"Slows the bleeding down, least ways does in me own kind." Maymon licked his lips and gazed up at Talos, a teasing expression in his dark eyes. "Tastes like turtle."

Maymon grinned then darted up off the couch to avoid the gray hand reaching for him. Wandering around the deck, he began to explore the various children's toys on the playground. Inquisitive and playful, he slid down a sliding board, but landed hard on his butt at the bottom.

Irritated at himself for allowing his personal desires to interfere with his job, Talos pulled Maymon up from the ground and snapped a pair of modern day handcuffs on him from his pants' pocket.

"No need for that, guv." Deflated, Maymon huffed and jangled the cuffs together, testing their strength and examining them. Finally, he merely shrugged and climbed onto a dragon-like rocking horse. It rocked suddenly under his weight and the pirate struggled to maintain his seating. After the initial surprise, he actively set the horse in motion, his dark, appraising eyes studying Talos from top to toe.

"Green."

Talos blinked, the slurred English accent and the unexpected comment throwing him off balance.

"What?"

Restless, tar-stained fingers danced in mid-air

82

from the silver manacles, indicating the whole of Talos' long, broad frame.

"Green. I imagined sea monsters what lived under the ocean to be green, guv. You're supposed to be green or maybe a lovely shade of sapphire blue. But not *gray*."

Maymon squinted and cocked his head to one side, making the beads in his hair clack and sway. "Though 'tis very silvery and shiny. A good look for you. Can you change the color of your hide as you please? Be any color what takes your fancy?" The fine-boned, expressive face changed from curious to confident. "You were definitely green afore."

"Before what?" Talos couldn't keep the frustration out of his voice. He took a small measure of satisfaction in the wide-eyed reaction his deep, grumbling growl managed to elicit.

The pirate's voice took on the patient, but tired tones of a parent explaining something to a simple child. "Afore, when I drowned." The dancing fingers did another number in the air, more rapid and expressive this time. "Tossed overboard by those scurvy bastards what stole me ship. Down to Davy Jones' locker, savvy? Where you found me."

Moving to investigate a teeter-totter, Aidan tried to figure out what it was supposed to do by sitting on one end. As the unbalanced seat hit the ground hard, Aidan grabbed his groin and hissed into the cushioned handles. Talos sighed and walked over to pull the bruised, hunched pirate to his feet.

Maymon's pinched face settled into a frown and then he shifted farther away from Talos. "Am I to be eaten, then? If I be a meal for the likes of you, I must warn you, there's not much meat on me bones and what there is 'tis likely diseased with all forms of the pox and such."

Leering, Maymon leaned forward and dropped his lilting tones to a conspiratorial whisper. "Like to frequent the wanton whores in town as often as me purse and me knob allow, guv. And both allows quite a lot, savvy?"

Talos gawked at the chattering, little thief and the pirate winked at him. Just exactly who was the fish out of water here? The kid should be quaking in fear, begging for his life, speechless with confusion. Instead, he was running the conversation and confusing the hell out of his captor.

"You're not dead, Runt. I took you from the water before you drowned. And I'm not going to eat you. That tradition's old history." He almost laughed out loud at the sudden click the pirate's jaw made snapping shut.

"Not dead?" The pirate's voice was tentative, just this side of believing. A slight frown marred his smooth face.

"No." The Hunter's patience was wearing thin.

"Didn't drown?" The frown deepened.

"No." The Hunter tone got a little tighter.

"Not shark bait, nor pickings for the fish and gulls?" Maymon clutched at his stomach and concentrated harder.

"No." Talos let the word roll off the short bones in his throat again, irritated at the persistence of the little shit.

"Drunk, then?" Aidan let a few seconds pass as he took stock of his present health. "Don't feel drunk. Least not *that* drunk."

"NO."

"Fevered?"

"NO."

"Hmmm." A glimmer of understanding began to show in the pirate's dark eyes. "I saw you just afore I died."

"Passed out! PASSED OUT! You didn't die." Talos was growing uncomfortable with the new reverence in the pirate's tone.

"But you saved me." It wasn't a question.

"Retrieved you."

"Retrieved?" The pirate's tone had a perplexed, thoughtful air to it and one scarred, dirty finger tapped at his chapped, dry lips.

Leaping onto a six-foot high jungle gym, Maymon swung his legs through the top bar and let them dangle by Talos' head.

"Acquired." Talos tried to make it clearer.

"Acquired. Well, now, you make it sound like I be some sort o' treasure, guv. What would the likes of you, a huge, bloody sea monster, want with me? What use be me if not for eating? Why take me to your den?" He rattled the manacles pointedly. "And chain me to your bed?" The pirate gave Talos' half-naked form a lingering once over, swallowing hard and then licking his lips when he came to the highly visible bulge at the Oracan's groin. "Have a preference for lads over lasses, do you?"

Talos couldn't decide by his tone if the pirate

was repulsed or interested, but the change in his scent told the Hunter the truth. The pirate's arousal filled the air between them and the small human's breaths started coming in frequent little pants. The old English sailor preference Talos had learned from his research of pirates for 'beer, 'bacca and bum' sprang to mind.

Oracans didn't have a gender preference. It wasn't necessary for reproduction of their species. In fact, Talos preferred male sexual partners to female ones. Carrying on the family name was his oldest brother's job, not his.

"My 'preferences' have nothing to do with this. It's business. You're business." Talos sincerely wished the human hadn't woken up before he'd had a chance to deliver him. *Damn those son-of-a-bitching Mercs*!

"In 1767 you made a map of where you hid a horde plundered from the Spanish vessel the 'Quedah Merchant'. No one has ever been able to find the treasure."

The wily little thief laughed, interrupting Talos with a saucy shake of his head and a flip hand gesture of dismissal the Hunter found both irritating and amusing. Talos reached up through the bars and tugged on Maymon's legs, pulling the pirate down. Maymon slithered to the floor and sat there looking up at Talos with an angelic expression on his face.

"Sorry to disappoint you, guv, but pirates don't bury swag. They spend it as fast as they can, on grog and common wenches and the like, savvy?"

Aidan wormed his way out from under the gym and sauntered to a swing and sat down. "Though I have to admit, that last load of Spanish pretties would have brought a nice bit of coin to me purse. Especially that heathen King's royal staff. Lovely red stones, the color of blood it was." The sassy pirate grinned like a Cheshire cat.

Talos smiled back at him then roughly yanked Maymon off the swing to stand in front of him. Holding him in place by the forearms, Talos towered over the smaller man and demanded, "Heathen King's staff? You mean like a royal scepter? One that glows red all by itself?"

Scowling, Aidan wiggled against the firm hold, but succeeded in nothing but having the Hunter increase the strength of his grip. "That's what I said, guv. Royal staff. Weren't on her ship's manifest. A terrible surprise it was, to be sure. Pity it's lost. It was a fine thing."

Talos eased up on his grip, but refused to let Aidan go. "I researched your whole life before I pulled your waterlogged, little ass out of that ocean. That treasure map is real. And that's what made you the bounty in this Hunt." His violet eyes held tight to the human's dark gaze until the black-smudged eyelids faltered.

"Bounty?" Maymon's eyes narrowed and his lyrical, accented voice hardened. "I have a price on me head? Even now?"

Talos grunted and fought back the urge to tell him yes. "Bought and paid for, Runt." Talos gave the young pirate a regretful glare. "You're the bounty in a legal Hunt within the outlines of the Official Details of Oracan. The prize for a man who wants you to decipher your own treasure map, which he now owns."

"I be the treasure now, eh?" Maymon shook his head in disbelief. "What gives you the right to buy and sell a freeman such as meself?"

"You're a thief, a murderer and a pirate. He had you declared a criminal, voiding your rights. You aren't a free man anymore."

"Pass judgment on a dead man and then bring him back to life to suffer the ill effects? Not very sporting, says I, guv." Agitated, Maymon pulled away then raced back, pointing a manacled hand in Talos' face. "And I never murdered a man who didn't try to do me own fine self in first. Never. Not once."

"You're not dead, damn it!"

Talos was surprised at the depth of the pirate's understanding and more than a little unsettled by his unique point of view. He hadn't allowed himself to think about the bounty's perspective when he retrieved a live prize.

"What does your mother call you?"

"My mother?" The connection eluded the Oracan. Only fathers choose the names for their sons in his culture.

"What's your Christian name, guv? You've made yourself privy to mine."

"I am Talos of Menalon."

"Well, my fine scaly friend, what's to stop me going after me treasure all by meself, Tals?" The fire of fresh rebellion burned in Maymon's dark eyes.

"Ta-los." The Oracan stretched out the pronunciation, making each short syllable twice as long as it really sounded.

Maymon nodded. "That's what I said, guv, --

Tals. What's to stop me, eh?"

The cartilage ridges over Talos' eyes arched and he titled his head to one side, listening for some elusive piece of missing logic.

"You mean besides the fact you're handcuffed, marooned, and you've been legally dead for centuries?" Talos shook his head. "It's been over 700 hundred years since you buried that treasure, Runt. Ocean currents have shifted and landmarks have changed. And let's not forget that you'd actually have to be on Earth in the first place."

"Ehh? Have to be in the 'Caribbean', guv, not 'Earth'. Seven hundred years?" A suspicious, calculating expression lit the pirate's dark eyes. "You said afore I weren't dead."

"*You aren't.*" The words were growled out between clamped teeth.

Maymon sat down and rested his head on his chained hands, eying the unfamiliar mechanism binding them. "Not dead, not drunk, you deny you be a sea monster and you says I be hundreds of years old?"

Talos nodded his head, relieved the pirate was finally beginning to understand.

"Well then," Maymon sighed, "that only leaves one thing to do." He began a vicious pulling and twisting of his wrists, trying to slide them out of the manacles. It took only a few twists before the pirate's wrists were raw and bleeding.

Talos grabbed both of the pirate's bare wrists. He held on tight trying to still the self-abuse. The pirate seemed unaffected by his grip.

"What the hell are you doing?"

89

"No problem, guv." Maymon redoubled his efforts. "It's not real." Despite his words, he gasped in pain. "These should come off!"

"Nearly drowning must have killed off more of your feeble brain cells than I thought, you knucklehead. Of course it's real." Talos couldn't resist shaking the daft human.

Aidan's earnest face leaned in close to him, a mere whisper. "No, 'tis just a dream, savvy? If I be in the future, chained to a silver god of a sea monster, neither drunk, nor dead, nor fevered, then I be locked in a dream of me own private wants, savvy?"

Maymon ran an appraising gaze over Talos' very large, very powerful, very close, desirable body, lingering longingly over certain areas of the alien's impressive physique.

"Didn't *know* I'd wants like these." Aidan looked up and batted his long, dark lashes. He had learned long ago to use every advantage he had in a fight. "Beginning to see the light of it though."

Unfazed by the manipulative flirting, Talos gripped the raw flesh under his fingers tighter and squeezed until the pirate squirmed.

"Does that hurt?"

"Aye," Maymon gasped. "A bit."

Talos lifted the pirate's light frame by his sore wrists until the human hung suspended off the floor. "Do you usually feel pain in your dreams?"

"Can't say as I rightly remember it happening afore, no." Maymon struggled against the increasing pressure. Talos could feel Maymon's bones grate against each other.

90

Details of the Hunt

"Then trust me, you're not dreaming. I'm real, it's the twenty-sixth century and you're alive."

Talos felt a shudder run the length of the pirate's body and the dark eyes held the first true shadow of panic.

"Can't be. I'll not be sold into slavery. Not without a bloody fight, I won't. Rather die first, guv, rather die!" Maymon struggled harder against the Hunter's restraining grip, trying to hide the growing fear Talos could smell on him.

"Understand this, Runt. You're mine. I own you. You can't get off this station without me and you have no place to go to if you did. In your world, your time, you're dead. And here, you don't even exist."

The words came out harsher than he had intended, but it was worth it to see the fire of rebellion in the pirate's eyes dim. Talos slowly lowered Maymon to the floor and let go of his bleeding, manacled hands. The smell of the pirate's blood filled his head and his groin danced under the thin fabric of his pants as the rich scent of the young man called to his mating instincts.

The moment his hands were free, the light of rebellion rekindled in Maymon's eyes and he swung both of his fists up to club Talos in the head. Taking advantage of having momentarily stunned his captor, he raced toward the exit and imagined freedom. Ten paces from the doorway, a massive weight landed on his back and forced him to the floor.

The air was squeezed from his lungs, but the pirate knew better than to allow it to stop his struggle. He twisted and squirmed under the huge Hunter's bulk, wrestling for an opening to wiggle away, landing an impressive number of good blows in the process.

Maymon suddenly found himself rolled over top of Talos and then lifted and bodily heaved through the air to land in the middle of the padded play area in front of the open observation window.

Catching sight of the view outside of the observation shield for the first time, Maymon froze in place, sprawled on the floor, mesmerized and stunned by the vision.

"Bloody hell. Me miserable soul's been cast out, all alone, not to Davy's grip, but into the black heavens above."

The power of the spectacle brought home the reality of the situation he found himself in, forcing the first tremble of fear to show in the dumbfounded pirate's voice. His wide, wondering eyes never left the view beyond the shield.

Moving to sit beside the stunned man, Talos was surprised to see moisture brimming at the rims of Maymon's eyes.

"'Twas I really so bad the Almighty's seen fit to abandon me here?" Aidan whispered, unable to pull his gaze away from the spectacular sight. He reached out a hand to touch the shield then hesitantly pulled back.

"You haven't been abandoned." Talos had a need to make the young man feel better, but knew the truth wouldn't do it.

"Been cast out, I have, like Adam from Eden. Cast out from my world."

"Your God doesn't have anything to do with this. There's no Judgement Day here, Runt. I took you, remember? Bounty in a treasure Hunt." Talos tapped the thin band of silver around Maymon's wrist marking him as Talos' bounty. "You belong to me. I brought you here, not some God."

Maymon glanced down at the bracelet then looked up, really seeing the massive, alien creature for the first time. He eyes flickered over the bloody wound on Talos' shoulder then back to the window.

"'Tis all real, isn't it? The future, strange creatures," he gestured to the transparent wall, "standing amongst the heavens without being dead?"

"Yes, it's real." Talos' tone was tender, his heart aching for the unsuspecting, lost soul he had thrust unprepared into his world.

A tear ran down Maymon's tanned, fine-boned cheek. "Can't go back, can I? Me mates'd burn me alive, a demon back from the dead and all."

He leaned closer to Talos, seeking out the other being's warmth and reassuring presence. A heavy arm slid across his bowed shoulders and Maymon immediately curled into the comfort.

"Then there's naught for it, I'm to be slave to another's whims and lash once more." Aidan's voiced dropped to a whisper. "Swore I'd never be there again." He looked up into Talos' face and pleaded, fingers digging into the fabric of Talos' weapons sash. "Don't suppose I could convince you to let me go? Or kill me? Tell his majesty I died in the taking of me?"

"The Details of the Hunt can't be altered. Even if the Hunt was suspended, there's no going back for you. You'd be 'relocated' by the Council."

"What's that? Relocated? Put someplace else?

93

With you?"

"You don't want to know. And no, I wouldn't be there."

Maymon swallowed hard and schooled his expression into one of acceptance, but his dark eyes betrayed him. Talos knew then that the young pirate would try to end his captivity any way he could before being turned over to the misery of a life of forced servitude.

"Come on. This little escape party of yours has cost me some valuable shut eye." Talos pulled Maymon up against him.

Shifting against the wall of gray-covered muscle, Maymon lurched to his knees, maintaining his swaying balance by bracing his palms on Talos' chest. The Oracan nearly purred at the unintentional contact with the sensitive nubs. Maybe it was a good thing other beings couldn't touch him, the human's constant handling was sending his hormones into overdrive.

Gracefully flexing his body, Talos stood up in one smooth motion. Beside him, Maymon tugged a the silver band on his wrist, then swayed and lurched to his feet, only accomplishing the move with the aid of Talos' belt loops. As they walked, he bumped into Talos' frame every few feet until the Oracan finally reached out and pinned him to his side, coordinating their movements.

"You can start sleeping it off as soon as we get back to my rooms. I have a call to make first."

"Call?" Maymon glanced around. "Aren't no one here to hear you, guv." He gestured at the empty space surrounding them and a sparkle of silver caught his eye. Noticing the Hunter's band on his wrist, he tugged at it, unsuccessfully trying to remove it.

A bright lopsided smile and a beguiling flutter of long lashes peered up at Talos. "But speaking of shiny things--."

"We weren't." Talos continued trudging toward the doorway.

"What say you to taking this little silver trinket off me arm? Chafes the wounds something fierce, it does. Got to be on the watch for infection and the like. If you could just take it off--"

"It's a tracker. It identifies you as my property." Talos added in a softer tone, "It'll help keep you safe."

Yanking harder on the band, Maymon grimaced and began dragging his feet. "Well, that's the point really, isn't it, guv. If you took it off--"

"No."

"Loosened it a bit?"

"No." Talos tightened his grip, nearly lifting the pirate off his feet.

"Just a wee bit? Metal makes me skin turn green, it does. A lovely color for you, but--."

"No." Not even breaking his stride, Talos wordlessly lifted Aidan in the air and swung him over his shoulder, the pirate's small pert ass high in the air.

Startled but determined, Maymon continued to plead his case. "If--"

Once out in the corridor full of travelers, a sharp swat followed by a yelp of indignant protest finally cut short the pirate's words, but only for a brief moment. "You really need to stop doing that, mate. People'll think you're odd."

Chapter Seven

Ever since Talos first laid eyes on Maymon during the mutiny onboard the *Jamaican Maid*, the small human had fascinated him. Maymon's adventurous, clever nature was very much like that of the Oracan's. But judging by his circumstances at the time Talos kidnapped him, not everyone was as charmed by the pirate's wiles.

Maymon would not have survived without his intervention, though Talos doubted his prize would be all that grateful. He knew how disoriented and lost he would feel waking up seven hundred years into the future, in another star system, in the company of an alien race, about to be placed into a life akin to slavery.

Talos resigned himself to the fact he was going to have one confused and unhappy pirate on his hands. He couldn't keep Maymon sedated the entire time it took to repair the fighter. Deep down, Talos knew he didn't want to keep the enticing young man unconscious.

Glancing into the bedroom, Talos watched Maymon through the open doorway. The pirate's boots, wrinkled sash and filthy pants lay in a heap on the floor. Clad only in his thin, worn white tunic, the pirate was asleep on the bed under a light blanket, manacles gone, his back to Talos. Torn shirt hitched up and askew, Maymon sprawled on one side of the large bed, wild, knotted hair fanned across the sheets. The blanket clung to every dip and plane of his lithe body, outlining the curve of his slender hips and the firmness of his pert ass. Talos' cock instantly reacted, stirring restlessly in his pants, forcing him to frown and turn away from the luscious sight.

Coming to a stop in front of the commlink in the living area, Talos tipped his head toward the bedroom and listened, sniffing the air. Smiling ruefully at the scent of hormones and strong emotions carried on the air, he turned back and activated the communications unit. Almost immediately Belith appeared on the screen in his formal Councilor robes and a stern expression on his long face.

Talos bowed and gestured with his fist, formally greeting his superior. "Honor and compassion, Principal Belith."

Belith returned the bow, and a glimmer of warmth lit up his eyes. "Honor and compassion, Talos. Council had not expected to hear from you so soon. Have you retrieved the bounty already?"

"Yes, High Principal, I have."

"Excellent work." The luminous rock that most of the Oracan structures were carved into shone in the background behind Belith. The familiar sight gave Talos a pang of longing for his home planet and intensified his growing feelings of isolation. He shook off the burst of loneliness and paid attention to his duty.

"I am honored." Talos paused, taking a moment to decide how much to tell the Councilor about the events that took place since acquiring the pirate. Belith was like a second father and he didn't like the thought of keeping anything from him. "My ship was attacked by Mercs the moment I exited the time flux."

Moving closer to the viewer, Belith looked both startled and displeased. "Was anyone harmed?"

"No. We're aces. I took care of the problem, but it will be a bit before repairs on my ship are completed." Restless stirring and a harsh cough came from the next room, interrupting Talos' thoughts. He paused, scented the air again then continued his conversation. "And Barlow broke the 'no contact' rule. He linked me here almost as soon as I arrived. He knew I'd captured Maymon practically before I did." Talos shrugged off a cold tingle buzzing at the base of his neck. "Something's up. He's too anxious."

"Unfortunate, but it is a minor offense. Humans have precious little patience, you know that. It is not unnatural for buyers to anticipate their bounty."

Talos snorted and shook his head. "I'll bet he's anticipating it. He forgot to mention there's a 'cursed King's scepter that pulses with the blood of a thousand men' in with the artifacts."

Caught off guard, Belith paused and narrowed his eyes. "The Arugalain Scepter? It is among this pirate's treasure? Are you sure?"

"Pretty sure. It fits the description the pirate gave me perfectly. He even had the ancient legend about it." Talos glanced at the open bedroom again, noting the faint, barely detectable sounds of movement repeat themselves. "Now we know where it's been for the last seven hundred years out of the millennium it's been missing."

"Its return will have a great influence with the Arugalain Council. Barlow's trade will improve dramatically if he has possession of it." Belith's frown deepened. "If its return doesn't start a war first." He sighed and pushed at several control buttons at the desktop he was seated at. "I'm beginning to see why Barlow is so insanely obsessed with this Hunt."

"There's one more thing." Talos paused until he had Belith's attention again. News of the scepter had been disquieting. "Barlow accused me of wanting to steal the pirate and his treasure. He actually threatened to buy a bounty on *my* head."

Bristling with rage, the spikes along Belith's forearms and shoulder emerged a full inch from beneath his skin before he was able to draw them back in. "Is he aware of the consequences of such an outrageous act of betrayal?"

"Yes, but he's crazy enough not to care," Talos stated, adding, "I'm betting he's responsible for the Merc attack on my ship, too."

Still outwardly seething, Belith retracted the bone spikes of his shoulders and arms. "Council will be informed of his threats." He gave Talos a commanding glare. "You will need to take extra care. You are both at risk, but the safety of live bounty is a great responsibility."

"I'll protect the bounty as my own, High Principal." A surge of protectiveness flowed through the Hunter since the moment he had seen Maymon throw overboard. Belith's cautions were unnecessary, but Talos lowered his gaze, hoping his personal desire

99

for the pirate wasn't apparent to the other Oracan.

"As it should be." Belith paused to study the warrior, then bowed and gestured. "Honor and compassion, Talos."

"Honor and compassion, Principal Belith." Talos returned the greeting. He closed down the channel and the screen went dark.

Relieved to be out from under Belith's careful scrutiny, he stripped off his trousers and sauntered towards the bedroom. On his side, facing away from Talos, Maymon appeared to be peacefully slumbering. Talos eased down on the bed, then reached back and quickly swatted the young man forcefully on his ass end.

Maymon yelped and jumped, turning onto his backside, one hand protectively guarding his assaulted butt cheek. "Bloody hell! What was that for?" No trace of sleep or drowsiness marked his sputtered speech.

"Eavesdropping. Now go to sleep -- for real." Talos stretched out on his back on the bed, roughly pulling his share of the blanket over his lower half.

"Ya've a highly suspicious interest in me arse, guv." Ruefully rubbing his butt, Maymon stared at Talos' partially displayed body, giving the Hunter's chiseled chest and hard packed stomach a lingering look that drifted down to Talos' bulging groin vaguely outlined by the blanket and stayed there. Maymon's dark eyes flickered up to meet half-open violet ones peering back at him.

The pirate wet his lips and murmured in a soft, seductive tone, "'Course, maybe you'd like to have a bit more than a quick hand on it, eh? Fancy something else?" When the Hunter didn't move or answer, Maymon licked his dry lips again and purred, "Might be able to make a bit of a trade, if you were of a mind for it. Say, my freedom in exchange for… well, let's call it a private boarding party, eh? What say you to that, guv?" Maymon leaned close and hovered tantalizingly near.

Talos stared at Maymon until the pirate's leering smile wavered, and then swiftly grabbed Maymon by the upper arms as the pirate bent closer. He pulled the young man partially across his own chest then froze, Maymon's lips only inches from his own. Hot puffs of breath flowed rapidly over his skin from Maymon's parted mouth and Talos breathed in the scent of pirate musk and sea salt and tar. His cock hardened and his own breathing turned shallow and fast. His grip on Maymon tightened and the urge to claim his small, warm mouth was overwhelming. Their eyes stayed locked together for what seemed ages, desire and need reflected back at him from the pirate's own dilated, sultry stare.

Calling on all of his restraint, Talos pulled Maymon to his chest and delivered two hard, solid swats to his bared ass before tossing Maymon back onto his own side of the bed. Pushing down his urge to ravage the surprised young man, Talos' tone turned icy and he struggled not to gasp for air. "I have that to say. I don't accept bribes, sexual or otherwise. Go to sleep."

Furiously rubbing at the spot the massive Hunter had targeted, Maymon glared and growled back, "You still need to stop doing that!" All pretense at seduction was gone, but there was a lingering disappointment in his eyes.

"No, what I need is sleep." Lying this close to the human was a challenge, especially after his offer, genuine or not, of sharing his warm, willing body. The constant desire to claim the young man was rapidly growing from wanton desire to a burning, absolute, undeniable need. Continually reining in his instinctive primal urges was beginning to wear on Talos' control. He was beginning to think it would soon be impossible to let the wily, treacherous creature out of his sight.

Looking for a distraction, Talos sniffed the air. "You need a bath."

Punching his pillow into a ball, Maymon threw himself down on the mattress and pulled the blanket up to his chin. He fussed with the wrist band and declared, "Was taking one when you met me, guv." His hip bumped aggressively against Talos' side as he curled into a ball beside his captor.

Talos snorted and closed his eyes. He tried to block out the feel of Maymon's warm flesh rubbing against his flank. "Drowning doesn't count."

"Fine," Maymon huffed. "When I wake up, you just point me in the direction of the nearest pond." He settled his head more comfortably and closed his eyes, restless fingers tugging at the silver band securely fastened around his wrist.

Talos watched the activity under partially closed eyelids. "And don't even think about slipping out on me again. I've sealed the door and I'm a light sleeper. Try anything underhanded and devious on me and you'll spend the rest of this trip unconscious in a sack, got it, runt?" Talos didn't even bother to look at

Maymon as he spoke, confident the pirate understood
his message.

A rumbled stream of unintelligible curses and
fairly impossible to accomplish phrases were uttered
under Maymon's breath, but he settled down under the
blanket and even rolled a little closer to Talos' side
before his breathing became the shallow, regular
rhythm of sleep.

Talos sighed and let his eyes close,
uncomfortably conscious of the warmth burning into
his side.

***

Hours later, having enjoyed the luxury of the
fine mist of warm water provided by his suite's large
shower, Talos emerged from the bathroom still naked.
His gray skin glistened in the subdued lights of the
bedroom as his porous skin rapidly absorbed the
lingering beads of moisture. He paused at the doorway
between the two rooms, taken by the sight of the young
pirate groggily rousing up from the bed.

Maymon's long hair wildly framed his slender
face and his lean, wiry-muscled body was nearly fully
exposed to Talos' lust-filled gaze. Maymon's torn tunic
hung open to reveal his scarred, hairless chest while the
grubby shirt tails fanned out behind him, showing
corded thighs, and a flat, taut abdomen. His skin was an
even shade of golden tan with no hint of any flesh left
untouched by the sun. Talos' gaze was unwillingly
drawn to the half-erect, curved, uncut cock springing
up from a triangle of thick, black hair between
Maymon's legs.

Obviously still half-asleep and disoriented,

Maymon peered groggily around the room, dark eyes darting here and there, full of questions and distrust until he saw Talos silently standing the doorway. Then that sudden, pleased smile the pirate had given Talos when he first laid eyes on him lit up Maymon's face again, and the distrust and fear vanished.

With just that one, beatific smile, Maymon stole the most unattainable and valuable object in the room, Talos' heart.

Talos swallowed hard and tried to think past the aching need in his chest, the overwhelming sense that the only important thing in the universe was right in front of him, sprawled across his bed. His cock responded by thickening and rising up from its nest of tentacles, curving up and out to bob impatiently in the air. Talos let the hot rush of desire flow through his veins until it reached the tip of his awakening cock. He savored the dull, almost-painful throb of unsatisfied passion assaulting his most sensitive nerves, knowing this was as close as he was likely to get to finding any sexual release in his desire for the young man.

Eyeing Maymon's worn, soiled clothing and tangled hair, he said, "We'll be staying here until my fighter is repaired. Get dressed and I'll show you around." He grabbed his trousers and pulled them on before Maymon had a chance to see his rising cock. A Hunter never revealed a weakness, never let his prey have an advantage over him. Talos refused to give in to his heart's emotions. The Hunt was his life. He would not surrender to the whims of his body or heart.

Maymon mindless of his own exposed body, slowly slid into his filthy breeches and boots, haphazardly bringing the edges of his torn tunic together before wrapping the sash around his small waist again. The effect left most of his chest exposed to the waist.

Peering around the room, Maymon investigated the corners, obviously looking for something. When Talos raised an inquiring eyebrow ridge at him, the pirate muttered, "Need to relieve meself, guv. Need a bucket."

Tugging the wary young man along by his shirtsleeve, Talos wordlessly took him into the bathroom and planted him in front of the sleek, unobtrusive commode, and walked back into the bedroom. He knew Maymon was clever, he'd figure it out. A moment later, Talos was rewarded with the familiar slight hiss of the commode emptying itself after use and Maymon's startled yelp and shout of, "Fancy that! A whirlpool in me bucket! Right clever, that!"

Talos watched Maymon exit the bathroom buttoning his breeches, the dirt and grime ground into the pirate's tar-stained hands. "Before you run wild through the crowds again, the Commander here insists you see their doctor. For your sake."

Maymon frowned and his lips pursed in a fine example of a childish pout. "Was lying about the pox, guv. Just said that to warn you off wanting to gnaw on me bones is all."

"Fine, then you've got no worries about seeing one. Besides, you cough when you're sleeping. A lot."

Maymon ran his hands through his hair, gathering it together and tying it off his face with a dirty rag from around his wrist. "That's just the 'bacca. Been

Laura Baumbach

coughing a bit since that last pouch I got off one of the Orient's finest."

Looking the pirate over from head to toe, Talos murmured, "That's probably not all they gave you."

Maymon looked hopefully up at Talos. "You wouldn't happen to have a bit of 'bacca on you to share, would you now?"

Maymon flopped down on the bed, back propped against the wall at the head of the bed, a beguiling, seductive smile on his dark pink lips. Surrounded by disheveled bed sheets that still radiated their shared body heat and smell to Talos' sensitive skin receptors and nose, the pirate was more alluring to the Hunter than ever.

"No. I don't poison my body with abusive substances. And neither do you anymore. Seeing a doc is a good idea. We'll get an idea how much damage you've already done to yourself."

Sitting forward, Maymon sliced his hand through the air. His voice dropped low, becoming thick, rich with dark emotion and conviction. "No drunken, old, flea-bitten, son of a goat with a rusty saw blade and a rancid bottle of ether is having at me flesh while I'm still using it." Maymon jumped up from the bed and casually edged toward the living area doorway.

Talos finished donning his boots and his usual array of light weapons, watching Maymon's every movement from the corner of his eye. He sensed the shift in the young man's intentions by the change in his scent even before Maymon rose up from the bed. Fear was one of the easiest odors to detect on humans. Panic was a close second.

"I doubt the doctors here are drunk or goats. This space station is owned and staffed by a very powerful corporation. They have the finest of everything, including doctors." He dropped all pretense of ignoring the pirate and began to match his movements. "And they stopped using rusty saws centuries ago. You'll be fine."

Fire in his dark eyes and a thin line of determination on his lips, Maymon edged closer to the door. His voice was soft and deep, belying his rising agitation. One hand automatically fumbled at his waist sash, but he found none of his usual weapons. Unsettled, he grimaced then raised a finger and pointed it at Talos' chest. "Won't go, guv, and no power on Earth can make me."

Talos chuckled and said, "Good thing we're not on Earth then, huh?"

They stared at each other for all of ten seconds then Maymon made a break for the outer door. Still keeping to the wall, he gained the outer living area, but hit a stumbling block when he crashed into a large fern-type planter by the small seating arrangement. Maymon stumbled to his knees, but lithely regained his feet. Despite having Talos on his heels, Maymon's mad dash to the sliding wall that would reveal the corridor ended abruptly when he spied a softball-sized, swirling gold and green sphere roll out from behind the now mangled plant he had tripped over.

"What's this pretty? Looks heavy." Fascinated by the shiny bauble, Maymon stopped and bent down, instinctively reaching out to touch it. He glanced up just as Talos made an abortive effort not to run over the crouched pirate. "Is it real gold?"

Maymon's dancing fingers brushed over the smooth, glowing surface of the ball just as Talos bellowed, "No, Aidan! Don't touch it!"

Diving head long across the room, Talos tackled Maymon to the floor and smacked the sphere from under the pirate's hand just as his fingertips made contact. A thick green smoke billowed from tiny holes in the surface of the metal ball. Instantly, frantic, computer-moderated alarms began to sound and the air was filled with fumes and chaotic noise.

Talos sucked in a deep breath while the air surrounding him was still smoke-free. He could feel Maymon panic and his ingrained protective instincts took over. He lurched forward and grabbed Maymon up off the floor with one beefy arm. He headed toward the only exit even though he knew it would be sealed by the computers to prevent the spread of the deadly gas.

Confused, Maymon struggled against Talos' grip, his fists rubbing furiously at his streaming eyes. "What the bloody hell is this? Can't navigate, guv! Can't see a bloody thing! I've gone blind!"

Unable to answer while holding his breath, Talos hefted Maymon over one shoulder and carried his writhing body to the exit. He rapidly entered the key release code into the lock panel, but the door didn't respond. The alarms began to wail in a higher pitch as the smoke permeated the air in the entire room, bringing the noxious fumes to a critical level.

Talos punched the non-responsive control panel

with his fist again and again until the mechanism finally loosened. Then he grabbed the exposed circuits and literally ripped them from the wall, ignoring the pain and shock to his hand and arm. The door hissed and opened an inch, then stopped in its track. The alarms wailed louder and an unseen blast of air blew hard in his face in an attempt to force the smoke back from the small opening.

Groggy from lack of air, Talos staggered and fell to his knees, refusing to take a breath. With Maymon still draped over his shoulder, Talos crumbled to the floor fingers prying at the small opening, struggling to remain conscious for as long as possible. He sat hard on the ground, back pressed to the door, Maymon squirming to pull free of his weakening grasp. His last lucid thought was a regret at having ignored his heart's desire, of never having the courage to surrender his heart and body to the human's touch.

Chapter Eight

Squirming out from under Talos' dead weight, Maymon wheezed and coughed, blearily looking around the thick, distorted room.

"Come on, guv! This is *not* the time for a nap." Shoving his smaller fingers through the tiny opening in the doorway, Maymon heaved and pulled. Bracing one foot against the doorframe he jerked back on the sliding panel, slowly forcing it open.

Alarms screeched at an appalling level and the door continued to attempt to shut on them every inch of the way. Maymon put his back to the door jamb and his booted foot to the door edge and shoved until Talos' propped-up body fell through the opening. He jumped free and grabbed hold of his fallen companion.

Straining under the burden of Talos' massive weight, Maymon pulled and stumbled, dragging the Hunter through the opening and out into the clear air of the corridor. Once free of their obstructing bodies, the door slammed back into place, sealing the gas inside. No trace of the deadly green smoke could be seen floating in the corridor air.

Near sightless, with eyes swollen and red, Maymon coughed and sputtered, still dragging Talos down the hallway by one arm unsure of where to go or when to stop.

"Might wanta be thinking about dropping a few stones after this." Maymon gagged and coughed, a deep rattling sound that echoed off the corridor walls. "Bloody hell, you're heavier 'an three whales and me ship's anchor!"

Once the air smelled cleaner, Maymon sagged against a wall, sliding his back down the smooth, cold surface to land in a heap on the corridor floor. He immediately fumbled over the contours of the Hunter's body, deft, anxious fingers searching for a pulse at the curve of Talos' neck and jaw.

The alarms continued their deafening blare, and Maymon was dimly conscious of a flood of shiny gray people brushing by him. Someone spoke to him, but he ignored the tinny sounding voice. All of his concentration was focused on the one solid reliable thing left in his life -- this massive beast of a creature who had saved his life and now owned his body and soul.

Finding a pulse despite his shaking hand, Maymon sighed audibly and relaxed against the wall, his hand moving down to rub absently over the smooth nubs of cartilage on the Hunter's chest. Maymon comforted himself with the slow rise and fall of wall of hard muscle beneath his hand, but the slight rattle and rasp of air as it entered and exited brought a deep frown to his tear-streaked face. After a few minutes, the rock hard body under his hand moved.

Wheezing audibly, Talos slowly roused, pulling himself upright, one hand grabbing onto Maymon's as it stroked over his chest. Virtually blind, Maymon felt

Talos heave to his feet. The Hunter called out, "It's tactan gas! Shut down the air flow."

Someone walked near them and Maymon heard a voice he didn't recognize answer in a tinny voice, "Got it." The footsteps moved away again and the voice added in a distant, clipped, professional tone, "Shut down Cabin matrix 12 delta. System purge already in progress. Secure the area."

Suddenly the alarms stopped. All Maymon could hear was the shuffle of feet and the labored wheezing of Talos' breathing. Nothing but blurred streaks of color and light penetrated his vision. He rubbed furiously at his burning eyes, desperate to have back the asset of sight in this bizarre, confusing world. He clung to the solid presence of Talos at his side, pleased the Hunter still had a firm hold on him.

A reedy swish of air brushed by his cheek and Talos' deep raspy tones rumbled in his ear. "Stop that. It'll only make it worse." His fists were gently stopped from grinding against his eyes by a larger, stronger hand.

Maymon allowed his arms to be pushed down and then immediately brought one back up when it was released. He felt Talos grab it again and hold on, silently forcing Maymon to leaving his face alone.

Maymon twisted slightly in the grip, more out of habit to test its strength than out of a desire to be let go. "What was that?"

Talos coughed and choked, the air making a tight hissing noise as he spoke. "A pellet. Mercs like them. Small, contained. Activated by sensors that can detect body heat. This one was filled with a poisonous gas, tactan."

Grimacing, Maymon placed both of his palms on Talos' bare chest and leaned close, voice loud and indignant. "Someone tried to *kill us*? Already? Just sailed into port, for Lord's sake!" Ruefully he added, "Usually takes a bit longer for death threats to come me way."

Talos walked away from the chaos in the hall, dragging a reluctant, stumbling, blind Maymon along with him. "Not *us*, me. Tactan kills Oracans, and about nine other species, almost immediately, if we inhale it. Ruptures our lungs." He paused to cough. Maymon could hear the big Hunter working hard to draw in a deep breath before continuing down the corridor. "It doesn't affect humans the same way. Your eyes, nose and throat will suffer some, but you'll be all right."

The world around Maymon blurred past in a rush of color and sound. Suddenly helpless and lost, he relived the rush of emotions that had nearly overwhelmed him when he had seen Sterns dead at his feet and his other loyal mates slaughtered by Perkins and his mutinous minions.

A cold wave of fear washed through his blood and Maymon realized how alone and isolated he really was in this strange place and time. The only connection he had to his former life was this hulking, possessive creature manhandling him through a noisy crowd of odd people he couldn't see, protecting him and taking him to a place of safety, caring for him in a way no one else had before.

Maymon fumbled his hands up the arm that gripped the front of his shirt, and latched onto Talos' thick wrist and forearm, thankful for the solid feel of the Hunter's presence. "Still can't see a bloody thing, guv."

"You need to see that doctor we were talking about." Talos took another a deep, rattling breath, adding, "Maybe we both do."

A resurgence of his earlier panic over the doctor surfaced. Maymon jerked and twisted out of Talos' grip. He squinted and blinked hard, unable to see which way to run. Turning, he took flight but ran straight into a corridor wall. Maymon never even hit the ground. A pair of familiar brawny arms grabbed him around his waist and he found himself deftly thrown over a hard-ridged shoulder once more.

Dangling upside down, Maymon scrambled for a secure hold, but found only the Hunter's bare skin. Legs and arms flailing in the air, he bellowed into Talos' naked back.

"Put me down, you over-grown, bloody son of a dung-eating sea serpent. You black-hearted bastard, you—." The sound of a swat echoed through the corridor before the sharp sting had a chance to register with the young pirate. Silence fell for only a moment before Maymon added in a quiet, exasperated voice, "You have *got* to stop doing *that*."

***

Striding through the double doors to the space station's medical unit, Talos paused to look around the unfamiliar room, a struggling, cursing Maymon still over one shoulder. Scenting the air, he let his nose lead the way. He shouldered past several stunned medical people to stand before a beautiful, if stern-looking, redheaded woman. Wheezing slightly, he grunted and tossed Maymon onto an empty medical bed directly beside her.

In her mid-thirties, Dr. Jaclyn Rice was slender, fit and well endowed. As the chief medical officer employed by the space station's corporate headquarters, she ran a tight, very professional department. Her sick bay was neat and tidy and organized. She frowned on her patients being dragged through the door, kicking and screaming, to be literally dropped at her side.

Breaking away from a conversation with a young, awe-struck nurse, Rice was just barely able to stop herself from grabbing the Hunter's hands and pushing him away from the young man he had just thrown down. She had never met this being before, but she knew an Oracan when she saw one and knew better than to touch him unprotected. She grabbed Maymon's shoulder instead. "What in heaven's name are you doing? Don't be so rough!"

Talos planted a hand in the middle of Maymon's squirming chest and pinned him to the bed. "He's been treated worse in his life. He'll be fine."

Grabbing a small pitcher of liquid from the bedside table, Talos sniffed it, then unceremoniously poured it over Maymon's face, targeting his swollen eyes. "He's been exposed to tactan gas." He watched as Maymon's struggles lessened after the splash of cold water in his eyes, but the pirate still pressed the heels of both hands hard into his eyes.

As seconds ticked by, Talos' instinctive need to protect the suffering young man, was apparent as he off-handedly jerked his chin at Maymon and casually suggested to the doctor, "You might want to do something about that soon before he digs his eyes out. Marius said you'd be expecting him anyway, so here he is, Doc."

Bleary-eyed and squinting, Maymon rallied long enough to mutter curiously, "Doctor? A wench?"

Talos and Dr. Rice both glanced at Maymon then ignored him to trade defiant stares. Rice turned away first to pry open Maymon's streaming eyes and flash a pocket light in them. Maymon yelped and flinched away.

Rice turned to the nurse she had been talking with earlier. "Get me an amp of epirylsone, please, Amy."

The nurse nodded and hurried off with more than one appreciative, backward glance at the two men.

Rice turned to Talos and demanded, "Was anyone else contaminated by the tactan?"

"Only me." Talos inhaled, but still felt the air struggle to enter his swollen airways. "The cabin's sealed and a security team was there. It should be under control."

Rice glared at him as if the situation was his fault. She broke away to check Maymon's eyes a second time. This time the pirate lay still under her touch, inhaling deeply when she leaned near. Rice didn't even notice, but Talos did. He couldn't blame the young pirate, as Rice's personal scent was fresh with a faint floral touch.

Brusque and all business, Rice demanded, "How did it get on the station? It's illegal." She made it sound as if he wouldn't know that.

Irritated by her attitude, Talos shrugged his

massive shoulders and sarcastically quipped, "That's the sixty-four dollars question, sweetheart."

Rice paused in her examination of Maymon and frowned at the unfamiliar phrase and the less than cordial endearment.

Taking advantage of the lull in interest in him, Maymon moved to get up. Talos glared at him and growled, "Stay put, pirate."

Rice looked from Talos to Maymon and back to the Hunter, her stern expression becoming even more closed and severe. "Pirate?" Her eyes narrowed and she almost spat her next few words out. "So you're the *Bounty Hunter*." She made 'Bounty Hunter' sound like a obscene, genetic mutation.

Bristling at her tone, Talos said, "Got it right on the nose, sister."

Maymon tried again to take advantage of their divided attention to ease off the bed. Glare focused on Rice, Talos still managed to instantly reach out and push the pirate back in place despite Rice's objecting yelp.

"Stop that! Get your hands off him."

Amy rushed back to the bedside and handed Rice a loaded injector, interrupting any further discussion or manhandling. Rice gave Talos a disgusted stare. She injected Maymon's arm, nearly missing the way Maymon flinched at the sudden unexpected jab of pain. "This will dissipate the effects of the poison." She patted Maymon on the shoulder comfortingly. "You'll feel better soon."

Glaring up at Talos, she harshly asked, "And this is your 'bounty'? A defenseless young man, a living being?"

Maymon's eyesight improved as the swelling of his lids rapidly decreased. Squinting, he tried to focus on the commanding, female voice beside him. "You're the doctor?" He stopped rubbing his eyes to peer at Rice, a leering smile brightening his tear-streaked face. When the doctor ignored him to turn indignantly back to face the Hunter, Maymon relaxed and watched the two argue over him.

"Defenseless?" Talos coughed and his wheezing turned audible again. "Listen, sister, I don't know who you've been talking to, but this 'defenseless young man' wasn't on this station thirty croms before he'd picked the pockets of a dozen people, started a brawl, destroyed a bar and broke more laws than you and I put together even know about."

Rice placed an audio magnifier over Talos' chest to listen to his lungs while he talked. A flash of concern marred her flawless forehead, then she readjusted her hypo to change the dosage and primly injected Talos' arm.

Drawing in a tentative, less-labored breath, Talos added, "If I were you, I'd be more worried about *your* sick bay than *my* pirate."

"*Your* pirate?" Rice's voice rose, her contempt easily heard.

Moving toe-to-toe with the five-foot six-inch tall woman, Talos leaned down and yelled back. "Yeah, sister, *my* pirate."

Undaunted, Rice frowned up into Talos' towering face, one finger stabbing at the fabric of his weapons' sash crisscrossing his broad, heaving chest.

118

"Well, *now* he's MY patient and I'll thank you to *leave* so I can get started on his exam."

"You'll be the one looking meself over?" Maymon leered at Rice through still half-swollen eyelids, and then shot a broad grin at Talos. "Thanks, guv. Should have said the doc was a beautiful lass. I take back all those things I cursed at you." A thoughtful look crossed his face, and he pursed his chapped lips. "All except that part at the very last." He frowned while one hand rubbed his right butt cheek. "You *gotta* stop hitting me stern."

Rice spun back to face Talos, outrage written all over her face again. "You *hit* him? You exposed him to tactan gas *and* you hit him?"

Giving a child-like, innocent pout, Maymon jumped into the conversation before Talos could comment. "Tis true, I'm sorry to say. m'lady. Could you check me body for bruises?" A sly, hopeful light danced in his blood-shot eyes while his young, smooth face remained the picture of fresh innocence.

Talos snorted and walked away, calling over his shoulder. "Call me when you're done with him, Doc. I'll be in the shuttle bay checking on my ship's repairs."

Maymon quickly pushed himself into a sitting position, panic replacing the innocent smirk. "Hold on there, guv!" He reached out and grabbed Rice's sleeve, tugging on it to get her attention as she continued to glare at the Hunter. "He said that vile smoke could kill him. Are you sure he should be leaving?"

Raising a questioning eyebrow, Rice studied the stoic Hunter, obviously waiting for him to tell her how he felt.

Smiling at the unexpected show of concern, Talos shrugged off the doctor's critical, questioning stare. He winked at Maymon, softly reassuring him "I'm fine." Darting a harder look at Rice, he added, "You just take care of the Runt, Doc. I'm used to taking care of myself."

Rice shrugged. "You like to play God with people's lives." She glanced down at Maymon briefly before staring Talos in the eyes. "I'm glad to see you include your own in that little fantasy."

"Yeah, playing God is fun." Talos gave her a mirthless grin. "I could almost be a doctor."

Wordlessly seething, Rice turned back to Maymon. She touched a pad at the head of the bed and the transparent walls surrounding them suddenly turned opaque, blocking Maymon from Talos' sight.

Turning back, Talos appeared at the open doorway to the cubicle and spent a few moments watching the out-of-place young pirate relentlessly flirt with Rice before interrupting. "Dr. Rice."

Startled, Rice spun around to face him. He nodded at Maymon and murmured, "Don't let him out of here on his own. It's not safe." He glanced at Maymon's swollen eyes, tear-streaked face and torn clothes. He warned, "For anyone."

Rice paused, then nodded in reluctant agreement.

"And Runt?" Maymon looked up at Talos expectantly. Talos' voice became soft and appreciative. "Thanks for back there." A glimmer of pride marked his tone. "You're one tough little shit."

Shrugging, Maymon tugged at the band on his

wrist and beamed at the Hunter. "Always pay back a debt. You save me life, I save yours, guv. True mates, eh?"

Slightly unsettled by Maymon's choice of intimate wording, Talos only nodded, then walked away. Listening to the sounds of Maymon's playful, flirtatious chatter with the medical staff as he walked, Talos ground his teeth until they ached. He never realized before how much like a disease guilt could be, growing and twisting inside a person. Or how invasive and powerful the desire to own another creature body and soul could be.

***

Once Talos reached the restricted area of the main docking bay, he checked over the remaining damage to his ship. The crew of human technicians working on it was small due the high level of security clearance required by anyone who worked on an Oracan vessel, so the repairs were going slowly. Any number of worlds would pay an indecent amount of riches to know how Oracan time-traveling technology worked on their ships. Talos would have had to do all of the work himself if any of the damage had been to the engines. As it was only the stabilizers, one weapons housing, and a portion of the hull had been severely damaged.

A new stabilizer element had been acquired and Talos had instructed the crew to leave it for him to install. He didn't like anyone inside the main workings of his fighter, even crew with the proper security clearances.

As it was, once this crew had finished with what

121

they could repair, he would meticulously inspect every inch of the ship to be sure nothing had been tampered with. The dangerous life of a successful Hunter left nothing to chance. They learned to trust others, even friends, only so far. That was a lesson his younger brother hadn't learned well enough.

While he worked beside the technicians, several small ships docked in at the far end of the bay, mostly small shuttles from nearby planets. Preoccupied, Talos ignored them all until one particular group of visitors disembarked from a larger, long-distance shuttle.

Attracted by an odor that made his nostrils flare and the roof of his mouth itch, Talos could tell from their heavy scent that the passengers were Venucian. One cloaked and hooded visitor paused to cast a furtive glance toward the Oracan fighter, then stalked away from the disembarking crowd and hurriedly walked out of the bay. Curiosity piqued, Talos scented the air again, but couldn't place the cloaked man's scent past the point that he was human. His sensitive nostrils were overwhelmed by the strong, dense smell of the musky Venucians.

Too far away to see the figure's shadowed face well, Talos pushed the mystery aside and returned to the business of repairing the *Dango*. He needed to get a certain pirate out of his life before his instinctive urges forced him to compromise his sworn oaths.

***

Sedated, Maymon lay naked on the sick bay bed, covered from the waist down with only a light blanket. Old knife wound scars and healed burns dotted his tanned skin, their ragged outlines raised and dark against his smooth, hairless skin. His long hair trailed over the edge of the bed and tiny spots of color tinkled here and there where numerous hidden glass beads reflected the harsh lights over the examination table.

Dr. Rice ran a handheld diagnostic scanner over Maymon's body while Amy assisted by checking the pirate's vital signs.

Rechecking the monitor's readings, Rice raised her eyebrows in surprise. "Well, that's impressive. Fourteen different diagnoses ranging from mildly incidental to near life-threatening."

She glanced down at the peacefully slumbering young man in her care. Relaxed and unguarded, his fine facial features showed his good looks and youth, despite the weathered condition of his skin. Rice felt a surge of protectiveness shoot through her and she gently pushed a lock of snarled hair off Maymon's brow. In a soft, maternal voice she complimented the young, flirtatious rascal. "Very impressive, Aidan."

Rice handed off the scanner to Amy and then rubbed her hands together, actually looking forward to the next part of the procedure. "Let's get him cleaned up. I'm curious to see what he looks like under all this dirt and grime." She fingered a stiff, twisted braid full of beads and bits of bright fabric. "I don't think there's any hope for his hair."

Shuddering, Amy cringed and shook her head. "Too many parasites, even if they are dead. I've never seen real lice and crabs before."

Rice chuckled despite the unpleasant task ahead of them. "He's an education, all right." She picked up a cutting implement and grabbed a length of matted hair.

"He'll thank us later." A sharp piece of metal fell out of one of the braids in her hand and two slivers of what looked like bone poked through near her fist. She glanced at Maymon's innocent looking face, and cautiously pulled the items from his hair. Examining a rough sliver of metal with a razor sharp edge, she muttered, "At least I hope so."

Rice cut while Amy gathered the hidden treasures they found in each new section of hair they removed and placed them in a transparent container for safe keeping. Rice couldn't help but think all of them belonged in some museum devoted to ancient Earth history, much like their owner.

***

Back in the docking bay, time passed quickly for Talos and soon the *Dango's* repairs were nearly finished. He released the maintenance crew once their work was completed then began the long arduous task of examining every inch of the ship, including every piece of equipment and system on board.

While outside of the fighter inspecting the hull repairs, the lingering scent from the large shuttle suddenly triggered a memory for Talos. Disbelieving what his own senses told him, the Hunter scented the air again then growled, "Christ! Now I remember who belongs to that stench." Dropping the tool in his fist to the ground, he set off in search of the prey that dared to invade his home territory.

Chapter Nine

The interior of the *Pink Tentacle* was dimly lit, the music was loud and the patrons were engaged in boisterous conversations at every table and corner in the room. The aftereffects of the recent brawl were obvious only in the cracked reflective surface behind the bar and the limited number of tables and chairs available for use.

A hunched figure in a dark brown cloak, face hidden by the shadows of his raised hood, sat at the bar. The man sipped a cylinder of green liquid and engaged the chatty bartender in conversation.

Micas, the amicable, portly, purple-skinned humanoid was both barkeeper and owner of the popular establishment. He enjoyed talking to all his varied customers, especially ones who tipped large credits like this one did.

Micas leaned one meaty hip against the edge of the lower sink behind the bar and wiped at a permanent stain on the countertop as he avidly answered the stranger's questions. "The Bounty Hunter? Who wouldn't remember him? Not many like that around here. Big. And deadly, too. Wouldn't want him on *my* trail."

The stranger nodded and nervously glanced

125

over his shoulder at the crowded room behind him. "Was he alone?"

"Nah." Micas pointed a towel-filled hand toward the upper levels of the station. "Came in with the Commander, but he left with that little thief of his."

The stranger leaned closer and casually asked, "Thief?"

"Yeah, that pirate he brought on board." Micas grimaced then laughed, gesturing at the damaged areas around the bar. "Little monkey had this place in an uproar practically as soon as he got here."

"Really?" The stranger's voice was smoothly sympathetic to the bar owner's concerns. "Then you'll be happy to see the last of him around here, I imagine."

"Hell, no!" Micas filled an order for a waiting server and then turned back to stranger. "He can drink in my bar anytime he wants."

"But you said he practically destroyed your place." The stranger glanced at a splintered barstool beside him.

"Sure did." Micas practically beamed with pleasure. "And now everyone knows this is the most entertaining place on the station. Business has tripled." He filled another order and moved off to wait on customers signaling him from the other end of the bar. Before going too far he paused to proclaim, "I just love those two," then hurried away.

The stranger sighed and sipped his drink, head bowed in thought, oblivious to the loud music and even louder patrons milling all around him.

***

Pausing just inside the grand open doorway to

the *Pink Tentacle*, Talos and Marius scanned the crowded bar. Talos scented the air as he moved through the throng of happy patrons enjoying each other's company. Halfway across the room, he pushed past two well-dressed businessmen who seemed out of place in the lower class lounge. The men openly stared at him for a brief moment, then immediately left the bar. Intrigued by their presence in the seedy bar, Talos visually tracked them until they disappeared from sight.

Turning back to the task at hand, Talos tested the air again for the scent he had been following since he left the docking bay, then strode directly to the hooded man hunched over at the bar. Marius followed at his side, taking his lead from the Hunter.

When they reached the bar, Talos yanked the hood down off the man's head, drawling, "Well, look what the cat dragged in. It's one of Barlow's chief rats. Who opened the sewers and let you out?"

Exposed, Barlow's personal aide, Sherman, paled and darted his wide-eyed gaze from Hunter to human and back again. Sherman fidgeted on his stool and tapped a random tempo out on the glass in his shaking hands. "Talos of Menalon, what a pleasure to see you again."

Talos moved close enough to brush his chest against the man's shoulder. "I'll bet."

Sherman slid off the stool, but remained in place at the bar. His glance darted around the room, lingering longingly at the exit. Finally he managed a weak nod for Marius. "And greetings to you, Commander Webb. Lovely station you have here." He plastered a false smile on his face. "Can I help you with something?"

"Mr. Sherman. Your processing papers said you were just passing through, picking up a connecting shuttle to the Delta Quadrant." Marius moved in closer to Sherman, blocking his route to the front door.

Sherman edged back, hemmed in by the two of them and the bar. "Missed my boarding time. I'll catch the next one. In the meantime, I was just enjoying a peaceful drink after my rather long journey."

Licking at his dry lips before venturing a glance up at the towering Hunter, Sherman straightened and boldly announced, "The bartender here was just telling me how good you've been for his business, Talos. You and your new companion, the young human with the colorful personality. The way he described him, he almost sounds like an old-fashioned pirate."

Talos glowered down at the smaller human and stepped closer, forcing Sherman to bend backwards over the bar to put a little distance between himself and the looming, unhappy face of the Oracan.

***

Outside of Talos' suite, the two businessmen from the bar stood in front of the lock panel. They both glanced up and down the deserted hallway, then one pulled a small gadget from his pocket and held it up to the retinal scan lock. When nothing happened, he adjusted the setting, then reapplied it to the lock. He repeated the change three times with no effect on the locking mechanism.

On the third attempt, a security team of four officers rounded the corner and spotted the men just as they spotted the officers. The senior officer stepped forward and called out, "Hold up there! Step away from the panel and drop the scanner."

Pocketing the handheld gadget, both men immediately ignored the officer's command, as they turned and ran down the opposite end of the hallway.

Weapons drawn, the security team instantly gave chase.

***

Still cowering under Talos' menacing presence, Sherman lifted his drink to sip it, spilling most of it on the bar.

"Listen up, you rat-faced flunky." Talos let his voice deepen and his r's trill, showing his displeasure. "You tell Barlow the Council's wise to him now. They know he's threatened a Hunter and your presence here is interfering with a legal Hunt."

When the aide slowly tried to slide out from under Talos' glare, Marius braced an arm on the bar making it impossible for Sherman to slip away. He held his back ramrod straight and presented the man with his best authoritative persona. "Threatening an appointed officer of the law, which all bounty Hunters are, is a serious offense, Mr. Sherman. You might want to remind Mr. Barlow of that."

Confronted on all sides, Sherman paled, flustered by the dual assault. He stuttered, his eyes darting back and forth between the two. "I-I'm sure this has all been a misunderstanding, Commander."

Bracing his arms on either side of Sherman, Talos breathed heavily in the man's face, smelling the fear radiating off him in waves. "Well, understand this. If Barlow makes one move toward my property before

Council gives the high sign, he'll be getting measured for a wooden box. That's if there's anything left of him to put in a box." He stared hard at the man. "And that goes for any of his flunkies that get in the way, too."

Barely able to manage a high-pitched croak of false bravado, Sherman demanded, "Are you threatening me?"

Making sure he touched only cloth, Talos punctuated each word with a tap on Sherman's chest. "No, I'm giving it to you straight, Sherman." The man flinched with each firm rap like it was a heavy blow. "Barlow tries to follow through on his threats and he'll find himself on the receiving end of a Ritual Hunt."

Gasping, a look of sheer terror crossed over Sherman's face.

Talos leaned closer to whisper in Sherman's ear, forcing the man to try and meld with the surface of the bar. "And they don't capture for bounty, they hunt *prey*. There won't even be enough left over to tell what species he was, let alone *who* he was."

Gathering his courage, Sherman jerked away, knocking over several stools in his haste to gain distance. His wide eyes shot to the timepiece on the wall behind the bar. "Well, look at the time. I'll need to rush if I don't want to miss that shuttle again." Sherman walked backwards as he talked, tripping slightly over the fallen stools in his path. "I'll be certain to inform my employer we chatted. Good day to you both." Sherman spun around and fled the bar, not even bothering to pick up his credits from the bar.

Standing side-by-side, Talos and Marius stared after him. Marius crossed his arms over his chest and sighed. "That went well."

Talos snorted and idly picked up the stool Sherman had been sitting on and placed it upright. "I thought so. He's still breathing, isn't he?"

Making his way toward the exit, Talos added, "Come on. I need to go check on the Runt. You can referee. Your doc hasn't warmed up to me yet." His gave Marius a suggestive smile. "She's got a great pair of big, brown eyes."

Frowning, Marius fell into step beside the Hunter. "Dr. Rice has green eyes. Very lovely green eyes."

Once in the outer corridor, they turned left and began the long trek to the other end of the station toward the sick bay. "Really? Haven't looked at her face yet."

Suddenly catching the ancient Earth slang reference for the doctor's well-endowed figure, Marius groaned. "Christ, She must just *love* you."

"Hard to believe, but I don't think so." Talos grinned devilishly and began striding faster down the corridor, adding, "Let's go ask her."

"Why do I think I should go back to my office instead?" Marius stopped in mid-stride and pressed a hand to the communications device in his right ear. Glancing up at Talos he said, "My men just picked up a couple of guys with a retina reproduction scanner near your suite. They were on the shuttle with your man Sherman."

"More of Barlow's goons. Too bad he hired a couple of boobs." Talos smirked and took off at a trot, calling over his shoulder, "And I ain't talking about the

Doc this time either."
Marius groaned and followed.

Chapter Ten

This time when Talos entered the sick bay he took time to look around the large, well-lit room. Taking up most of the room were twenty-four individual beds placed in a semicircle, all easily viewed from a central monitoring station.

Transparent walls separated the beds on three sides, with large sliding doors on the end facing the station. Each unit boasted an array of high tech equipment. The cubicles were bright and sparkling clean, but cold and sterile. Talos doubted many human patients found much comfort in these surroundings. He hoped the staff made up for the bland atmosphere.

On one wall hung a colorful poster proclaiming "Support bacteria. It's the only culture some people have." He experienced a sudden stab of guilt at having left Maymon alone here.

Striding to the bed where he had left his pirate, Talos was surprised to find a scrubbed-clean, very young-looking man asleep on the bed. The human's hair came only to his hairless chin, and it's rich black color shone in the harsh light. Talos reached out and ran his hand through it, marveling at the silky texture. The heat radiating out from the man's scalp warmed his fingertips and ignited a fire in his chest. The human's

133

Laura Baumbach

scent had altered somewhat, but the underlying odor he
recognized as Maymon's own was stronger than ever.
Though he had been powerfully attracted to the wily
little human in his previous odoriferous, grime-coated,
disheveled state, this newly sheared and scrubbed
version was even more appealing.

Talos inhaled deeply, savoring the spicy musk of
Maymon's body, and letting it imprint itself on his brain
again in its purest form. The smell filled his senses and
his body automatically responded. His heart raced, his
groin tightened, and his eyes dilated as surges of
physical desire pulsed through him. Impossible as it
was, he wanted nothing more at this moment than to
claim the pirate as his own, brand him with his family's
mark, and permeate his flesh with his own scent.

Before Talos could act on his instinctive urges,
Marius joined him at the pirate's bedside. The
Commander let loose a low, amazed whistle. "Wow. If
I'd seen him outside of here, I wouldn't have recognized
him at first."

Growling between clenched teeth as he pushed
down his desires, Talos said, "I would have."

Before Marius could comment, Dr. Rice walked
out of an adjoining office. She spared a cold stare for
Talos. "I see you've returned for your property." Then
turned to warmly greet the Commander. "Hello,
Marius."

Talos noticed that Marius' smile reached both his
eyes and his lips, transforming his face into a softer,
more amicable expression. "Jaclyn."

Ignoring the mildly flirtatious conversation
between the other two, Talos demanded, "What'd you

do to him?"

Rice folded her arms under her ample breasts and glared. "I cleaned him up. His skin was tar-stained to the point of toxicity, and his hair was matted, full of dead lice and filth." She looked regretfully at the unsuspecting young man still peacefully sedated. "We *had* to cut most of it off."

Shaking his head, Talos continued running his hand through the shorter locks of hair on Maymon's head. The clean strands fell like warm water over his sensitive fingers. He stared down at Maymon, murmuring, "He's not going to be happy."

Both Marius and Rice did a double take, glanced at the gray-skinned hand embedded affectionately in Maymon's hair, and then stared at the massive, stoic Hunter.

Talos' eyes narrowed. "You think I don't care about his feelings?"

Rice looked at the gentle stroking of Maymon's head and frowned, her gaze steady and unflinching when she finally turned it on Talos. "It's not what I'd expect from one of your kind."

Removing his hand from Maymon's head, Talos planted his fists firmly on his hips and loudly asked, "What is it with you humans? No one else around this galaxy's allowed to have a heart? And if they do, they have to wear it on their sleeve? Wise up. Scientists proved a long time ago Earth wasn't the center of the universe. Humans just still think it is."

Marius raised a placating hand and patted the air in a calming gesture. "Just calm down. I'm sure Dr. Rice just meant that someone... like you... who...."

Cutting in before Marius could talk the dark cloud of anger off the Hunter's face, Dr. Rice flatly explained her earlier statement. "I meant, a cold-hearted species like yours."

"Oh, that helped." Marius sighed and threw his hands in the air, stepping to one side out of the verbal firing range.

Talos and Rice stood toe to toe, each glaring into the other's face from close range. Talos towered over the woman, but Rice met him head on.

Bellowing, Talos demanded, "Who the hell cut the kid's hair off without a thought about how he might feel about it?"

Arms crossed tightly on her chest, Rice yelled back, matching Talos' increasing volume. "He's all I was thinking about. What's best for him. Just like I thought about him when I had to repair the damage to his liver from the lethal doses of alcohol he's been drinking," she counted off each medical problem on her fingers, "the tuberculosis in his lungs, and remove his intestinal tumor." She shook her fingers in Talos' face. "I made a pound of lice disappear, along with a huge colony of crabs." Bright spots of red glowed in her cheeks and she was breathing hard.

"Are you saying I'm fit or I be dying, Doc?"

Startled by the rough, slurred, cockney-tinged voice, Talos stopped in mid-rebuttal. He and Dr. Rice blinked at each other a moment before it registered who was doing the interrupting. They both turned to look down at the object of their argument.

Appearing marginally awake, Maymon lifted his head from the thin pillow and surveyed his surroundings and his own physical body. He shut his eyes for a few seconds then forced them wide in an obvious effort to focus. Groping at the thin blanket covering his lower half, Maymon groggily lifted the edge of the blanket and peeked under it. He looked surprised, then confused, and then faintly pleased at his naked state.

Speech slow and heavily slurred, he looked pointedly at Rice. "I be naked. I can only hope me present state of undress means something meaningful," he paused to forced back open his falling eyelids, speech nearly indistinct, "has passed between us, m'lady."

"Of course not, Aidan." Rice blushed and self-consciously tugged at the open collar of her lab coat.

Talos moved closer to Maymon's side, drawing the pirate's flirtatious attention away from the doctor. "Hey, runt."

A bright smile lit up the young man's face. "Morning, guv." Talos thought he could see a shadow of relief in the black eyes, as well. "Hoped I'd be seeing you again."

Maymon leaned sideways, almost tipping himself off the bed. Talos caught him and pushed him gently back into place. Maymon chuckled and then whispered to Talos, shooting a questioning look at Rice. "I think me virtue's been breached."

Talos smirked at Rice, but turned a neutral expression back to face Maymon and innocently asked, "That upsets you?"

Maymon's eyes popped open, an offended tone in his rough, sleepy voice. "Course it does, man!" Both

Laura Baumbach

hands gestured futilely in the air, vaguely pointing in Rice's direction. "I weren't awake for it! How can a man brag about it if he don't remember it!"

Rice blushed deeper, but she stepped forward and put on her best professional persona. "I assure you, Aidan, nothing unseemly happened while you were sedated. Removing your clothing just made it easier to attend to your needs."

Winking at Talos, Maymon whispered, "Told you, guv!"

Exasperated, Rice gritted her teeth and forced her voice to stay level. "Your *medical* needs."

Despite the light, playful lilt to the pirate's tone, Talos could smell a level of fear radiating from the young man, an uncertainty about what had been done to him while he was asleep and at the mercy of strangers.

Suddenly protective and impatient, Talos turned to Rice. His voice dropped lower and there was an automatic note of unintended menace in it as he demanded, "Are you finished with him?"

Slightly taken back by the abrupt change, Rice frowned and cast a troubled look at Marius, who appeared to be content to just watch the interplay between the three. Marius just lifted an eyebrow in response to her glance, but his eyes darted to the Hunter's hand as it gently stroked through the young pirate's hair again.

"Just about. I want to talk to Aidan about a few things first." Rice waved a hand toward the doorway, dismissing Talos without a glance. "You can wait outside."

138

"I'll stay." Talos' deep voice thundered in the room. Talos paused, surprised by the sound. He made a visible effort to calm down, one hand casually stroking over his chest once.

Rice blinked several times at the unexpected response, but refused to back down. The tension in the room between the two immediately escalated.

Marius and Maymon both remained silent, but observant as the argument went back and forth like a heated game of catch.

"This is confidential, between doctor and patient," Rice snapped, unused to being challenged in her own sick bay.

"I'm responsible for him." The menace hadn't disappeared from his voice completely, but suddenly conscious of it, Talos had it under better control. "I'm staying."

Rice narrowed her eyes at him and pulled her full, pink lips into a thin line. "No, you're not."

Talos tapped the cloth of her shoulder lightly with one finger. "No dame is..."

Mouth dropping open, Rice shifted her weight on her feet and took on a more aggressive stance, one well-manicured, but less than gentle, finger punching the thick webbing of the Hunter's weapons sash in return. "Dame?" Her voice rose with each new word. "What the hell is that?"

Widening his own stance as if preparing for a frontal assault, Talos planted his fists on his hips and snarled, "I'll tell you what it means, sister! I..."

Abruptly, a placating hand waved in the air between Talos and Rice, taking care not to touch either one of them. Talos glanced up to see that Webb had quietly moved to stand beside the two possessive combatants, a look of quiet concern mixed with a fair amount of amusement on his face.

Marius shrugged and suggested, "Maybe we could settle this by asking the patient what *he* wants."

Staring first at Marius, and then at each other, the Hunter and the doctor both turned to look at Maymon, the looks on their faces clearly showing they had almost forgotten he existed for the moment.

Ruefully, Rice smiled and laid a comforting hand on Maymon's bare arm. "Aidan, I'd like to discuss a few things of a very personal nature with you. I'm sure your *'friend'*", she shot a dismissing glare at Talos, "would understand if you wanted him to wait outside."

Speech still slow and indistinct, Maymon beamed and announced, "Got nothing to hide, Doc. Seems just about everyone here except maybe his Lordship here," Maymon gestured vaguely in Marius' direction, "has seen me whole self, including me pieces parts."

Brow furrowed in a confused frown, Marius murmured to no one in particular, "Pieces parts?"

Waving his hands over his lower torso, Maymon pointed at the small bulge between his legs. "The important parts of me body, mate, pieces of me privates. Me pieces parts." Fingering the edge of the bright white sheet, he lifted it and glanced under, a cheeky smile on his face. "Want a peek, me Lordship?"

An ominous rumble purred from Talos' chest and Marius carefully and quickly stilled the billowing fabric with a hand, staying far away from the pirate's groin. Barely able to hold back laughter, Marius cleared his throat and reassured Maymon. "I'll pass, thanks just the same."

Shrugging his acceptance, Maymon's attention darted back to Rice. "Then chat away, m'lady, I'm all yours." He folded his arms on his bare chest and planted his head firmly in the pillow, the picture of a man at ease with his surroundings. It only took a moment before he began to rub his left thumb over the first two fingertips of his left hand in a nervous, fidgety tempo. He twisted Talos' silver band on his wrist.

Noticing a change in Maymon's scent, Talos immediately moved closer to the pirate's bedside. He watched the rubbing motion increase in tempo the longer he waited for Rice to start talking and the stronger the smell of fear grew in the young pirate.

Rice shot an unhappy look at Talos, but didn't comment on his nearness. "Very well."

Voice softening, she looked at Maymon. "Aidan, I did an intensive examination of your body." Blushing, she ignored the adolescent, drugged leer he gave her. "All the way down to the cellular level. You've obviously had a hard life..."

Maymon jerked his head once in agreement and shrugged. "Been at sea since I was nigh on eight or thereabouts. Woulda gone earlier but a buccaneer's life didn't set well with me mum. I signed on the day after she died."

Taken back, Rice asked, "My lord, why?"

Maymon's speech was growing less slurred. He spread his arms open and raised his empty palms to the air in a "why else" gesture. "Hungry. Alley scraps don't fill a growing lad much. Need a trade to make your way in the world on your own. Sailing's a hard life, but better than most, as long as the Captain doesn't take a shine to using the cat too often." He flicked a hand in the air to illustrate his point.

Frowning, Rice looked from Marius to Talos for an answer. "The cat?"

"Flogger." A faint frown marred the doctor's beautiful face and Maymon searched for a better word to describe his meaning. "The rope, miss." He flinched and twisted to one side to show the thin tracings of rough-edged scars crisscrossing his back. "Hurts something fierce, it does. Leaves a bloody fine scar or two besides." He twisted back around then popped up to sit with his arms around his sheet-covered, bent legs, becoming more awake and restless with each passing sentence.

"I wondered what made those marks." Rice stepped around to look at his back closer, examining the old wounds with a new fascination. She lightly traced one scar down his back. "You were flogged?"

"Aye." Maymon cheerfully acknowledged the offense. "But not since I took over me own command. Though me first captain didn't take too kindly to repeating hisself." He tapped the side of his nose. "Turned into a right quick learner under his sail, I did."

Stuttering, Dr. Rice stepped away from the bed and pointed at Maymon's curved, lean, scarred body. "That's barbaric, you were only a child."

"Humans have a long history of mistreating their young." Talos rested a hand on Maymon's shoulder, earning him a bright smile from the pirate.

Rice bristled, but remained silent as Maymon proclaimed, "What don't kill you, makes you a stronger man." He shrugged and looked dubiously around him. "I lived."

"You *are* a strong man, Runt." Talos ran an affectionate hand down Maymon's bare back, enjoying the satiny feeling of the warm flesh.

Startled, Maymon stared at him a moment, a puzzled look on his face, then smiled and winked at the Hunter.

Rice huffed and pointedly ignored the increasingly intimate interaction between the two. "You may be a strong man, but you're not a well one." Smoothing out her lab coat, she crossed her arms over her chest and donned a serious expression. "And that brings us back to my original point. You're malnourished. Both your teeth and your eyesight have suffered from it, as well as your bone growth. I adjusted the astigmatism in your eyes while you were asleep, but I still need to finish repairing the damage to your teeth."

"She can do that?" Wide-eyed and open mouthed, Maymon turned to Talos, who merely nodded. Flummoxed, the pirate blinked several times and squinted, trying to focus on something across the room. He glanced up apologetically at Rice. "It's my misfortune to tell you, m'lady, I think you might have made a wee bit of a mistake with me eyes." He repeated his overly dramatic attempt to focus. "Everything's blurry and all wavy like." He suddenly snapped his head around and narrowed his eyes at Rice. "Was there rum in your potion what laid me out?"

Rice struggled to hide a laugh. "No, no rum,

Aidan. The medicine I gave you earlier was a sedative. You're still feeling its affects. Your vision will be perfect when it wears off." Rice turned away to check her equipment. "And this next part will only take a moment."

Still smiling, Rice looked at Marius and they exchanged amused, fond glances before Rice began selecting pieces of equipment to work with.

The rush of hormones in the air sizzled down Talos' spine with every breath he took. The air was ripe with the smell of his and Maymon's mutual attraction for each other, but the added stimulus of the other couple was almost too much for the Hunter to bear. He wanted to shut down his sense of smell, but it was one of his best defensive weapons. His need to protect the pirate was reaching overwhelming levels and his body refused to dampen any of its instinctive, primal functions.

Nurse Amy returned to the bedside, taking readings from the monitoring equipment using a small, glittering crystal device then pocketed it. The blinking, shiny gadget drew Maymon's attention. He frowned in disappointment when she slipped it into her pocket while she helped Rice prepare tools from the small selection on the bedside tray.

Talos engaged Marius in a quiet conversation, keeping one eye on Maymon. Amazed at the young man's behavior, he watched as the pirate did what came naturally to him.

Using the sheet to cover his slight of hand, Maymon casually and expertly picked Amy's pocket, relieving her of the bright, shiny object. Unfortunately, once he had it, he suddenly realized he didn't have anywhere to hide it. Startled by Amy as she unexpectedly moved away, he hurriedly slid the crystal under the sheet, hiding it in the bulge between his legs.

Amy only got a few feet away before she stopped and tapped her index finger in the air, obviously remembering something. She reached into her pocket and turned back around, a puzzled frown on her face. She bent down to examine the surrounding floor and looked under the bed.

Just as Maymon was about to pop the crystal into his mouth and swallow it, Talos stepped forward and took it away, prying it out of Maymon's unwilling fingers. Talos handed it back to Amy who gave Maymon an exasperated frown as she readjusted its settings. Talos wordlessly smacked Maymon's hand and forcefully shoved it under the sheet just as Rice turned back to the bed, a new hypo in hand.

Eyeing the array of medical tools yet to be used, Talos said, "While you're at it, Doc, maybe you can tell me why he's the only human that can touch me."

Attracted to the silver instrument, Maymon tried to take the hypo out of Rice's hand. Attention riveted on Talos, Rice calmly moved the hypo from Maymon's reach as if she was dealing with a curious, overactive toddler.

"He's probably the only one that wants to," Rice snapped.

"Listen, Sister..." The growl was back in the Hunter's voice but this time it was more aggressive than protective.

Marius immediately stepped forward. "Talos,

145

maybe you and I should wait outside. They're almost done here, right?" He looked hopefully at Rice.

"That won't be necessary, Marius." She turned to Talos. "I'd need a tissue sample from you if you really want to know why he's apparently the only human your skin doesn't burn."

"Fine. Take whatever you need."

"It'll be a pleasure." She handed the hypo to Amy. "Amy, would you finish up with Aidan for me while I peel some flesh from his keeper?"

The nurse flashed Maymon a smile. He flirtatiously returned it, adding a wink and a lopsided leer. Amy laughed and said, "Certainly Dr. Rice. I'd be happy to."

"Thank you." Rice leaned down and checked Maymon's still heavy-lidded eyes. "I'll be right back. While I'm gone, Amy will take good care of you, Aidan."

Maymon leered drunkenly up at the nurse. "I'll take that as a promise." He looked blearily at Rice, a serious expression falling over his now shockingly young-looking face, concern clouding his eyes. "I'll be thanking you to be kind to me 'keeper', m'lady. He's all the kin I got left now."

Rice frowned and swallowed hard, her eyes misting over slightly at the implied message from the stolen young man. "Aidan --."

Maymon fussed with the silver band on his wrist, interrupting her. "Says so right here. Meself belongs to him, so 'tis only just he belongs to me, too." He nodded solemnly and jerked his head in Talos' direction. "Be kind to him."

Rice patted his shoulder and pulled the hem of the sheet down on one corner, absentmindedly tucking him in. "For you, I will, don't worry."

Satisfied, Maymon turned his attention back to the waiting nurse. As he walked away with Marius and Rice, Talos glanced over his shoulder and his eyes met Maymon's dark ones staring back at him, a soft smile on the pirate's lips. Their gazes stayed locked together until Amy insisted Maymon lay down and give her his attention as she worked on his stained and decaying teeth.

Rounding the corner and entering the adjoining room, Talos took a seat on an exam table. Marius lounged in the doorway, one eye on Maymon and one on Rice.

Preparing her equipment, Rice approached Talos with a scalpel-like instrument extended in one hand. Her other hand held a small, clear plastic disc. "Open your mouth wide. I'll try to be careful and not make you gag." She gave Talos a challenging, amused smirk. "Too much."

Snorting his disdain, Talos said, "Don't worry, lady. Oracans don't have a gag reflex like humans." He leaned closer to her and let the menacing quality rumble back into his tone. "Lets us swallow things whole."

Rice inserted the instrument into his open mouth and quickly scraped a few cells off the lining of one cheek. "Why would you want to?" She wiped the cells onto the disc.

"Tradition. Oracans believe a person's soul rests in their heart and liver. In ancient times, they would eat those organs from fallen enemies. They had to be swallowed whole to preserve their power."

Adding a preservative to the disc, Rice paused and gave Talos a questioning glance.

Pleased by her shocked expression, Talos added, "Hearts are easy, but have you ever tried to swallow an entire liver?"

Turning back to her disc, Rice sniffed and said, "That's barbaric."

"Really? Several of your planet's civilizations practiced similar rituals." Talos jutted his squared chin toward the main sick bay and Maymon. "Even the Runt's ancestors had blood sacrifices. Probably still do."

Unable to deny it, Rice busied herself with the disc and silently fumed.

Idly playing with an array of small items lying on the counter by the door, Marius cocked his head toward Maymon. "Seems you and your pirate are a lot more alike than people might think." He glanced over his shoulder through the archway at the lively chattering young man in the next room. "Maybe he's right. Maybe you are 'kin'."

Feeling an odd burst of pride, Talos straightened and nodded. "In spirit, the Runt is a lot like an Oracan."

Rice glanced out the door, too, and shot back at both of them, "Well, in reality, gentlemen, he's a lot like an abandoned child."

Scoffing, Talos snorted, "You *are* a crazy dame. He's at least twenty years old and I doubt there's an innocent bone left in his entire body."

Leaning against the counter behind her, Rice shook her head. "In terms of life experience, maybe, but he's completely naive to this world and its inhabitants."

Moving to stand beside the doctor in a wordless show of support, Marius sighed and cast another glance over his shoulder at Maymon. "I have to agree with Jaclyn, Talos. Larceny and immoral inclinations aside, he's still an innocent here."

Frowning, Talos stood up from the exam table and stretched, flexing his body. "He'll do fine. I'm taking care of him. He can handle it."

A bellow of outrage from the outer room shattered the air. Marius and Rice exchanged stunned looks while Talos ran from the room and raced back to the pirate's side. He found Amy trying to calm down a nearly hysterical Maymon.

Standing naked at the bedside, Maymon stared into a hand mirror. He ran his fingers frantically through what was left of his hair again and again. Looking up, his anguished eyes locked on Talos as the Hunter entered the room.

"She stole me hair! Scalped me, she did." The doctor arrived at Maymon's side and anguish turned to anger as he rounded on her. "Why would a body do such a bloody awful thing?"

"That's what I asked her." Talos tossed Rice an 'I –told-you-so' glance then nodded toward the pirate's naked state, surprised by his own reluctance to have others see the young man unclothed. "You might want to grab the sheet, Runt, you're catching a breeze."

Maymon looked down, shrugged and then wrapped himself in the discarded bed sheet in a rapid series of jerky, forceful whips of the fabric. "Got nothing to be ashamed of, guv."

"Please, calm down, Aidan." Rice laid a hand on

his shoulder and he instantly shrugged if off. A flash of regret registered on Rice's face then she schooled her expression into a neutral frown. "I had to cut it. It was full of parasites." His wrinkled brow and angry, squinted eyes clearly said the pirate had no idea what she was talking about. "*Dead bugs* and it was tangled far beyond saving."

Devastated, Maymon danced away as she reached to console him again. A fair distance from her he clutched the sheet to his waist with both fists held so tight his knuckles turned white. "But it was me hair, a living part of me. And the beads were the last of me mum I had. What other parts did you cut off while you had me drugged and at your mercy?"

Maymon blanched white and frantically pulled the sheet around his middle open to double check that he was still completely intact. He shamelessly bent his knees and swayed his hips to be sure all of his dangling bits were still hanging there. His sigh of relief was audible to everyone in the room.

Marius covered his mouth with one hand to hide the smile tugging at his lips. "Dr. Rice was only looking after your best interests, making you healthy."

Snorting in disgust, Maymon vowed, "If healthy means having part of your spirit cut off, then I'll thank you to be leaving me on the sickly side of things." He tried to add his normal wild hand gestures to the conversation, but found had trouble keeping the sheet in place at the same time. He finally decided on using one hand to hold the fabric low on his hips. Then he stalked over to the Hunter and slapped Talos in the middle of his broad chest with his free hand. "Told you doctors couldna be trusted."

Concerned, Rice pleaded, "Your beads are here. We saved them." She offered Maymon a clear container of brightly colored pieces of round glass. He snatched it from her hand and held it close to his chest, scowling at Rice when she tried to console him. "Aidan, I --."

Spinning around, Maymon raised one finger in the air to silence her. Taking on an imperious attitude, he lifted his slender nose in the air and told her, "Be wanting nothing more from you, m'lady. Nothing at all."

Maymon gathered the sheet more tightly around his body then realized it belonged to the doctor. Belligerently, he released his hold on the sheet and stiffly handed it to Rice, indifferent to the stares of the milling staff and Amy's smothered giggle in the background. After a defiant glance at Talos, Maymon stalked out of the sick bay and into the busy corridor, completely naked, jar of beads in one hand.

Talos couldn't suppress a smirk as he followed his feisty pirate to the door. "Smart-mouthed little shit, isn't he? Maybe we are related." He winked at an open-mouthed Rice then glanced at Marius. "You still prime for watching him for me while I lam out of here later?"

Marius nodded. "I'll keep an eye on him." He let the suppressed smile from earlier spread across his face. "If not for you, then for my station's sake."

"Thanks. I owe you." Talos glanced at Rice. "Be seeing you, sister. You've been a *great* help. Tell the other broad thanks, too."

"Why you arrogant--." Picking up a percussion hammer off the instrument tray, Rice took a step toward the Hunter. Marius grabbed her arm and wrestled her back. Amy took advantage of the moment to quietly slip away with the rest of the lingering staff members, leaving just the three of them in the main bay.

A satisfied light in his violet eyes, Talos strode confidently out the door intent on catching up with Maymon as soon as possible. As capable of handling himself as Maymon was, Talos was uncomfortable with the thought of the young man wandering naked through the corridors of the station.

The sick bay doors slid shut, leaving Rice and Marius alone. Rice tossed the hammer back on the tray and sighed. "Where is he off to?"

"Oracan Council meeting. He needs to make some sort of declaration in person." Glancing around the deserted sick bay, Marius sauntered closer to her. "He didn't go into the details."

Raising an eyebrow, Rice finished up with the instrument tray and turned to face Marius. "So you're taking care of Aidan while he's gone?"

"I was hoping that would be 'we'." Marius waved a teasing finger back and forth between them.

Making a disgusted noise in the back of her throat, Rice shoved her hands in her pockets and leaned against the empty bed. "I doubt Talos will like me being anywhere close to his 'property'." She darted an angry look at the closed doorway where the Hunter had departed. "He is *so* rude."

Marius chuckled and ran his hands up her tense arms, planting his feet on either side of hers, locking her in place against the bed. "He learned English from watching 1930's Earth movies. He has a whole package of gangster attitude and slang at his disposal. I think it lends him a certain..." Marius rolled his eyes searching for the right word, "air."

"Yeah, one that smells," Rice huffed.

Taking advantage of the soft lighting and the empty room, Marius lightly rubbed her shoulders, trying to soothe away her bad mood. "He's taking his responsibilities toward Aidan very seriously." He thought about the Hunter's affectionate, possessive behavior in the exam room and cautiously added, "He obviously cares about him."

"Like a pet, not a human being." Rice snorted and leaned into Marius' hands, then groaned and rolled her neck before straightening up and indignantly asking, "Was he actually petting Aidan's head in there?"

Being aware of the Oracan sexual propensity for either gender, Marius made a non-committal noise. He decided to shy away from discussing the intimate direction he suspected the other two males might be headed in. "You're being too hard on him. If you want to be mad at somebody, be mad at the lowlife who convinced the Council to take the Hunt." His hands moved further up the doctor's neck and he softly kneaded the tense muscles bunched at the base of her skull.

Rice moaned appreciatively, eyes closed in pleasure. Mocking the Commander's newly influenced speech patterns, she smiled and teased, "The 'lowlife'?"

He stepped closer, lightly shaking her shoulders and chuckled, "I must be spending too much time with Talos. He's infectious at times." He smiled at Rice and murmured convincingly, "Why don't you save me from any more immediate exposure and have dinner with me?"

Pushing off the side of the bed, Rice moved in close until their bodies touched chest to chest. "Well...", she playfully drawled, running a fingertip seductively down Marius' chin and neck, "I suppose it would be all right, since I'd be saving a life."

Sweeping her into his arms, Marius embraced her. The gentle, exploratory touch rapidly grew into the hungry, aggressive kiss of longtime lovers. Breaking apart, Rice breathlessly stated, "Forget dinner." She licked along the path her fingertip had traced down his flesh. "I think some intensive mouth-to-mouth is called for in this situation."

Equally breathless, Marius closed his eyes briefly to enjoy the feel of her hot wet tongue along the sensitive curve of his jaw then whispered, "I always follow my doctor's advice." Grabbing Rice in a firm embrace he pulled her in for another deep, arousing exchange of lips, tongues and air.

Lips clamped to Marius' questing mouth, Rice fumbled one hand along the wall until her fingers could activate the wall privacy panel. The transparent walls instantly dimmed to a gray opaque.

Chapter Eleven

In the small observation lounge on the south side of the space station, Sherman hunched over a view screen in the far end of the lounge. His eyes darted from the view screen to the surrounding people in the sparsely occupied room, making sure no one was close enough to overhear his conversation. On screen, he watched his employer pace, Barlow's bright waist sash flashing back and forth like a gaudy light show. Sherman inwardly sighed and repeated for the third time. "I'm positive. It's the pirate, sir."

Increasingly upset, Barlow halted and whipped around to face the viewer. "And now the Council has summoned me for a meeting. This Talos is trying to steal my treasure, I just know it." Nearly vibrating with agitation, Barlow venomously spit, "He's stolen my pirate and now he wants my gold as well."

Attempting to placate the man, Sherman contritely reminded, "Technically, sir, the pirate *is* his until the Council grants you rights to the bounty."

Resuming his furious pacing, Barlow hissed, "I've paid a fortune getting this deal off the ground. There's ten lifetimes worth of gold in that treasure." He paused to slam a fist down on a nearby desk. A computer panel rattled and a small round disc fell off the surface with a tiny clatter and plink.

A glint that Sherman knew promised nothing good sparkled in Barlow's eyes as the man added, "I won't be cheated. That pirate is *mine* and I intend to have him, with or without the Council's approval."

Swallowing nervously, Sherman quietly protested. "The Details promise severe consequences for anyone who interferes with a Hunt."

He had backed up Barlow's sundry harsh and shady business deals in the past, but none of them had involved Oracan bounty Hunters before. The Oracan race was not a group of beings he was willing to have take a personal interest in him if Sherman could help it. He liked living and when he did die, he wanted all his body parts left intact.

Smiling maliciously, Barlow stopped his pacing and looked directly at Sherman. "But they would have to prove it was my doing first. And that won't happen." The smile was erased in a split second, replaced by a hard, calculating look that pinched the corners of Barlow's eyes and lips. "Are the others in place?"

Hesitating for an instant, Sherman licked his dry lips and took a deep breath before contritely nodding. "Yes, sir. They're ready."

"Excellent." Barlow began pacing again, occasionally pointed a long, thin finger in Sherman's direction as he schemed. "And make sure the Hunter knows you've left. I want him to relax his defenses."

Scoffing slightly, as much as he dared, Sherman ventured, "I highly doubt my presence has made *him* tense." He felt a surge of icy coldness sweep through his body as dread and anticipation battered at his sense of self-preservation. "Besides, I don't think this particular Hunter relaxes -- ever." Darting a nervous glance at Barlow, Sherman risked asking a skeptical question. "Are you sure about this, sir?"

Barlow narrowed his overly bright, dark eyes and growled, "Are you questioning me, Sherman?"

"No, s-sir. Of course n-not." Quick to reassure, Sherman cringed slightly when he stuttered over his words. He flipped a quick glance around the lounge again before whispering, "But using Betovan mercenaries!" He felt a wave of nausea roll in his gut and he hoped he could finish the conversation soon. Outlawed, branded mercenaries and Oracan Hunters were bad enough when faced separately, but together they made Sherman worry about losing control of his bodily functions. He leaned in close to the screen and implored, "You know their reputation. There's a good reason they're outlawed in every known galaxy."

Snapping, Barlow sneered, "They're necessary to do the job." He swaggered back and forth, one hand propped on the hilt of his pirate sword and one hand clenching and unclenching a frustrated, murderous fist. His voice rose and a manic gleam lit his eyes. "I'm sick of these arrogant, Oracan peacekeepers denying me what's rightfully mine! I won't tolerate interference from anyone!" He pinned his aide in place with a meaningful stare.

Cowed, Sherman hunched forward and pulled his hood further down his face. Voice quietly resigned, he said, "I understand, sir. I'll make sure your interests are well-served, as always."

"See that you do, Sherman." Barlow hissed then

smiled in anticipation. "I'll be expecting a full report on your return." He gleefully rubbed one hand down the hard length of the sword at his hip. "I want to hear, in detail, all about my precious pirate." He gripped the hilt and demanded, "Make me happy."

"I'll do my best." Sherman bowed and raised a shaking hand in a placating gesture. "Thank you, sir." As Barlow's expression remained severe and unforgiving, he hastened to add, "I appreciate the opportunity to serve --." But Barlow cut off the transmission, leaving Sherman talking to empty air. Cursing under his breath, Sherman said, "Crazy bastard. You're going to get us all killed."

He closed his eyes to compose himself and visions of murderous Mercs and vengeful Hunters danced in his head. Sighing, Sherman hung his head and reviewed his options. "I think I need to explore new employment opportunities."

***

Trying to keep the sexual hunger from his gaze, Talos openly stared as a nude Maymon paced the confines of their suite. The young pirate was still swearing up a blue streak, hands fidgeting with the silver band on his wrist when they weren't flinging through the air in time to his colorful, loud cursing and condemnation of the station's medical chief of staff.

"Accursed woman! Devil in an angel's corset, she is!" Maymon stomped one foot, setting his genitals to sway and tensing the muscles in his small, rounded butt. Talos' breath caught in the back of his throat as the slender cock firmed and mushroomed a few inches from the nest of black hair between Maymon's creased groin. Oblivious to his state of partial arousal, Maymon threw a small pillow from an armchair at the wall and ranted, "Evil, she is, with a black-heart under that glorious bosom."

"Better find something to put on, Runt." The Hunter's cock hardened and squirmed against the silky fabric of his trousers. Despite the urge to give into the rush of emotions and hot flare of desire and need, he tried to block out the scent of the pirate's hormones wafting through the air. A tingle of jealousy ripped through his gut as he muttered, "Half the people we passed out there were offended and the other half were interested."

Voice strained, but with the same throaty edginess from before, Maymon demanded, "With what?" He stopped and spun to face Talos, arms held wide and body fully and unabashedly on display. "That she-devil took all me clothes. I've got nothing else to wear." Speculatively, he eyed Talos' extra large frame and sparse clothing. "Don't think nicking anything from you will help much either, guv."

Deliberately turning away, Talos went to the view screen. He casually shrugged and stated in a voice that was steadier than his pounding heartbeat, "You needed new ones anyway. There's a shop on the third level that delivers." He sat down at the screen and hit a few keys and the computer sprang to life. Glancing over his shoulder at the trim, naked, wild creature still fuming and pacing behind him, he off-handedly quipped, "Not that I'm objecting to the scenery, but I'm going to be gone for a little while and you'll have visitors." He heard the sharp catch of the pirate's breath and the smell of fear touched his nose, and for the first time, it affected his heart, as well. Moved, he hastened to add, "I have to go visit my people."

Maymon froze in place; his agitated pacing replaced by a look of dread. Voice soft and a little shaky, he quietly asked, "Turning me over so soon, guv?"

"No." Talos was quick to reassure. "I just need to straighten out a few things." He turned back to the screen and busied himself with the keypad. "You're staying here."

A bright spark of mischief lit up Maymon's eyes. He strode over to Talos' side, asking hopefully, "On me own?"

Talos snorted and chuckled, eyes still focused on the view screen. "Hell no. There wouldn't be a station left for me to come back to." He glanced up at the waiting pirate and added, "Marius has agreed to look after you."

Eyes full of suspicion and distrust, Maymon plopped his naked backside on the edge of the console desk and let his tanned, lean legs swing free a foot above the floor. His thigh nudged Talos' arm and his half-hard, little cock poked up seductively from between his splayed thighs, reminding Talos of an over-sized Nubian sandworm he played with as a child.

Maymon hunched his shoulders and dropped his face enticingly close to Talos' head, his musky arousal and natural scent permeating the air all around the Hunter. Maymon's warm breath caressed Talos' cheek as the pirate asked, "His Majesty, the Commander?" his dark eyes clouded over and a frown marred his full lips. "I'll be locked in his brig then?"

"No." Maymon grinned. "You'll be locked in here." Maymon's grin fell.

"I'll starve to death, mate."

"Marius will make sure you're fed and watered. I won't be that long. You just behave yourself." Talos went to the view screen, to call up the shop and order several things.

Maymon watched, fascinated by the computer and the flashing images on the screen, over Talos' shoulder. Several times he tried to tap the keyboard while the Hunter was busy reading selections, disrupting the entire process. Eventually Talos figured out sizes and picked clothing styles that he thought would please the young pirate.

When Talos grunted in satisfaction and pushed away from the viewer, Maymon looked warily at him, an indignant pout on his slender, handsome face that made him look like the innocent both Rice and Marius claimed he was. "Don't have nothing to pay you back with for the finery, guv." The pout deepened. "You and his majesty, Lord Marius made me give back all the pretties I found yesterday."

"You didn't find them, you stole them." Talos said ominously. "They didn't belong to you."

Maymon tugged at the silver band on his arm. "The way I belong to you?" Indignation colored his tone. "You nicked me and you get to keep the spoils. Where's the difference?" He jabbed a newly scrubbed and trimmed finger in Talos' face. "Rules are only for those what got no say in the matter?"

Brusquely pushing the accusing finger away,

Talos pushed back from the viewer and stood. "They aren't the same thing."

"Says you." Maymon jumped down off the desktop and stood toe-to-toe with the massive Hunter, his still half-hard cock bobbing against Talos' thigh. The pirate gestured sharply in the air with his hands while he talked. He put his slender nose in the air and jutted out his chin in defiance, harshly proclaiming, "Looks the same from my side of the manacles, guv."

It was Talos' turn to shake an insistent finger, his fiercely possessive stare meeting Maymon's angry one head-on. "That band is for your protection as much as anything else."

"Protection is it?" Maymon's eyebrows arched, disappearing under the shaggy remains of his thick black hair. He planted his hands on his naked hips and leaned forward until his chin almost touched Talos. He tapped an impatient fist against Talos' rock-hard chest, punctuating every few words with a firm smack. "Where I come from, them what's got the most say in things takes a hot iron to any freeman such as meself what has the misfortune to be taken alive, marking him as a criminal and a slave. They called it 'protection', too, for the rest of the fine ladies and highfalutin gents."

"I know." The faint smell of fear had popped out on the young pirate at the mention of the branding custom and a shadow of mistrust clouded his dark eyes. Talos' own anger abated, replaced with concern and a nagging desire to banish all traces of the pirate's fear. He pushed the emotion away and acknowledged, "An influential trading corporation used to brand a 'P' on a pirate's forehead when they caught them back then."

162

Maymon's eyes glittered brightly as anger overtook his ingrained fear of the East Indian Trading Company. "Aye, they do...did...whatever!" He stuttered, overwhelmed and angry. "As I see it, guv, the only difference between their 'brand' and your 'band' is the 'r'."

Maymon stormed off into the bedroom. Once there, he huffed and paced, obviously looking for a door to slam. Unable to vent in his usual manner, he picked up a vase from a nearby table and smashed it on the floor, then threw himself on the bed, back to Talos.

Talos watched the tantrum from the living area then followed Maymon into the bedroom, the need to protect, claim and keep the young man warring with his duty to turn the pirate over to the Council. By the hormones lacing the air of the bedroom, he could tell Maymon was aroused by his presence and he knew he had seen interest in the pirate's eyes the day before when he had offered himself in exchange for freedom. Talos clamped down on his personal conflicting desires and prepared to shower before leaving for the Oracan Council meeting.

Ignoring Maymon's pouting stare, Talos stripped off his weapons sash and hung it up then removed his trousers and forcefully flung them into a corner of the room. His cock stood out at half-mast from his groin, still a healthy seven inches of thick shaft, stiff and rigid, and needy. As he moved to leave the bedroom for the shower, Maymon's gaze drifted to his cock and the look on the young man's face grew wanton and hungry.

Maymon had been eyeing the Hunter from the bed, tracking his every movement since the moment he had slipped out of his clothing. Now the pirate's dark eyes were dilated and his breathing was coming in short, little pants, releasing warm puffs of pirate-flavored air into the room. Talos' senses grabbed onto the stimulus and his sexual urge to take the man pounded through his veins, forcing him to remain in the room as Maymon slid off the bed and advanced on him.

The lithe pirate normally had a swagger to his hips that Talos assumed had been cultured over years of balancing at sea on the rough sailing ships, but now the swagger had a new seductive purpose. Talos followed the sway for the few paces it took for Maymon to reach him, then his eyes moved to the rapidly growing shaft curving out from the pirate's lean flat, lower abdomen. It bobbed slightly, too short to stretch too far from his body, but long enough for the hooded tip to extend past the top of the tanned hand Maymon wrapped around it, yanking it to full engorgement with a practiced, efficient motion.

Moving in so he was close enough to nudge one of Talos' taut, thickly-muscled thighs with his cock, Maymon tipped back his face and seductively dropped his sultry gaze down to look pointedly at both of their straining cocks, then raised his dark brown eyes to stare into Talos' own violet ones. He slowly moistened his lips with the tip of his tongue and let his still stroking hand 'accidentally' brush repeatedly against Talos' thick, stiff shaft.

Breathing heavily, Talos remained still as stone, watching the seduction play out. He wished the pirate's overtures were being made for the same reasons that he would like to accept them, but he knew it was part of a game to the child-like man. A game to gain the upper hand, a position he would have to keep all to himself if he was to safeguard the Hunt, Maymon, and his own heart.

Talos felt a restless stirring in his groin and knew his instinctive drives were responding involuntarily to the musky odor of sexual arousal radiating from the pirate. He marveled at the level of hormonal release the small human was capable of and nearly groaned out loud when a sharp blast of rich, spicy musk filled the air as pre-cum leaked from the wrinkled folds of Maymon's cock. Glancing down, Talos watched and hungered as the slick, bulbous tip of the human's cock began emerging through from its fleshy hood with each downward stroke of his tight fist.

Unable to stop himself, Talos reached out and took hold of Maymon's upper arms, drawing him to his chest so that the pirate's warm flesh rubbed the cartilage nubs on his chest. Fire burned through Talos' body and made his blood sizzle with passion and need. A warm hand closed around his shaft and gave a few rough yanks before Maymon spun himself around in Talos' light grip to crudely present his backside to the Hunter.

Maymon leaned over and rested his free hand on his knee, the other furiously working over his cock. He looked back over his shoulder and muttered, "Well, come on then, guv, bugger me arse. It's what you've been wanting. It's there for the taking. Just remember to use a bit of spit, if you will. That main mast you got sailing there is a bit more than I've boarded afore."

Maymon hung his head and waited, but when no movement occurred behind him, he was forced to look back over his shoulder again. One look at Talos' grim face and Maymon straightened, dropped his hand from his shaft and turned around.

Indignation and hurt flitted across Maymon's expressive face. "What?" Chest heaving with angry, rapid huffs of breath, Maymon turned back to Talos again. "After all of this manhandling me bones and groping me arse, you've decided I'm not good enough for ya, guv?"

Hiding his own pain, Talos shook his head and gently cupped his hands around Maymon's angry face. "No. If I wanted to bed a whore, I could find one I didn't have to wake up to in the morning down on the tenth level. What I want from you isn't a quick fuck and an impersonal handshake."

Confusion pulled a frown onto Maymon's face, furrowing the normally baby-smooth skin and clouding his sparkling dark eyes.

Talos stroked one large hand down Maymon's soft cheek. "What I want, Aidan, I don't think you know how to give." He leaned down and tried to kiss Maymon's lips, but the skittish pirate pulled his head back at the last minute, just the way Talos knew he would, confusion and panic written all over his young face. Talos gently patted Maymon's flushed cheek and swiftly went into the bathroom, leaving the open-mouthed pirate with a dwindling erection and an uncertain expression.

Stepping immediately into the huge, open-walled shower, Talos adjusted the multiple sprays to beat a heavy rhythm on his unsatisfied and aching body. He stood, silent and still, under the pounding waterfall and tried to let it wash away his bitter disappointment and the addicting, heady scent of the delectable pirate. His cock slowly relaxed to sway in the warm, moist air, luxuriating in the sensations the warm spray provided. It squirmed and coiled, seeking out the promised gift of gratification.

Talos slowly stroked himself, and tried to soothe away the ache in his chest. He wanted Maymon, but he couldn't have him while he still belonged to the Council and he didn't want him at all unless he had the young man's stubborn, wild heart as well as his lithe, sturdy body. Half a heart wasn't enough to last a lifetime.

Chapter Twelve

Staring at the empty opening where Talos had disappeared into the lunatic washroom that acted as if it was alive, Maymon thought over what the Hunter had said. He knew the Hunter wanted him. He saw it in his oddly colored eyes every time the massive creature looked at him. He saw the hesitation and the longing and he knew where they came from.

And it wasn't a one-sided attraction. He thought the beast was a right handsome gent, better looking than any pirate he'd ever sailed with. Rated higher than even Giselle or Abigail at the *Charred Horse,* as well. Smelled better, too. Like the first sunny day after the hurricane season blew through the islands, rich, warm, clean and full of the promise of hidden adventures yet to come.

And if the Hunter knew what to do with the impressive knob Maymon had groped a moment ago, the adventure would prove to be right filling and worth the pain and effort. But Talos had rebuffed his advances. Not because the stoic beast didn't want him but because he wanted something he said Maymon wasn't capable of giving him.

And that was ridiculous, because Maymon had just offered the bloody bastard his most precious possession, himself. Or had he? He offered his willing body, but the Hunter wanted something else, something more. What more did a carefree spirit like his self have to give to a beast to whom he owed his very life? A creature who still sheltered him and protected him in a world so different than his own that at times Maymon thought he'd gone completely crackers and this was all some sort of Almighty punishment for his past misdeeds. All of which were grave misunderstandings, mind you.

If Talos didn't just lust after his body, what more could he want? Surely the massive Hunter didn't want them to be a...a couple, did he? Was it acceptable in this bizarre and highfalutin time for two males to be more to each other than a quick bit of relief in a dark corner? Was his sea serpent savior asking for his affections and not just his arse? The attempt at a kiss would lead a body to think that, but the Hunter had yet to say an affectionate word to him or do anything more physically suggestive than slap his arse. But he did *that* a lot.

Talos was as hard to understand as everything else here was. He was demanding something from the pirate that he seemed to hold in high value, but Maymon had the feeling that whatever cost the Hunter asked of him, it would be worth it to pay. The beast was a formidable warrior and his only ally in this dangerous and confusing place. And Maymon was attracted to him, more than simply attracted, if he was honest about it. But sodomy was a criminal offense in his time. It was hard to shake off the specter of the hangman's noose and openly express more than a momentary interest in

169

another male. Even on board ship for lonely months on end, couplings were rough, fast and never spoken of in the light of day. They certainly didn't include gestures of affection before or afterwards and there was never talk of emotions involved outside of relief of one's body's needs.

The idea of having more than a fumbled exchange in the dark intrigued Maymon. It stirred a strange feeling in the pit of his stomach he couldn't put a name to. It made him short of breath and his limbs trembled. A rush of anxiety raced through him and his chest ached while at the same time, his cock hardened and his fingertips went numb and tingly.

Maymon suddenly realized he still standing stark naked in the middle of an empty room while the object of his anxiety and desire was naked in the next room. He'd never been a coward before and he wasn't going to be one over bedding a creature of his own wanting. Even if it was a the spitting image of a Cemi sea god.

Not one to let any opportunity for pleasure or gain pass him by, Maymon took a deep breath to steady his quivering legs and followed Talos, feverishly hoping he wouldn't be rebuffed a second time. Obviously he needed to alter his approach. He hated to do it, but possibly the big beastie would appreciate honesty instead.

Rounding the corner into the cavernous washroom, Maymon hesitantly approached the open threshold and the four feet tall half-walls surrounding the large place where Talos stood, his back to Maymon. He knew the Hunter was aware he was there by the way the muscles of his broad back suddenly tensed. Maymon didn't understand how, but tiny waterfalls erupted from four different contraptions on the walls at various heights, showering the massive Hunter with thin rivers of water, hot water by the amount of steam and heat in the room.

Although Talos had tensed on Maymon's arrival, he hadn't moved, remaining perfectly still, waiting, as streams of clear water cascaded over him to disappear down a hole in the floor. Maymon guessed it all ran down to someone else's bath next.

When Talos refused to acknowledge him, Maymon slowly moved into the shower to stand a few feet from Talos and he quietly addressed the solid, unflinching wall of sculptured, gray back.

"Was thinking 'bout what you said out there. 'Bout wanting more...more than...what I was offering." Maymon eased a step closer, the heat and the thick air making him lightheaded while it coaxed his flaccid erection back to life. As he neared, the tiny pinpoints of hot water pelted his skin and he flinched back until the sensation registered as exotic and pleasant.

"I thought about it...and I..I know," he licked his lips and a newly-acquired, sincere pleading note made his whiskey-roughened voice quiver. "I know what you're talking about...looking for." Maymon nervously pushed his wet, shaggy hair back from his face and pressed his palms together in a gesture of supplication. "You 'ave to understand, guv, gents only get together when there be no wenches about and when they do, it's for a quick bit of buggery or a fast swallowing to polish off an aching knob."

He took another tentative step forward, but jerked to a halt when Talos slowly turned around, his violet eyes darting over Maymon's every feature. Maymon knew the Hunter was reading him, scenting him, practically tasting him in the air.

Maymon bit at his lower lip in an uncharacteristic show of anxiety, and then tentatively said, "And even if a body wanted more from another gent," a long hidden desire filled his tone and touched his eyes, conveying what he was having trouble putting into words, "sodomy is a hanging offense...and no one looks good with a noose round his neck, guv." He swallowed hard, letting his own eyes drift repeatedly down and then away from the grip Talos had on his own long, thick shaft. He forced his lust-filled gaze to lock on Talos' guarded expression and softly, hopefully asked, "I'm hoping the rules might have changed a bit in the last seven hundred years or so, have they?"

He stared at Talos, neither one moving, both gauging each other's sincerity.

Nostrils flaring and breath coming in short, hard puffs, Talos appeared to be restraining himself. The stone-hard muscles of his body quivered and his speech was little more than rumbled growl from deep in his chest as he demanded, "I want forever."

Maymon's eyelids fluttered and his mouth hung open, stunned by the statement. No one had wanted him for more than a day, and then he was paying for the privilege with a hefty piece of coin. Never for just the pleasure of his company, for just himself. But forever was a long, long time.

He glanced away and huffed out a series of

rapid breaths to clear away the confusion all this talk of love and commitment was causing. The heat of the room and his own rising desires served to compound his distress. He decided to throw all caution to the winds and go with frank honesty again. "I can't promise forever, guv." He saw the light of hope start to fade from the Hunter's startling eyes and hastened to add, "but I'm willing to let you convince me of the profit in it."

Talos covered the distance between them in one long stride and lifted a stunned, flustered Maymon off his feet, pinning him against a wet shower wall. Their chests met in a thud, driving the air from Maymon's lungs and slapping his head against the slick surface behind him.

Talos looked directly into Maymon's wide, black eyes and growled, "The rules *have* changed, Aidan."

The rumble in the Hunter's chest vibrated into Maymon, shaking him all the way through to his wall-plastered spine. He saw something dark and lustful click in Talos' beastly eyes. A white hot blast of terrified passion flared in his blood and burned throughout his entire body until he thought his very heart and soul had been set on fire. The flames fanned higher and hotter when Talos butted his chin up with one gray, satiny cheek and darkly declared, "Now...now you're mine."

Maymon's cock hardened painfully as the Hunter's rich, deep voice claimed possession of him. He was surprisingly thrilled to be so desired, thrilled and frightened. He knew this would mean problems for the Bounty Hunter. He was the coveted prize meant for others, but right now, as usual, all the young pirate was interested in was the moment and the overwhelming, unfamiliar emotion of being desired for more than his arse.

Oh, he was sure his arse was going to be the center of attention at some point soon, at least he hoped it was, but he also realized the great beastie wanted *him*, not just his hot, snug hole. Not only did the Hunter desire him, but he felt something shift inside of him each time he looked at the massive warrior. He had since the first time he laid eyes on Talos down under the murky, green sea. It felt amazingly different knowing that. His heart seemed to grow in his chest and his breathing became rapid and shallow. Everything felt more intense, more tantalizing, more stimulating, more untried to the young pirate.

So preoccupied with discovering he had feelings for the Hunter that went beyond mere sexual gratification, he was taken by surprise when a set of thin, warm, wet lips grazed across his own.

Maymon instantly jerked his face away. He felt a strong, massive hand grab onto his skull and gently but firmly hold his head still, soft supple lips working their way over and up and down his jawline and neck.

He weakly protested between grunted puffs of shallow air. "Gents...gents don't kiss, guv. Be like kissing ...ah," a long wet swipe of Talos' tongue lapped over his Adam's apple making him squirm against the unrelenting hold on his head. "Kissing, oh, my,...," another unexpected assault of lips and tongue began on the tender flesh behind one ear and Maymon gasped and arched his back in response. "Like kissing a swine's arse...rancid and coarse and hairy and....," satiny lips kissed his closed eyelids and rained small touches down his cheeks, stopping to linger over one corner of his talking mouth. His own tongue automatically responded to the seductive sensations, tentatively poking through his parted lips between stuttered words. "Not something...I...I want to...do."

Up until now, Maymon's hands had been latched onto Talos' brawny forearms, each new assault by Talos' talented silky lips made his hands clench and unclench as passion fought with his outdated prejudices. As Talos' lips skated over his mouth a second time, Maymon gave up the battle as he surged up within the gently confines of the Hunter's hold. He locked his lips firmly onto the insistent mouth exploring his face, arms wrapping tightly around Talos' stout neck, drawing the Hunter impossibly closer in a harsh, insistent embrace.

The passionate, almost violent kiss lasted for several long, breathless minutes as the two devoured each other. Maymon wrapped his legs around Talos' waist and hung on, running his hands over the hairless scalp and silky smooth skin of his lover. He broke away only when he found he was breathing so hard he was lightheaded and dizzy.

Pulling back in amazement to stare at Talos through half-lidded, passion-glazed eyes, Maymon sputtered in disbelief, "Brandy. Bloody hell, you taste like *brandy*. Better even than the bottle I stol—liberated from that last merchant ship." He licked his swollen, tender lips, delighted and aroused by the way Talos' eyes hungrily followed the simple movement. "Shoulda listened to you before, luv," Maymon smoldered.

175

"Remind me of that now and then." He dove back in for another blistering kiss, undaunted by the click of clashing teeth and the lack of sufficient air.

Through parted lips, Maymon tentatively tasted Talos, his own tongue darting out to lap at the long, slick muscle invading his mouth. Their tongues dueled, then stroked each other, the Hunter's longer more agile tongue wrapping around Maymon's tongue, caressing and drawing it into his, only to release it and capture it again.

Talos' lips felt like smooth satin, but wet and warm. They latched onto Maymon's and refused to allow air or sound to escape as they ravaged him, sucking and working their sultry way over his mouth, alternating their attention between his lips and his face, leaving a burning trail of passion behind in their aggressive wake.

Maymon gasped and heaved against his captor, reveling in the sensations he was free to indulge in, overwhelmed by the sheer novelty of being able to let his urges and emotions have free-rein in this taboo relationship he desperately desired. Buggery was nothing new to him, but making love to a man was. Being made love to was even more startling and disturbing yet, but he was willing to have the Hunter convince him of the pleasure of it.

Wanting to taking in all the sensations demanding his attention, Maymon consciously registered each one assaulting his body. One large, meaty hand still held his head arched back, the thick fingers of Talos' hand kneading his scalp and entwining the fine strands of his thick hair tightly around them.

Talos' chest rubbed over his own, the soft cartilage nubs running across his broad frame becoming more supple and warmer as their passion grew more intense.

Legs wrapped around Talos' hips, Maymon squirmed against the massive, strong hand supporting his left hip and butt cheek, amazed by the sheer power of the Hunter he could feel through the firm grip. Maymon's scrotum lay on the bed of soft, tubular appendages surrounding Talos' cock and he couldn't resist the urge to shift back and forth on their spiny surfaces, gasping at the tingling buzz of pleasure the action generated in his balls. The buzz traveled to the base of his stiff, straining cock and he began to leak, barely able hold back a climax that sizzled at the root of his shaft as he pictured himself linked to his new, voracious lover.

He reached down to fist his cock, but before his hands were free of Talos' neck, his cock was gripped in a warm massaging caress. As the caress stroked him up and down the length of his rod, a slightly coarse pad rubbed over the leaking tip of his cock as his scrotum was gently kneaded and tugged.

Maymon groaned into Talos' mouth and feverishly prayed for his teetering climax to come crashing down on him when he realized that neither of Talos' hands had moved from their hold on his head and his arse. His eyes flashed open and panicked, he pulled his mouth away from his lover's to glance down between their plastered bodies. Talos eased back and let Maymon watch as the Hunter's snake-like cock continued to curl and uncurl around the pirate's shaft, milking it and stroking it, its full fifteen inches coiled snugly up against Maymon's own seven inches of proud flesh.

"Bloody hell, luv. You *are* part sea serpent."

Maymon's eyes turned wide and his panting mouth hung open as the soft tubular fingers moved over his balls, the tiny suction cup-like tips gripping his sensitive flesh then pulling off to move to a new patch of skin, leaving a burst of pleasure and a fiery tingle behind each time.

Passion and delicious excitement overrode any of Maymon's few remaining inhibitions. He embraced his new lover's special attributes with an open mind and a starving libido. Arching into the firm grip, he squirmed and bucked, driven to near madness by the oh-so-near-but-unobtainable-climax dancing at the edge of his consciousness.

Grimacing at the intense, building pain/pleasure, Maymon strained and heaved then suddenly froze in place as the sensations around his cock changed again. The exposed tip of his cock was suddenly enveloped in a blanket of heat, his cock tugged down straight from his groin. Unwilling to escape the passionate nuzzling of Talos' wordless, affectionate, sucking kisses being rained down on his neck and chest, Maymon ducked his head slightly and cocked it to one side to see what was happening next to his captive jewels.

"What the bloody hell?" The hand holding his ass yanked and Maymon slid closer to Talos' groin as the Hunter's long cock began to disappear up inside the massive Oracan, drawing Maymon's still clenched shaft along with it. "Lord almighty, you're the devil's own spawn, you are, luv."

Maymon groaned in pleasure-drenched bliss and panted through the overwhelming sensation of sinking his shaft into the Oracan's lava hot body. Multiple bands of muscles rippled over and around his shaft and the outside tubulars latched on his body and scrotum as soon as his cock was completely seated inside. Even though he was being milked and stroked without moving a muscle of his own, Maymon's hips automatically joined the ancient rhythm and he rocked and bucked, held securely in the Hunter's unyielding embrace.

With one massive heave, Talos slammed their bodies together harder against the wall embedding Maymon's cock as far it would physically go. He made a soft 'ta-ti' sound and plastered them together and began a relentless assault on Maymon's mouth, stealing the pirate's every breath. He pinched and rubbed at the tiny nibs of dusky flesh on the pirate's hairless chest and kneaded the soft skin of his lean waist. Following the flow of Maymon's curved hips, Talos ran his hands down the pirate's ass and groped both cheeks, separating them and exposing the sensitive ring of muscle to the warm water and cooler air.

Talos rumbled that odd, new noise at the back of his throat again, emitting "ta-ti" in Maymon's ear.

The pirate gasped, "What's that? That noise you keep making –tat-ti? What's that? A curse?"

Nodding slightly, Talos grunted, "Yes, a curse." He growled softly and added, "It means 'I love you'."

Maymon moaned and squirmed, his hips jerking in minute spasms. His mounting climax had reached mind-blowing portions and his head buzzed with the need for release. Even as he was sure he could not be pushed any further into the flames of passion, his desire rose another notch and his flesh seemed to sizzle on his very bones.

Just when Maymon though his heart would burst from the strain, Talos nuzzled his head to one side, shoved a thick, oily long, finger up his ass and growled a raw "Mine" in his ear as the most powerful climax of his lifetime roared through his arched and vibrating body.

It could have been the multiple stimulation, or the sudden penetration, or the fact that it had been days since he'd had any sexual relief, but Maymon suspected it was the intense declaration of ownership whispered in his ear that sent him spiraling over the edge of the cliff. He felt like a gull flying through an ocean gale, buffeted by the rain, surrounded by the sizzle of lightning, but supported by the strong wind as he soared through the eye of the storm and gently glided down to earth, exhausted and battered, but exhilarated by the awe-inspiring ride.

"You've damn near killed me, luv." Boneless and dizzy, Maymon slumped against Talos, a devilishly pleased grin on his dazed face.

He let the Hunter pull his head gently back and responded in kind when his lips were kissed, no longer the least bit concerned about locking lips with another male. If Talos was right and he really wasn't dead, then he'd found a piece of glorious heaven floating free in the stars he was marooned in and he intended to claim it as his very own.

Details of the Hunt

He wrapped his arms around Talos' neck again and pulled himself up to get the upper position in the kiss, his tongue down the Hunter's throat and his lips actively rewarding his lover's generosity and sexual skill. His cock slipped out of the cocoon of warmth and he shivered at the stream of water that ran down his groin and splashed over his partially flaccid member, grunting a moan into Talos' hungry mouth as it hardened and poked at the Hunter's ridged chest. At twenty-three, his libido was the one thing he counted on to be ready at a moment's notice and it didn't fail him now.

Deep into the harsh and hungry kiss, Maymon felt a tremor of restrained power quake through Talos vibrating both their bodies. Maymon ran a hand over the nubs on Talos' chest and deliberated tickled the edges of one while pressing his palm against it. The response was immediate and more violent then he expected, taking his breath away in more ways than one. He was grabbed by the waist and heaved higher by both of Talos' hands holding his ass cheeks.

Maymon latched on harder to the lips under his own mouth, grunting deep in the back of his throat when his cheeks were spread and his ass was impaled on a thick, hot cord of flesh that reached to the core of his insides, poking at the wall of flesh at his belly button. Something ridged and bumpy scraped along the sensitive walls of his rectum and the rings of protective muscles at the opening and higher up.

He threw back his head and cried out when it raked across a sensitive spot inside, the like of which he had never experienced before. Writhing and twisting to

Laura Baumbach

recapture a burst of wild euphoria, Maymon pounded his fist on Talos' chest, pushing and groping at the chest plates that helped fuel the Hunter's already soaring sexual drive. The sensation repeated along with a flutter of movement deep in his abdomen, and Maymon flushed a deep red and screamed out again.

***

Buried deep inside of his mate, Talos braced his body against the smooth shower wall to prevent crushing the small human. His cock traveled deep inside the tight hot entrance to Maymon's body, stretched to its thinnest diameter for ease of passage and the desire to penetrate as fully as possible.

Once completely seated inside his young lover, Talos let his cock thicken, shortening the shaft and unfurling the nubbed collar around its leaking, triangular head and at its base. With snake-like grace and agility it turned on itself, making the pirate feel impossibly full, and then, lead by the scent of hormones, it found Maymon's prostate gland. There it raked the ridged collar over the pea-sized swelling until Maymon bucked and screamed. Talos allowed the slit in the tip of his cock to open wide and the end of his cock latched onto the tiny gland and sucked, sending his young lover into a frenzy of explosive need.

Pinning his vocal, writhing lover to the wall, Talos hunched his spine so he was low enough to grab onto one of Maymon's swollen, taut tits with his mouth and suck on it. He used his head to clamp Maymon's trunk to the wall while both his hands held the pirate's body in place as his cock danced inside of his lover. The feel of the young man's hot, moist body squirming on

182

his cock and bucking against his hold drove his need for release higher, but Talos knew this first time had to be overwhelming for both of them.

This was the ritual claiming, the bonding, the no-going-back moment in their impulsive, savage relationship, whether the pirate knew it or not. This moment would define their sexual life together, tie them to each other on a chemical plane as well as an emotional one and neither would be the same again after this.

Maymon's sperm was already being absorbed by Talos' unique system, the human's chemical structure was being embedded deep into the Hunter's neurons and sensory stations. Maymon was a part of Talos, now and for all time.

Talos would never be free of the human, the instinctual need to have him, touch him, care for him, make love to him and no other until his death would rule his thoughts and body from this day on. He knew if he couldn't convince Council to void the Hunt and let him claim Maymon as his own, he would turn rogue to keep the young pirate for himself. There was no turning back now.

Flushed with the new buzz created by the changing chemistry levels in his body, Talos growled around the swollen nub in his mouth and demanded, "Surrender." When no answer came except a gasped grunt and a frantic, defiant twisted of Maymon's hips, he raised his head. Grabbing Maymon by the hair, he pulled their face together, lips only centimeters apart and softly rumbled, "Surrender to me, my desire."

Maymon pushed against the hand holding him

in place and grimaced, eyes glazed with burning passion and lust. He grunted through tightly clamped teeth straining and arching against the barrage of unseen caresses Talos' cock was lavishing on his most sensitive and responsive hidden recesses.

Maymon's eyelids fluttered at a seductive half-mast and his full lips huffed tiny, hot breaths of sex-laden air in Talos' face. He gasped and looked Talos in the eye while declaring, "Be happy to luv...Be the first time...I ever been...victorious in me own defeat."

Letting loose all the restrained passion and power he had been containing, Talos roared out a victory call. The tip of his cock snapped free of Maymon's prostate and unfurled, undulating up and down Maymon's passage, ridged collar flared. Each undulation sent a spasm through Maymon's body and Talos shivered in delight as the young man vibrated and moaned in his arms.

Maymon cried out and arched his frame, his stiff, moisture-covered body glistening in the dim lighting of the steamy shower stall. Spurts of thick white cum shot out of his purple knob, coating the two of them and showering the tubulars attached to his scrotum and surrounding flesh with its gift. The tubulars moved to suck up the beads of fluid before the water washed it all away. Maymon sagged and slumped against his lover.

Tight spasms gripped Talos' thick rod as the scent of Maymon's cum and throaty murmurs pushed the Hunter over the edge to climax. He gripped Maymon tightly to him and shot his cock out to its full length, burying his shaft, forcefully ejaculating his release as far into his mate as it would go. The wide collar under his cock's head expanded and locked itself in place like an open umbrella, ridged nubs tightly embedded in the snug channel preventing the loss of the Oracan's seed until Maymon's fluid-depleted body absorbed every molecule.

Cock still locked inside his mate, Talos turned off the water, gently rotated Maymon's body on his shaft and carried his semi-conscious, newly claimed lifemate out of the shower and into their bedroom.

Gently laying their joined, wet bodies down on the bed on their sides, Talos cradled Maymon to his chest and pulled a light sheet over the pirate's rapidly cooling skin. He pushed Maymon's wet hair off his flushed cheek and nuzzled at the exposed curve of the man's slender neck, licking the newly formed sheen of sweat from the pirate's skin. Detecting the faint flavor of his own body in the salty moisture, Talos savored the new taste. He inhaled Maymon's distinctive, spicy musk, and let the combined mixture permeate his senses.

Satisfied by the knowledge his seed had been absorbed by his lover's body, Talos relaxed and allowed his cock to soften. It slowly withdrew from Maymon causing the man to moan in protest and press his ass back into Talos' groin.

Maymon half-twisted in Talos' embrace to stare up at the Hunter through glazed, sleepy eyes. He smiled and muttered in a slurred, drunken voice that reminded Talos of raw whiskey poured over crystalline rocks, a rough but mellow sound that made his cock quiver in delight.

185

Laura Baumbach

"Got to hand it to you, luv, never knew a gent could make me feel like this." he tried to raise his hand to touch Talos, but his arm fell bonelessly back on the bed halfway through the movement. "I'm beginning to see the profit in maintaining our relationship. You keep this up and I'll never have to drink rum again to lose all the feeling in me body. I'd prefer to get drunk on you. Brandy's me new favorite drink." Maymon leered at the Hunter and grinned, but his eyelids fluttered shut.

Smiling, Talos ran a comforting hand down Maymon's shoulder and arm and pulled the covering up to his chin, then reminded the pirate, "I have to go to Oracan for a Council meeting. I want you to stay put and behave. Marius will check on you."

Maymon hummed an answer, mumbling something unintelligible. Talos scented him to detect if the pirate was misleading him, but the human's scent and the slow regular rise and fall of his chest marked him as truly asleep. If Talos was lucky, Maymon would sleep through most of his absence and lessen the amount of frustration he knew he would come back to after leaving the inquisitive young man locked up for the duration of his trip.

Talos gently pulled away, tucking the edges of the covering loosely around the pirate's naked body. He rose effortlessly off the bed, his powerful frame taut with a rippling, raw strength, his energy renewed by the fierce coupling.

He made a humming sound deep in his broad chest and grinned, reminding himself that the nicest part about Oracan bonding rituals were that custom demanded they be repeated frequently. Then he remembered that depending on how the Council meeting went, Maymon and he would either have a lifetime together or no time at all.

Donning his trousers and weapons, Talos strode out of the room without a backward glance. He knew he would be coming back for the pirate, he just wasn't sure if it would be as an honored Oracan Hunter or a disgraced rogue warrior.

He retrieved the package containing Maymon's new clothes from the delivery transport slot in the wall and laid the clothes on the dining table where the pirate would find them easily.

Wiping the security panel that operated the door, he programmed the locking mechanism to allow only Marius and himself entrance to the suite. He paused, glanced at the open door to the bedroom, then re-keyed the panel and added Dr. Rice to the retinal scan codes. Maymon would need both protection and comfort if something unexpected occurred and Talos was unable to make it back to his displaced, culturally naive lover again.

Taking a final, deep breath of the pirate-scented air, Talos left to publicly claim what he had already taken. And may the Gods of Juninus protect any who tried to thwart him.

***

In an isolated corner of the secluded docking bay, two hooded humanoids, pitted and grisly under their tattered cloaks, watched from the protective shadows of an unoccupied shuttle as Talos entered the bay and immediately left in his fighter alone.

Mercenaries from a distant planet, Betovans

were an entire species that had earned a permanent bounty placed on their collective heads from the Oracan Council for heinous crimes against all known species. Only a huge reward could lure these creatures out into the open of a human-operated space station.

As soon as the *Dango* left the hanger, one Betovan, Zrac, pushed the hood back from his face and pulled a handheld communication device out from under his cloak. "The Hunter's left the station. Alone."

Barlow's clipped, distinct voice clearly vibrated from the communicator. "Alone? Are you sure?"

Zrac ground his jagged, yellow teeth together and flared his flat, disfigured nostrils in disgust before firmly replying, "Positive. The Hunter was traveling light, no luggage, no companions."

"The Council meeting." Barlow's tone turned angry, his voice laced with suspicion. "And he's not bringing my bounty with him." He muttered in a voice that seemed more for himself then Zrac. "They're not going to hand him over, the cheating monsters. There's no other reason to leave the pirate behind." His voice rose until it sounded like he was practically spitting his words. "Damn it, I've paid dearly for him."

There was a pause filled with nothing but the sound of several deep breaths being drawn, then Barlow harshly demanded, "I want that pirate, no matter what the cost."

Throwing an evil grin at his partner, Garn, Zrac reassured his employer. "You'll get him, don't worry."

In a challenging tone, Barlow taunted the Mercs. "You're sure you can best a Hunter?"

Zrac snorted, but his eyes narrowed dangerously

as a sneer further distorted his unattractive, swine-like face. "No one can track a trail that isn't there, not even an Oracan bounty Hunter."

"Make sure of it," Barlow barked. "I'm paying you both a king's ransom. *No one* can connect this to me."

Grinning, Zrac nudged Garn with his shoulder then spit on the floor of the docking bay. "You just make sure the rest of our credits are ready when we hand over your new toy."

Letting an unspoken threat travel over the void of space, Barlow warned, "And make sure he's in good condition when he arrives." Without waiting for an answer, Barlow broke the connection.

Zrac and Garn exchanged amused glances while Zrac pocketed the communicator and checked that his sidearm was close to hand.

Garn frowned and hissed, his speech impeded by his missing lower lip, "Crazy human."

Nodding, Zrac grinned. "Rich, crazy human."

Needing to one up his partner, Gran added, "Disgusting, rich, crazy human."

Zrac paused, a thoughtful expression on his twisted face, then announced, "I like him."

"He pays well." Gran dropped his frown and returned the grin. "He'll do." They exchanged a glance then shrugged and stepped back into the shadows.

Chapter Thirteen

On arriving Talos immediately entered the familiar hall where the Oracan Council Chamber had made its home for the last several millennia. The thick, rock wall, bold design and luminous hallways had always given Talos a sense of pride in his race and in his career choice of ritual Hunter, but now the impressive structure looked forbidding and harsh, more like a prison then a sanctuary.

Inside the main chamber the Council was in full assemblage. Talos took his place at one of the highlighted circles on the patterned floor, ignoring everyone else in the hall except for the Council members. His blood raced through his veins like fire. The scent of Barlow standing only a few feet away from him made his instinctive urges to protect his newly claimed mate vibrate his very bones until his chest ached and his fists clenched in an involuntary urge to strangle the insane bastard. In the background he could smell Sherman in the crowd and he flared his nostrils in an attempt to track both men's movements without looking at them.

All around him muted chanting floated on the heavy, moist air of the room, its tone different from the previous meeting, sounding more ominous and primal.

190

It sent a shiver of unease down Talos' spine. Before this, before mating to his life partner, nothing threatened or unsettled the Hunter, but now he had another who depended on him, one he wasn't willing to risk losing for any reason.

Seeing everyone in place, Belith sat behind the Council's broad, smooth table, and formally began the proceeding. "This gathering between the Council of Oracan, procurer Agustus Barlow and Bounty Hunter Talos, son of Menalon, is at the decree of Council to address grievous claims against the procurer."

The lights on Talos and Barlow brightened, making both figures the focus of attention. They stood several feet apart on separate circles carved into the intricate pattern of the stone floor.

Barlow's distinctive smell intensified and Talos turned to glower at Barlow, the bright color and bizarre pattern of the man's always present pirate-style sash grating on his sensory system.

Violet eyes riveted on Barlow, Belith continued his opening remarks, declaring, "A claim of interference with a Hunt has been given against you Agustus Barlow. How claim you?"

Looking pious and confused, Barlow answered, "I claim innocence, High Principal Belith. While it is true one of my employees did visit the station on which Talos is presently staying, the meeting between them was purely accidental."

Belith stared at the man for several uncomfortable seconds, then moved his hard gaze to Talos. "Talos of Menalon, what say you?"

"His aide was found interrogating the station's

staff about this Hunt's bounty." Talos looked at the crowd of spectators behind him, pinpointing Sherman's location by his scent. He stared hard and long at the man. "He knew I was there. He should have avoided the station at all costs." Talos turned his attention back to the Council. "The Details of all Hunts clearly decree no contact until the Hunt has been declared final by Council."

Sherman sank further into the shadows at the back of the crowd of watchers.

Barlow ignored his aide, addressing Council, his tone placating. "My deepest apologies, High Principal. My aide was poorly informed and certainly not acting with my approval. I will see to it that he is made more aware of the Details in the future." Barlow lowered his gaze. "No harm was intended, I assure you."

Belith glanced around the table as each Council member made a small move with their hand. Tone still unyielding, Belith nonetheless proclaimed, "Apology admitted into chamber memory, Mr. Barlow."

The low undertone of chanting in the deep Oracan guttural language suddenly took on a threatening tone. The members of the Council all stared at Barlow and the atmosphere grew thick with anticipation.

Leaning back in his seat, slowly enunciating each word, Belith stated, "Claim of death threats to a Hunter have been given against you Agustus Barlow. How claim you?"

Barlow took several rapid breaths through his nose and his lips quivered so slightly it was barely visible. Sweat popped out on his upper lip. "It was a

misunderstanding. I never truly meant it." Barlow
managed to look contrite, eyes lowered and voice
softening. "I was excited and overwrought by
anticipation, High Principal." He extended an open
hand in askance toward the Council members. "The
magnificent job of recovering the pirate by this
outstanding Hunter was cause for elation." He
indicated Talos, unaffected by the Hunter's piercing
glare, then smoothly continued. "The pirate is of great
significance to my people. Surely, you can understand
that."

Seemingly unaffected by the man's heartfelt
speech and plea for understanding, Belith shifted his
appraising glance to the Hunter. "Talos, what say you?"

Talos bowed respectfully at the Council, but
darted his eyes back to Barlow as he spoke. "Barlow
accused me of trying to steal both the bounty and the
treasure he is seeking. When I refused to discuss the
Hunt, he then threatened to procure an illegal Hunt,
with me as the bounty."

A ripple of angry discord ran through the room.
The chanting swelled then ebbed, the thudding beat
echoing off the cavernous rock walls and ceiling. Every
eye in the room was trained on the two occupants in the
opposing spotlights.

Barlow jerked and tilted his head to one side,
narrowing his eyes for a moment before stepping
forward off the carved disc toward the Council. "Again
my apologies, to all of Council. I had been drinking at
the time. I wasn't--."

"Enough." The single word echoed in the room.
Exchanging looks with Council, Belith nodded as each

Laura Baumbach

member set forth a yellow stone in front of them on the table.

Beside Belith, Zeban silently studied both Barlow and Talos. He scented the air then snapped his gaze up to lock on Talos.

Talos didn't move a muscle or bat an eye, well aware his elder brother would be able to detect the change in his scent. A change that happened only when an Oracan takes a mate. He knew the pirate's scent was different than any species' scent in their world and Zeban would know it, too. In all of recorded and remembered history no Oracan had ever mated with a human before. It was impossible before this. There had never been a human who could stand to be touched by an Oracan before Aidan Maymon.

Zeban lowered his gaze and closed his eyes briefly. Talos let out the breath he had been holding, but remained tense and on guard. His whole future and that of his lover's rested on this moment and the Council's decisions today.

Belith recovered his usual neutral demeanor and spoke. "Council is united. The Details of this Hunt are stricken. All claims to any bounty already obtained in the Hunt are revoked."

A murmur of faintly hostile agreement washed through the audience. All twelve of the Council remained silent, but Talos noticed that the bone spikes of several had raised marginally on their forearms.

Barlow ignored the agitated crowd. His tone was placating and low, but his eyes narrowed and his stare turned harsh. "High Principal Belith, please!"

Belith ignored the interruption and calmly

continued with the remainder of the sentencing. "All credits paid are forfeit."

"This is extreme, High Principal. I've already invested a fortune in this Hunt." Barlow sputtered and fumed, but Talos couldn't detect any real scent change telling him the human was truly upset by the verdict.

Belith rose and stood, towering up to his full height of seven feet. His thin, satiny robes flowed around his massive physique like swirls of luminous dust, and clung to his brawny frame, outlining the powerhouse body all Oracans possessed.

The High Principal's voice trilled on the r's and hissed over the s's, adding a menacing, guttural quality to his naturally deep, smooth tone. He stared Barlow in the eyes until the human faltered and lowered his gaze to the floor, accusing, "And you have violated its terms and offended the honor of all of Oracan society."

Recovering, Barlow glanced around the room, including every Oracan present in an attempt to smooth over the discord. "I greatly apologize and... I accept your decision without reservation." Barlow bowed his head slightly and waited for Belith to continue. His fingers drummed on the hilt of his pirate sword, making an irregular rhythm that thudded annoyingly at the edge of Talos' hearing range.

"Know this Agustus Barlow, if you make any attempt on the life of the Hunter, Talos of Menalon, or the bounty, Aidan Maymon, there will be severe consequences to pay." Resuming his seat, Belith let his words hang heavy in the air before adding, "Ones that will cost you more than just your precious credits."

Barlow curtly nodded and bowed, his back stiff

and his gaze indifferent. "I understand completely, High Principal."

Giving the human another appraising glance, Belith stated, "I greatly doubt it." He shifted his attention to the witnesses present and stated the next portion of the decision ritual demanded.

"Regretfully, as this is live bounty, Council will accept ownership of the pirate Aidan Maymon until relocation." Belith quietly addressed the Hunter, confident the usual answer would be received. No Hunter had ever claimed live bounty before, none needed or wanted the burden and to sell it for personal gain was forbidden. "Are you agreed, Talos of Menalon?"

"No." Without hesitation, Talos faced the full Council and firmly addressed them, looking each member in the eye one by one as he spoke. He ended at his brother, holding Zeban's gaze for an additional few seconds before respectfully turning to Belith. "No, High Principal. I do not agree."

Silence fell over the room and Talos became the center of everyone's attention, Oracan and alien alike. Talos could hear the sharp intake of air Barlow drew and held, apparently waiting for Council's reaction.

Perplexed, Belith paused, glanced at Zeban's closed face and then studied Talos again. "You're making claim of this pirate? This human?"

"I am, High Principal." The spikes on Talos' arms and back rose to half-mast, causing a ripple of hushed murmuring to run through both the crowd and the Council table. "I proclaim my rights as set forth in the Details of a Stricken Hunt, taking ownership of all procured bounty. For life."

Several Oracans scented the air and then shifted nervously in their Council seats. Outwardly, Talos ignored them, but he was pleased they were reading his serious intentions correctly, even if they were confused by his odd new scent. "There will be no relocation. I accept responsibility for him. He will become part of my family's cache."

A wave of excitement and surprise flowed through the room. Zeban touched Belith's sleeve and the High Principal leaned his head toward Talos' brother and listened. A flash of something Talos couldn't interpret flashed across Belith's face then morphed into sly understanding and reluctant acceptance. That was something Talos recognized. His brother was wearing the same expression.

Straightening up in his chair, Belith made an oddly tuned, slight humming sound deep in his chest. Every Oracan witness and all of the Councilors snapped their heads around to stare at Talos in wonder, all startled by the ancient ritual hum covertly announcing a newly mated male to his brethren.

Belith drew a deep breath and returned his focus to the matter at hand. "Very well. It is your right." He raised his voice and announced to all, "Proclamation admitted into Chamber memory. The Live Bounty, the human Aidan Maymon, is harbored to Talos of Menalon, as his property and that of his cache, to protect and care for from this time forth until the human no longer exists."

The subdued chanting rose and then abruptly stopped, leaving the chamber eerily silent and suddenly feeling twice as large as before.

"Council is ended." Belith moved a black stone to the center of the table.

Body held taut and insides churning, Talos slowly expelled the breath of anticipation he had been holding. His mind reeled and his chest felt like it had just been released from a vise. With one word, he had been given back his future, his life and his lover. The spikes on his body recessed a few inches, just high enough to break the surface. The smell of Barlow was too near for him to relax completely.

The entire Council rose as one, bowing to Talos, fists over their hearts. "Honor and Compassion, Talos of Menalon."

All twelve let out a small, oddly pitched hiss, each acknowledging Talos' change in status from single male to mated partner. One or two were marginally slow in coming, but all were given freely.

"Honor and Compassion." Talos respectfully bowed and saluted. Shifting his feet to widen his stance in a preemptive battle move, Talos added a low, sharp, challenging hiss of his own to the ritual greeting. The spikes on his arms and back rose fractionally letting the other males know he would battle any that objected to his change of status. No one answered his challenge and a thread of elation ran through the Hunter. This was the first big step to having his unusual choice for a mate formally accepted by his people.

The thrill of the moment dulled slightly as Talos detected the stench of Barlow coming up behind him. He turned and his faintly wild, hormone-induced, possessive glare bore down on the antiquities dealer, making the man abruptly stop several feet away.

Doing a fair job of hiding his insecurities, Barlow smiled and shrugged. "No hard feelings, I hope." A tiny band of sweat beads on the man's forehead and a distinct change in his scent told Talos the man was unusually uneasy in his presence, more so than Barlow had been during the last Council meeting.

Talos' natural suspicions were awakened and he had to wonder what the devious human was up to now. "You giving up just like that?"

"I don't see that I have much of a choice, have I?" Barlow's smile turned hard, then he abruptly pivoted on one heel and stalked away, nearly colliding with his own aide who stood waiting to one side as he always did.

"I'm truly sorry...about...all of this. Please remember that." Sherman flashed an apologetic look at Talos, then hurried after his employer, throwing several conflicted glances over his shoulder at the watching Hunter as he walked.

Talos' thoughts on Sherman's odd behavior were interrupted when his elder brother approached him, a wry, faintly concerned look on his expressive face. "I hope you know what you're doing. This is going to be a difficult joining to maintain."

"The ritual called to me." That single sentence justified everything. No Oracan warrior refused the call of their instinctive, biologically motivated drive to bond when their finely tuned systems came in contact with a suitable mate. Guided by scent, taste, and their body's chemical response to these factors, a decision to take Ritual-chosen mate was unquestionable.

"Ah, I see. Then the cache will welcome your pirate. Father will be pleased to have another in his domain." Zeban studied Talos for a moment, then quietly added, "The cache has missed having a troublesome little brother in its midst since Bakus' death. Your young pirate will be an interesting addition."

Pain flickered across Talos' face then disappeared. "He has spirit. His soul is that of an Oracan," he fiercely proclaimed. The he sighed and admitted, "It's his morals that need work."

Suppressing a smile, Zeban asked, "He really is a criminal then?"

Talos shrugged. "Pirate, rogue, pickpocket, flirt, thief, drunk --."

Amused, Zeban interrupted. "I understand." He rested a reassuring hand on his brother's shoulder, tactfully avoiding the still protruding spikes. "And I look forward to meeting him. When will you present him to the cache?"

"Soon. I need to...talk to him about a few things first. He's...unused to the current way of life and completely ignorant of Oracan society." Talos gave his brother a tolerant grin. "Aidan has a tendency to steal *everything* bright and shiny he comes across. We need to...reach an...understanding before I let him loose in public."

"Ah, domestic chores." Zeban let out a low, trilled chuckle of understanding.

Still hyped and wary, his mental readiness always partially in Hunter mode, Talos relaxed marginally, at ease in the accepting presence of his brother. "More like finding a leash and collar."

Glancing around the slowly emptying meeting chamber, Zeban lowered his voice, eyes suddenly serious and bright. "Does he still wear your band?"

Nodding, Talos reluctantly said, "Not happily, but yes."

Zeban gave an abrupt nod of approval and removed his hand from Talos' shoulder to tap one finger on the Hunter's chest, just over his heart. "It is for his protection. Given the circumstances of his bounty status, he will undoubtedly need to wear it all of his life."

Talos' voice grew rough and slightly resentful. "He sees it as a sign of slavery."

Surprised, the older Oracan frowned. "That's an interesting and complex way to look at it. It is meant to be a mere labeling system, to prove ownership of an item if it were to become lost."

"Well, he's lost most of the time, but he definitely doesn't like being 'owned'."

"Then you have much to attend to, my brother." Zeban saluted and bowed. "Honor and Compassion."

Talos returned the gesture and hurried away from his brother and out of the chamber, ignoring the remaining Oracans who boldly scented him as he passed.

Chapter Fourteen

Dr. Jaclyn Rice's bedroom was moderately large and very comfortable. The room was decorated in pale shades of pink and red, with a modern artistic touch to all of the paintings and furniture. A slim bedside chair was covered in discarded clothing of a decidedly masculine cut and a pair of heavy service boots lay askew on the floor at the bottom of the bed's platform.

Under a thin layer of dusky pink sheets, Marius and Rice were sprawled together, their nude bodies comfortably entwined in sleep.

Slowly awakening, Rice blinked away the early morning fog and groggily focused on the sharp luminous green 0700 that showed on the time meter built into the bedside stand. Slipping out from under Marius' resisting arm, she wiggled out from under the sheet and leaned over to grab her robe off the end of the bed.

Eyes still closed, Marius snagged her arm and pulled her back for a long and lingering kiss, a satisfied and appreciative moan coming from deep in his chest.

Rice hummed a response and drew back, her hands making light circles of contact on his muscled chest. "Hold that thought." She kissed him again, quicker this time then sat up on the edge of the bed and pulled her robe on.

Marius groaned and struggled awake. "Where are you off to so early?"

"I want to take Aidan some breakfast and apologize for yesterday." She got up off the bed and walked into the adjoining bathroom to start the shower then popped back into the bedroom, brushing the snarls made from last night's lovemaking out of her long red hair.

"Apologize? For cutting his hair?" Marius pushed himself up on one elbow, but his eyes were still at half-mast and struggling to shut.

"No. For not understanding." Rice's voice was muffled, her head bent down as she ran the brush through the underside of her hair.

"Not understanding what?" Marius lost the battle as his eyes fluttered closed.

Rice threw her head back and tugged the tie to her robe tighter. "His whole world's been ripped apart, Marius." She crossed her arms over her ample chest, grimacing. "My medical exam must have been the ultimate violation for him."

Marius fell back onto the pillows and mumbled to the ceiling. "He didn't seem too upset over anything except his hair. He's a pirate. I'll bet he's had worst things done to him in his short life. He's a survivor. He'll be fine."

"That right there is the problem." She pointed an accusing finger at Marius, but it lacked impact when he didn't even lift his head to see it. Thwarted, she made a humphing sound and shook the end of the mattress, rousing Marius enough that he opened one eye and

Laura Baumbach

looked at her.

Once she had his attention she said, "I think everyone shrugs off his feelings because he appears so unaffected by it all. And that can't be true. Look what he's been through just getting here. Attempted murder, kidnapped, drugged, captured by an alien warrior, examined and violated. It's too much for any normal person."

Rising an eyebrow, Marius quipped, "I think normal may be the key word here, Jaclyn."

"Marius!" Rice's eyes flashed wide and her lips formed a thin line of disapproval.

Relenting, Marius turned to face her and sighed. "Okay, okay. You really don't believe he's fine?"

"No, I don't." Rice sat down on the edge of the bed next to Marius and rubbed his bare shoulder. "And I'm going to go apologize for not seeing it sooner."

Dropping a chaste kiss on Marius' willing lips, Rice darted off the bed and sailed toward the waiting shower. A backward glance showed her Marius as he planted his heavy head back on the pillows. She could hear her lover snoring before she had even stepped under the hot spray.

***

Standing outside of the Hunter's suite, Dr. Rice carefully balanced a large covered tray with one hand while she unlocked the door using the retinal scanner in the wall. When the door obediently slid open, she walked boldly in and started to call out.

"Aidan? I brought-augh!" Her startled scream echoed off the walls, the sound muffled by the swish of the door as it swiftly closed behind her. She had to scramble to keep her precarious hold on the heavy tray as Aidan popped off from a chair moved close to the door, brandishing a large object over his head.

Seeing whom his visitor was, Maymon hastily jumped down and quickly placed the heavy Oracan statue out of sight on the floor behind a potted plant.

Rice choked back the severe rebuttal she had on the tip of her tongue. "Good Lord, Aidan, you nearly scared me to death."

Maymon self-consciously raked his fingers through his short hair, reminding her of her offense. "No need to curry favor with titles, m'lady." He sniffed and his chin rose in the air. "'Specially since I'm not sure if I be wanting *your* company just yet."

Taking in the pirate's new clothes, trim body and athletic build, Rice was suddenly struck by how attractive and young Maymon was. Not only was he now clean and well groomed, but he had a flushed glow about him she hadn't noticed before and couldn't place. He looked healthy, full of energy and high-spirits if the way he blithely jumped from table was any indication.

Rice smiled and lifted the lid off the food tray. "Really? I thought you might be hungry. And please, call me Jaclyn."

Maymon sniffed again, this time sampling the aromas wafting up from the open tray. His stomach growled and Rice could see his stiff resolve melt a little.

"Well, maybe just a wee bit." He glanced at her then his eyes darted back to the food. "Jaclyn." Maymon hesitated for split second then grabbed the tray, taking it to the small dining area. Plopping down on a chair he propped his feet on a corner of the table and began to devour the meal.

Ignoring the silverware, Maymon shook a handful of scrambled eggs in Rice's direction and said between bites, "Been extra hungry since yesterday. Whatever happened to me whilst I were in your wicked care, it made me appetite heartier than it's been in some time." He picked up a mug, sniffed it, then put it down, frowning. "Did you bring any beer? Or maybe some of that blue grog from the inn?"

Shocked, Rice sat down in the chair beside Maymon and delicately replaced a piece of toast that had slipped off the plate in Maymon's enthusiasm. "Of course not! It's breakfast! You shouldn't be drinking alcohol this time of day."

Maymon paused mid-bite and asked around a mouthful of ham, "What should I be drinking if not grog?" He chewed and swallowed, picking up the discarded mug again to suspiciously glance in it a second time. "Most everything else gives a man the runs." He sniffed at the fluid inside the mug, obviously thirsty, but just as obviously unwilling to trust her.

Disturbed that the young man was so uneasy with her to not even drink, Rice sighed and tried to reassure him. "Not any more. Things are different in this age." The furrows between Maymon's brows lessened a little. "As your doctor, I'm telling you water is the best thing for you." The dark cloud settled back in Maymon eyes and his frown deepened again.

Apparently reassurances from a doctor had the opposite effect in the eighteenth century than they did now. Rice tried to salvage the moment. "But that's orange juice. It's good for you too." He stared at the mug then back at Rice. She smiled and encouraged him to try something new like she would a small child. "Go ahead, try it."

Maymon sipped it suspiciously then greedily drank it down, slamming the empty mug on the table in loud bar-behavior satisfaction. "A tasty bit of drink that." He smacked his lips and rubbed his new shirtsleeve over his mouth, leaving a small smear of orange behind. "A body could get used to that, it could." He shoveled another handful of food into his mouth, adding in a niggling, hopeful tone, "If it had a little rum in it, that is." He waited for a response, dark gaze flirting with the doctor.

Suppressing a grin, Rice shook her head no and Maymon immediately went back to eating, unfazed. Rice watched his uncouth habits for a moment, worried about how he was going to fit into his new life. "You know, Aidan, there are a lot of things here you're going to have to get used to."

"Know that." He never stopped eating, but a guarded expression suddenly clouded his face. "Tals is showing me," he said quietly.

"I'd like to help too." Rice leaned forward and rested a hand on Maymon's arm. "If you'll let me." She smiled and added sourly, "If your keeper doesn't mind."

The vaguely guarded expression on Maymon's expression hardened and instantly shut down. He stopped eating and slowly got up from the table, gently removing Rice's hand from his arm in the process. "Must be the strange eats." His voice was low and neutral, but Rice heard the hurt and forced distance he put into his words. "I'm feeling a wee bit like me sails have lost all their wind." He stepped back and made room for her to have a clear path to the door. "It might be best if I were on me own just now, m'lady."

"Aidan, I'm sorry." Realizing she actually knew nothing about Maymon and Talos' situation except her own feelings about the aggressive, annoying, sexist Hunter and the taking of live bounty, Rice backpedaled. "Please sit back down and finish eating." She tugged at his sleeve and drew him back to the table to sit. "I came here to apologize for yesterday, not to make matters worse between us."

"Apologize? For cutting off me hair?" Indignant and hurt, Maymon sat but folded his arms defensively across his chest.

Patting his shoulder in a gently petting motion to soothe him, Rice explained, "For not understanding how difficult this has all been for you."

Maymon remained silent and standoffish, but his gaze flitted to meet hers.

Gesturing helplessly, Rice huffed out a deep breath and said, "I just don't understand why this Talos means so much to you. He's a bounty Hunter. He kidnapped you. He's ruined your life. I'd hate him if I were in your place."

Maymon shook his head and smiled sweetly. "That's where you'd be wrong, m'lady." He hunched forward, leaning in close to her, a light of joy and wonder in his eyes. "He saved me. Rose up out of the ocean's depths and snatched me dying body and soul right out of the mouths of a horde of cold-blooded devils, both above and below me."

He shook his head and looked off into the far corner of the room for a moment. "Me mum's people believe the dead turned into water spirits called the Cemi. After a raid, I'd always throw a piece of our swag overboard to honor them, to honor me mum." Conviction filled his words as he confidently proclaimed, "'Twas what saved me."

Listening with a new sense of awe for the young man's resiliency and survivor instincts, Rice got caught up in his enthusiasm and wonder. "Saved you? How?"

Maymon's eyes sparkled and his entire body vibrated with energy. The flush on his cheeks deepened and a glimmer of amazement colored his words. "There I be, tied to a barrel, floating face down in a sea of gray-finned devils all looking to have me guts for lunch, and what is the last thing I sees before me senses leave me? A huge, bloody sea serpent with a near-human face and a body the size of me own jolly boat swimming up from the ocean floor to greet me." He gazed off into the distance, obviously seeing the event all over in his mind again. "Me own Cemi come to save me."

His gaze snapped back and he pinned Rice down with a determined stare. "The sacrifices were worth it, every last gold piece and gem." He threw himself against backrest of the chair and propped his feet back up on the table again, a satisfied, oddly sated smile on his lips. "I won't be hating him, m'lady. I owe him me life." He grabbed an apple from the tray and bit into it, speaking while he chewed. "And I'll not be forgetting it."

"Even if that means allowing him to hand you over to Barlow?" Rice wanted Maymon to think past the

moment the pirate was always living in and to look at
his impending future.

Maymon hesitated, then cocked his head and
raised an eyebrow. He quietly murmured, "I guess that
be the part where I have to trust him to do right by me
again and save me life a second time." He studied her
face for a moment then cautiously added, "'Specially
now that we're lovers and all."

"What?" Taken by surprised, Rice tightened the
grip she had on Maymon's arm. "You're...lovers? With
an Oracan?"

Startled, Maymon shook his arm away and
pushed his chair away from the table, boots smacking
the floor hard. Defensiveness in his every movement, he
stared hard at Rice, his eyes shifting over her apparently
trying to read the reasons behind her reaction. "Aye, we
be that and more. Was content to warm his bed in the
dark, but he says that's not the way it has to be
anymore. Tals says two men can be together, in the
daylight, in front of everyone, and no one's got to hang
for it."

"Aidan, if he's taking advantage of you--."

"There be none of that, m'lady." Maymon shook
his finger in her face as he sternly declared, "Was me
what went to him. I offered, and he refused, unless I be
willing to match the rest of my days to his." Maymon
fiddled with the band on his wrist, his insistent tugging
and yanking on the silver strip less aggressive than
usual. "Seems the massive beast's the 'ring and forever-
promise' type of mate, he is." Maymon's tone was
petulant, but still obviously pleased at the same time,
apparently peeved only about the insistence for

commitment.

"He doesn't ...hurt you at all when...I mean, he's so much bigger than humans...," she blushed, but forged ahead, "as a doctor, I just have to...worry about...things." Rice stuttered her way through, searching for a subtle way to make sure the small man was truly comfortable with this unheard of human and Oracan pairing.

A blinding sparkle lit up Maymon's dark eyes and the grin on his face showed every one of his gleaming white teeth. "True, he's a huge brute of lover. And he outmatches me in strength and stamina, but," his expression turned shy and his voice held a note of awe, "I've never afore experienced the things he does to me head and me heart." Then his grin was back and he waggled his eyebrows at her. "Not to speak of the delightfully wicked things he did to me knob and me arse." He wiggled his butt on the seat cushion to make his point and added, "Weren't sure I could sit this morning. Buggered me senseless, he did." When Rice colored a bright red and covered her snickering mouth with one hand, he sincerely asked, "Do you know how enjoyable it is to kiss? I mean really kiss? To *want* to kiss another person's mouth?"

His eyes were wide and his voice held a note of such wonder and delight that it made Rice think of her first time with a thoughtful lover. She smiled and reassured him, "I think I have a good idea, Aidan." She winked at him and added, "I've kissed a few men in my time. Though I'll admit, none of them were ever a muscle-bound Oracan Hunter."

Suddenly realizing Maymon may not be as naive

and helpless as she thought, Rice stood up and ran her hands maternally through his shortened hair, ruffling the fine strands. "You're an amazing young man, Aidan Maymon."

Never one to let a compliment or an opportunity pass by, Maymon asked, "I don't suppose that would convince you to let me wander a bit?" He batted his devilishly long eyelashes at her.

Rice laughed and messed up his hair even more. "No. In this instance, I have to answer to your Hunter the same as you do." Turning serious, she conceded, "He strikes me as the protective type. I think it's best if we humor him for awhile, especially now that you two are...close."

Maymon snorted and casually tossed the apple core into the corner of the room. "You find a sense of humor in him, save it for me." He picked at the remaining fruit on the tray, popping a few grapes into his mouth, outwardly pleased with their strange, new flavor. He threw the grape stems after the apple core. "I'll be needing it more than the likes of you will."

Rice laughed. "I'm sure you will." Shaking her head, she reseated herself at the table and popped a grape into her own mouth sharing a grin with Maymon.

A light crackling sound filled the air and a segment of the room erupted in a shower of bright sparkles and a shimmering field of energy. Zrac and Garn stepped through the energy field. Heavily armed, with weapons drawn and aimed directly at Maymon and Rice, they advanced on the startled pair.

Surprised, but used to thinking fast on his feet, Maymon instantly reacted by grabbing the silverware off the table and then flipping the small piece of furniture in the air, showering the Mercs with dishes and uneaten food. Throwing a dinner knife with the practiced eye of the keenest of assassins, Maymon was able to stagger Zrac for a moment, but the Merc's weapon's beam hit the pirate dead center. Maymon crumpled, unconscious before he hit the food-strewn floor.

Rice grabbed the nearest object and winged it at Garn, but the brawny mercenary just batted it aside and leveled his gun at her. Rice made a dive for the commlink, but she crashed to the floor midway through her jump, a beam of ghostly white light striking her directly in the middle of her chest.

The room shimmered and the crackle of energy filled the room again. The last thing Rice saw before the room went black around her was Maymon's limp body roughly lifted from the floor.

Laura Baumbach

Chapter Fifteen

Restless, feeling the nagging need to return quickly to his rambunctious lover, Talos straightened in the cockpit chair and refocused his thoughts. Activating his ship's recording device, he replayed the video of the day he rescued Maymon, reviewing the underwater rescue and then the attack on his ship by the marauding Mercs fighter. A sudden realization hit as he watched the attack and he slammed his fist down on the console.

"Son of a bitch! Barlow, you lousy, deceptive, power-hungry bastard!" Checking the time, one long, large hand darted up and hit the commlink, opening a channel to the space station and directly into Dr. Rice's suite.

***

The chimes sounded twice before Marius Webb dragged himself out of bed and walked to the view screen. He grunted in acknowledgment of Talos' familiar identity code flashing on the screen, then grabbed a nearby robe and shrugged into it. He slumped down into the chair in front of the screen and activated the link, blinking hard as the image of the Oracan Hunter filled the viewer. His voice was sleep-roughened, but alert. "Webb."

Giving the Commander a moment to orient

himself, Talos quipped, "You sound like you're still visiting with the Sandman, Marius."

Marius frowned and rubbed his eyes. "Don't know anyone named Sandman. I was asleep." He looked for the timepiece Jaclyn kept on her desk but couldn't find it among the various feminine articles on the stand. "What time is it?"

"Later than I'd like it to be," Talos said forebodingly. "I just figured out Barlow's next move."

Starting to dressing as he continued listening, Marius paused in the act of zipping up his uniform shirt. He instantly snapped from casually interested to wide-awake and unhappy. "I'm not going to like this, am I?"

"You got it right on the horse's nose, buddy. He sent Sherman and then the other two idiots so I wouldn't be watching for a third." The Hunter's eyes flashed and the second layer of transparent eyelids snapped in place making him look even more startlingly fierce than before. His pupils were hidden by the bright yellow covering that fell into place to protect his eyes. His body was automatically getting ready to do battle, responding to the hormonal jump in the Oracan system that said his mate was in danger. "And I fell for it."

Dressing faster, Marius added, "If he's after Aidan, Jaclyn is with him. She took him breakfast and hasn't come back yet."

"Then they're both in danger." Talos' voice vibrated, trilling his r's. The spikes on his back flared into place, the white smooth bone gleaming in the cockpit's harsh light on the screen.

"I'll meet you at your place." Marius grabbed his handheld personal stun weapon off the bedside stand.

"Docking now. I'll be there in less than three." Talos hit the console of the fighter and the view screen went blank.

Marius didn't even pause to shut down the commlink before he raced out, mentally calculating the fastest way to navigate three levels and about a mile of corridor that stood between him, Talos' suite, and the two endangered people under his sworn protection.

***

Marius arrived outside the Hunter's lodgings seconds after Talos teleported into the public corridor. Several people in the hallway stumbled and hurried out of the Hunter's way as he stormed up to the retinal scanner and activated his door. In full assault mode, with spikes erect, eyes glowing and muscles bulging, the Hunter was terrifying to look at even without the barbed mace and torpedo-phase cannon he held cradled in his capable hands.

Hyped and ready to defend his home and lover against any and all foes, Talos was greeted with only the silent devastation of the chaotic remains of an unseen battle. Entering the living space, he surveyed the mess, knowing by fading scents in the room that neither Maymon nor Dr. Rice was there.

An unfamiliar, male scent assaulted his system and he grimaced and growled under his breath at the pungent, sickly smell that clung to the olfactory receptors in his palate. He spat into the mess of fallen food in an effort to remove the foul taste the odor left in his mouth.

Details of the Hunt

Coming up behind Talos, Marius took one look at the suite and ran to the wall commlink. He wasted no time snapping open the station-wide intercom. Punching a series of numbers into the keypad, his voice urgently boomed through the entire station. "This is Commander Webb. Security alert -- alpha-vector-kia-delta. I repeat -- alpha-vector-kia-delta. This is not a drill. I repeat, this is not a drill."

Several unformed station personnel ran by them, all hastily returning to their posts.

Talos backed out of the suite room, frustration mounting and hunting instincts on full alert. He joined Marius and without a word, they took of running for the docking bays.

They both knew there was only one way to leave the station and it would have to be in a shuttle. Although Talos had teleported into the corridor, he had done it from the docking bay after landing. The station had an energy field that prevented outside teleportation for security reasons. Whoever had kidnapped Maymon and Rice would have had to take them to a shuttle and exit the station the standard way. Talos knew Marius' Security forces had started preventing shuttles from taking off, but he didn't know if they had been quick enough to catch the kidnappers.

"How long has the Doc been gone?" Talos sprinted in place beside Marius, impressed the Commander could keep up, even if the docking bays were fairly close to his quarters.

"Less than ten minutes. They hit hard and fast, whoever they were," Marius said. They rounded a corner and entered the main docking bay. It was filled

217

with shuttles, large and small.

A crowd milled around waiting for the security alert to be lifted, their distant chatter telling Talos they were curiously speculating about what could have happened on such a quiet outpost, but not much else.

"Their scent is only a few croms old." Coming to a stop, Talos scented the air again and looked sharply around the bay at all the dark corners and hidden nooks. "They have to still be on the station."

Marius shook his head at the size of the task ahead of them. "There are dozens of ships here. We'll have to do a ship by ship search."

Talos moved toward his fighter and opened the secure hatch, heading into the bright interior of his ship. He paused at the doorway and said, "Don't need to. The Runt's banded. It's a homing device. Plus we're chemically bonded now. I can track his little ass through a forest fire in hell if I have to." He stared at Marius, and pointed a stern finger at him. "I'm going to jump ahead in time by two croms. If they're still here, I'll find them."

He raised his shoulder and back spikes even higher and commanded in a soft, deadly tone, enunciating each word clearly despite the trilled r's and serpent-like hiss. "Wait. Here." Then he turned and disappeared into the *Dango*.

***

Unused to being ordered around on his own command and curious about how the time link worked on the fighter, Marius couldn't resist. It was his job to know everything that happened on the station and Talos was his best friend. The Hunter would understand. Eventually.

Details of the Hunt

Marius eased through the open fighter's doorway and peeked around the lip of the hatch. He was sure his aggressive friend wouldn't kill him for just ignoring the command to wait. Pretty sure, anyway.

In the center of the small cockpit, the massive Hunter stood stone still, eyes closed and face calmly composed. He almost looked like he was asleep on his feet to Marius, if it weren't for the tight hold he had on his weapon. Marius was just about ready to pull back when Talos murmured a deep, relieved, "Got you, Runt," and blinked out of sight right in front of the Commander's eyes.

Astounded, Marius stood staring at the empty space where Talos had been, jaw hanging open. He scanned the interior looking for some unseen device or trigger, but found none.

Sudden insight struck and he fell back against the hatch framework, muttering to himself. "You don't use a time link device. You *are* a time link device. The ships are just a ruse!"

Marius swallowed hard and anxiously looked around to be sure no one was within hearing distance as he told himself, "Christ! No wonder no one can duplicate Oracan technology."

He glanced out at the open hatch again. Sitting down on the steps to the opening, he pursed his lips and slowly blew out a long shaky breath as all the implications of this forbidden knowledge came rushing up to greet him. Damn his curiosity. Maybe Talos would kill him after all.

Making a quick decision, Marius turned his back to the fighter and patiently waited, resolving to deny he saw a thing, quietly declaring, "And that's one more little secret I never learned. No matter who asks me."

***

On board the Mercs' shuttle, Zrac began to pilot the craft while Garn strapped an unconscious Maymon to a low pallet beside an already restrained, limp Dr. Rice. Once the job was done, Garn hurried forward and took the empty seat across from Zrac.

A tractor beam shot out of the station towards the sleek, black ship, freezing the vessel in place. The ship lurched and Talos appeared in the center of the shuttle's cluttered cargo bay for only a millisecond, then he blinked out as the shuttle unexpectedly broke free of the tractor beam's hold and jumped into hyper warp.

In the crackle of warp energy distorting, Talos suddenly reappeared inside the *Dango*. He fell to the floor of the fighter, stunned.

Alerted by the electric hum and snap, Marius bolted into the cabin and rushed to Talos' side. He helped his friend up, careful to only touch clothing and not skin. "What happened?"

Slightly dazed, the Hunter shook his head and strode forward to the cockpit. "They warped out at the same time I linked in. The warp phase knocked me back. Aidan and the Doc are both on board a shuttle." He sat down and began strapping himself in, alternating between readying systems and securing the craft. "The kidnappers are Betovans," he hissed, disgust readily heard in his voice. "They smell as rancid as they look."

Talos hit a few more switches then stopped to glare at Marius as the Commander began strapping himself into the co-pilot's seat. "What the hell are you doing?"

Giving Talos an innocent glance, Marius activated the view screen and linked to the control center to get emergency clearance for take off. "Going with you."

"Since when do you get involved in an Oracan Hunt?" Talos hit a control and the outer door to the fighter slid shut and sealed.

"Since kidnappers took off with the head of my medical staff." Marius settled back and checked his hand weapon. "Corporate headquarters won't be happy about that."

Talos openly scented the air around Marius. "And headquarters is the only one that will be worried?"

Coloring slightly, Marius primly answered, "Dr. Rice is a brilliant physician. She'd be hard to replace."

Smirking, Talos punched a button and piloted the fighter out of the docking bay at the first flash of the 'all clear' from the center. "For the dame's sake, I hope the Betovans know that."

Marius frowned and demanded, "What the hell are Betovans?"

Flying out of the bay, Talos took them a safe distance out then engaged the energy drive engines, shooting into light speed. "Mercenaries from the far side of the galaxy. They can teleport, but not time travel."

His eyes narrowed and his tone turned dark, menace vibrating the short bones in the back of his throat as a passionate hatred bloomed in his chest. The mate he had put his life, his honor and his family on the line for had been taken from him, and possibly injured, and he knew the bastard who was responsible for it. "*Barlow* must have paid a nice piece of change for those jackals to come out of hiding."

Marius absently studied the array of lights and buttons on the touch pad console as he asked, "How can you be sure it was Barlow?"

Talos sniffed then grimaced. "I could smell him. His putrid sweat was all over those deadbeats."

Remembering what Talos had said earlier, Marius frowned. "Why do these guys stay in hiding? That ugly?"

"Yeah, they are, but that's not the reason." Talos paused and decided maybe now wasn't the best time to update the Commander on the graphic, shocking history of violence and crimes the Betovan race was guilty of. "The entire race has a permanent bounty on their heads." He dropped his voice and gave Marius a knowing stare. "Long story. Just drop it for now."

After giving Talos a long thoughtful stare, Marius relented and sat back in his seat. "Okay, then." He needlessly checked his weapon a third time and then drummed his restless fingertips on his thigh. "Where do you think they're taking them?"

"Where else? Earth and the Runt's treasure. Barlow will have to move fast." Talos stared straight ahead and thought of all the different ways he could kill the antiquities dealer, selecting the most painful one to add to a short list of possibilities. "He knows I'm coming after him."

Chapter Sixteen

The primitive, but practical chemical torches cast crude, dancing shadows over the uneven rock of the tiny outcropping of volcanic stone. A single tropical bird called out its displeasure at being disturbed in the crisp night air. A light breeze ruffled through the sparse grasses and the few palm trees near the center of the bare land mass. The dark blue, Caribbean waters rose higher on the beach with each new gentle wave and the soothing sound of the ocean's unending movement swirled around the small band of intruders spoiling the serenity of the island.

Barlow's sleek, expensive shuttle sat to one side, barely supported by the thin stretch of white sand that ringed the entire place before giving way to ancient lava stone and ragged bursts of tall grass. A huge bonfire was surrounded by several high-tech lighting posts, turning a small area beside the craft from delicate island paradise into a harsh segment of daylight.

Four human guards with sleek, gleaming weapons dotted the brilliant space, all business and deadly intent in their measured, pacing and alert stance.

Barlow sat on a flat rocky outcrop, his clothing more pirate styled than usual. Knee-high, black boots glistened in the firelight, while his tight pants clung to

his frame revealing an athletic body that his usual
flamboyant robes hid. His crisp white ruffled shirt was
open to his waist and a layer of curly dark hair dotted
his well-developed chest. The only familiar piece of
clothing he still wore was the brightly patterned,
blindingly yellow sash wrapped snugly around his trim
waist. Strapped over the whole outfit was his prized
pirate sword, hilt polished to gleaming shine with its
finely honed blade encased in a jeweled sheath. Barlow
sat patiently waiting, a sated smile on his face, watching
the figure on the sand in front of him.

Still unconscious, Maymon lay sprawled at
Barlow's feet. To one side, Dr. Rice sat on the sand,
unrestrained, but with Zrac and Garn standing over her,
one on either side. Zrac periodically grabbed a handful
of her thick, tousled red hair and yanked on her head as
if to remind her they were close.

The attention of everyone in the group shifted to
Maymon as the young pirate groaned and slowly rolled
over, one hand going to his chest where he was hit with
the stun pulse and the other searching uselessly at his
waist band where he had kept a weapon for most of his
lifetime. Finding nothing, Maymon clenched his empty
hand into a fist, uttered a few unintelligible curses
under his breath and groggily, sat straight up and
looked around.

***

Maymon smiled wanly at Rice, frowned severely
at the Betovans, merely ran a passing glance over the
four perimeter guards and then turned to Barlow,
instinctively zeroing in on the man he knew he had to
negotiate with for his life. Too many years as a pirate on

the high seas had taught him how to determine who was in command by the airs the man presented.

Smiling widely, Barlow tipped his head in greeting, a mocking gleam in his eyes. "Finally, Captain Maymon. I was beginning to think my men had been too harsh with you."

Maymon grimaced and rolled his aching shoulders, making the wide opening of his wrinkled, food-smeared new shirt gap all the more, revealing his darkly tanned, smooth chest all the way down to his low-riding, tight, black pants.

Maymon eyed his new captor and frowned, instantly recognizing barely suppressed lust in the man's piercing glare. "Had more enjoyable reasons for a rough sleep." He pushed himself up in one graceful leap to a stand, stance still slightly unsteady. He rubbed at his chest again, inspecting the exposed flesh looking for a wound. He raised his eyebrows and then shrugged when he found nothing but old scars and unblemished skin.

Remaining seated like a king on his throne, Barlow introduced himself, bowing marginally from the waist, careful not to disturb the lines of the yellow splash of silk bound around his middle. "I am Agustus Barlow and I'm very pleased to finally meet you."

A half-lidded, calculating look of distrust flickered across Maymon's face. He murmured a low sultry sound and responded in a blatantly flirtatious tone. "Ah. The man what wants to own me, eh?"

Barlow's eyes roamed hungrily over the lithe pirate's lean frame, taking in Maymon's slim hips, half-naked chest, provocatively pursed, full mouth and

Laura Baumbach

challenging stare. He moistened his lips before answering. "On the contrary, Captain. I'm the man who gave you a second chance at life."

Barlow offered his hand in a gentlemanly welcome. Maymon easily accepted the offer, not bothering to wipe the wet sand and beach debris from his palm first. Frowning, Barlow grimaced and delicately rubbed his hands together to remove the gritty mess.

A light smile tugging at his lips, Maymon ignored Barlow's disgusted reaction. He stepped back a pace and planted one hand on his waist, surveying the beach in greater detail as he talked, smugly taunting the pompous man who was a large part of the turmoil in his life.

"Been giving all that credit to a rather large, gray, sea monster what plucked me drowning self from these very waters." He sauntered nearer to Rice, a suggestive swagger in his stride that had Barlow's attention riveted to Maymon's ass and not his actions. As he drew near to the doctor, Zrac pushed him away and Maymon graciously backed off to continue wandering around the small campsite.

Shifting on his rock throne, eyes glued to Maymon, Barlow bristled, a look of hatred and disgust darkening his sallow complexion even more. "The bounty Hunter might have been the one who transported you, but *I'm* the one who paid for the trip." He stabbed a finger in Maymon's direction and seethed, "Make no mistake who you owe your life to, Captain."

A knowing smile lit up Maymon's face and his eyes glistened brightly in the flickering firelight. His

226

voice was throaty and misleadingly seductive as he softly declared in a mocking tone, "Oh, I have a fair notion about the right of things, mate."

Barlow's eyes narrowed, but he continued to try to entice the young pirate to see the advantage of working willingly with him. "If you cooperate, I can offer you a future like you have never dreamed of. Riches and comforts beyond your imagining."

Still circling the camp, Maymon searched for some avenue of escape. With no lorry or slip in the waters he could find, and knowing the mainland was too far to swim out to, he was at a loss as to how to right the present, unfortunate situation he and the fair doctor were in. He suddenly wished Talos was here to fight at his side and he realized the big beastie of a lover of his would be looking for him. All he had to do was stall this pompous arse long enough for the Hunter to track him down once more and save his life. His heart ached and his confidence soared. Now he just had to keep the doctor and himself alive long enough for a rescue.

Stopping directly in front of Barlow, Maymon cocked his head to one side and suggestively drawled, "I've a pretty big imagination, mate. Don't need much past a dry berth, a cup of grog, a full plate and a solid ship under me feet." He winked at Barlow, noting the way the man's breathing sped up when his eyes appeared to be glued to the way Maymon licked his lower lip between sentences. "I wouldn't turn me back on a fit bed partner neither."

"I'll see to it that you have the finest ocean-going ship available." Barlow stood up and swung an arm at the wide open, crystal-blue waters behind them. "The best crew, the finest sails and the most beautiful women."

Appearing to contemplate the generous offer, Maymon crossed his arms over his chest and tapped one finger at his lips, drawing Barlow's gaze back to his pouting mouth. "Just how does me own fine self earn such swag? I own nothing but what you see before you." He spread his arms wide to show he had nothing but the clothes clinging to his sand-dampened body, an alluring sight in the flickering shadows as a light tropical breeze ruffled through his long dark hair and waved the open edges of his disarrayed clothing in a come-hither dance.

Barlow swallowed hard, then pulled his lust-filled gaze back up to Maymon's face to find a mocking smile. His stare hardened and he was all business again. "Tell me the location of the cargo from the 'Quedah Merchant'. Treasure hunters have searched this island for 700 years without finding a trace of it. You and you alone know the secret to its location." Barlow moved closer to Maymon, an impassioned plea in his voice. "Share it with me."

He dropped his voice seductively, leaning in close to whisper in the pirate's ear. "You'll have anything your heart desires, whenever you desire it. You'll truly be a free man. No Navy to Hunt you, no rivals to attack you, no port will be closed to you."

Taken by surprise, Maymon sincerely asked, "Pirating's legal now?"

Frowning, Barlow pulled back slightly and harshly barked, "Of course not. You won't need to steal other people's riches. You'll have enough of your own."

"I ask you, mate, where's the pleasure in that?"

Leaning in close again, Barlow let his shoulder rub against Maymon's arm as his hand traced the curve of Maymon's spine up to his neck. "You'll have everything you've ever wanted, my boy."

Unfazed by the man's lecherous touch, Maymon calmly returned the seductive whisper. "Well now, that sounds wonderfully delightful, it does. Anything I want?"

Maymon paused, tapping his lips thoughtfully with a finger. "What me blood-thirsty, pirate heart is fast becoming most desirous of is. . .," he winked at Barlow, "...seeing the likes of you dancing at the end of a merry rope. Mate." He pulled away and let all of the distaste he held for the sleazy buyer show in his face and tone. "I have no taste for doing business with the likes of you. I don't bargain with gents what deals in the buying of human flesh. Never have, won't start now."

Barlow stalked over to the Betovans and jerked his head at Dr. Rice. His venomous tone was full of pleased anticipation. "Very well."

The two Betovans dragged the struggling Dr. Rice up between them and brought her over to stand in front of Barlow.

Finding her voice for the first time since awakening, Rice let their attackers know exactly what she thought of them. "God damn, shit eating, sons of a Druillian whore! Let go of me!"

Garn shoved her back down to the sand and both he and Zrac pressed their weapons to either side of her head. Rice froze in place as Maymon jumped and attempted to go to her. Barlow stepped between them bodily forcing the young pirate to halt.

"Here now." Maymon glared past Barlow at the Betovans. He dropped his worried gaze down to Rice's scared, wide eyes and gently asked, "Be you all right, m'lady?"

"I'm fine, Aidan. Don't worry about me." Recovering her spirit, Rice elbowed Zrac's knee and shoved at Garn's leg. Surprisingly both Betovans backed off a pace, but kept their weapons directed at Rice. Heartened by the shift, Rice slowly stood up, tossing both guards an evil glare. She brushed the sand from her pant legs and reassured the young man. "I can take care of myself."

Chuckling mirthlessly, Barlow drolly said, "As competent as she is, I doubt even the good doctor can heal herself should any real harm befall her." He nodded at the Betovans and casually commanded, "Shoot her."

"Wait!" Panicked, Rice raised her hands to uselessly ward off the attack. Zrac restrained her arms while Garn menacingly raised his weapon and aimed it at her chest.

"Hang on there, you bug-eyed, pus bucket of a pox-ridden snake." Maymon struggled against Barlow's surprisingly strong grip, attempting to go to her aid.

Suddenly Barlow's prized antique sword loomed in Maymon's face. Maymon tentatively fingered the fine-honed edge of it, jerking back when blood coated his fingertips. He sniffed in disdain and shot Barlow a pouting glare. "No need for rough trade, now, mate. The lady's got nothing to do with this."

Barlow's gaze grew confident, knowing he held

the upper hand. "She does if you won't cooperate."

Turning his frowning pout into a seductive flutter of long eyelashes, Maymon changed course and coaxed, "What say we have a drink and talk about this, eh?" He tried to walk toward the shuttle and away from Rice, but Barlow held him in place. "I could use a pint about now. Been a long day, it has." Maymon grimaced, and twisted his arm in the painful grip.

Sneering in Maymon's face, Barlow ground out his demand through gritted teeth. "Tell me what I need to know and the good doctor will remain unharmed." He shook Maymon hard and hissed, "Deny me what's rightfully mine and she'll pay with her life."

"Don't listen to him, Aidan." Rice called out, struggling against Zrac's continued hold. "He plans on killing us both when he's done anyway."

Ignoring the outburst, Barlow eased closer to Maymon. "You, my dear pirate, I will keep." He leered, leaning in close to Maymon and breathing hot puffs of air on the pirate's exposed neck. "I couldn't care less about the good doctor. She doesn't mean anything to me. Don't give me a reason to rid myself of her annoying chatter any sooner than necessary."

Incensed, Rice yelled, "You're a vile, bastard, Barlow. You won't get away with this."

Pretending mild surprise, Barlow kept a hold of Maymon as he turned to face Rice. "My, my." His eyes darted to Maymon then back to the doctor, disdain and amusement on his face. "And he calls you a lady." His smile widened. "I suppose according to his crude, eighteenth century standards you are slightly more couth than a common wench." His smile twisted

Laura Baumbach

becoming ugly and perverse. "But only slightly."

Forsaking all lady-like decorum, Rice lurched forward and spit at Barlow's feet. "If anyone would know about 'crude' and 'common' it would be a scumbag, lowlife like you." Maymon grinned with a new appreciation for the feisty doctor.

Zrac dragged Rice back and shoved his weapon painfully into her neck. He buried one hand in her thick hair to hold her head in place.

Barlow abruptly shoved Maymon to the sand and advanced on the doctor, arm raised to strike.

"There's no call for that, you heartless blackguard!" Maymon jumped to his feet, throwing sand and seaweed in all directions in his haste to stop Barlow. "Leave off the lass."

Turning quickly, Barlow finished his original intent, violently slapping Maymon instead of Rice. The force of the blow sent Maymon tumbling to the ground again and he sat there, wisely giving a moment of peace to the situation.

Barlow suddenly drew his weapon and threatened Rice with the edge of his gleaming sword, but his gaze remained on Maymon. "Then give me the coordinates of the treasure." The flickering torches were reflected in his eyes, showing the fanatical glint shining in their depths.

"Don't need to, mate." Still seated on the wet sand, a bright red hand print outlined on his one cheek, Maymon stared into Barlow's twisted face, then darted a quick comforting look at Rice. "You have the map."

It had grown increasingly darker. Firelight flashed off the metal of the weapons and the sounds of the surf pounded in the background, all heightened by the enfolding darkness closing in all around them. Even the call of the sea gulls had disappeared to be replaced by the surge and slap of the restless ocean.

With a frustrated growl, Barlow grabbed Maymon by the scruff of his neck and dragged him up off the ground, pulling him close to snarl in his face. "Yes, I have the map. The coordinates don't work. This entire island is nothing but rock. There's no way you buried anything here." He shook the young pirate and bellowed, "It's not real!"

Zrac pressed the tip of his weapon deeper into Rice's neck, causing her to gasp and hiss as the edge of the gun pushed painfully against her windpipe.

Maymon's gaze darted from Barlow's burning stare to Rice's pinched grimace and back again. He let his voice fall to the low, throaty, flirtatious tone he used whenever he needed to get his own way and coaxed, "Course, they are, mate. You're just missing one wee bit of information."

Rice's gasp turned into a choked groan. Barlow lowered his sword, allowing Zrac to handle the doctor alone and turned his full attention to the pirate.

Maymon eased his arm out of Barlow's grip. "Never said I buried it." He batted his long lashes at Barlow and gave the man a seductive, teasing smile. "It's hidden." Barlow began to raise his sword again and Maymon hastened to add, "In a cave."

"That's rubbish." Barlow's tone was disdainful, but his eyes still held a gleam of fervent desire. "Every pit and crevice on this rock has been searched countless times. No trace of a treasure's ever been found."

233

Barlow eyed Rice and nodded at his men. Garn instantly twisted her arm behind her back, ignoring her anguished grunt of pain.

Satisfied, Barlow narrowed his eyes at Maymon and mused, "Maybe there never was any treasure."

The ominous sound of a stun weapon charging to full fatal capacity came from the direction of the mercenaries.

Maymon shifted slightly in Rice's direction. He didn't know what the sound meant, but from the increase in the doctor's struggles to get free, it couldn't be good.

Smiling a thoroughly charming and suggestive pout aimed at Barlow's libido, Maymon swaggered away from the uncertain man. He knew Barlow's vile eyes would be on his arse, not his destination as he moved closer to Rice's position.

Having gained several feet unchallenged, he turned back to face Barlow and drawled, "Well now, you don't believe that or me own fine self wouldn't be standing on this spit of godforsaken rock." He jerked his head at the kneeling figure of Dr. Rice and demanded, "Release her and I'll tell you what you want to know."

Eyes narrowed to mere slits, Barlow appeared to contemplate the offer. He nodded at Rice's captors and the mercs immediately released her.

Falling forward onto her hands and knees, Rice choked and coughed a few times, then rubbed gently at her bruised windpipe. She sat back and blessed both Zrac and Garn with a venomous glare. Both mercs chuckled and exchanged pleased looks.

Details of the Hunt

Gesturing to Rice, Maymon called out, "Come stand by me, m'lady." He glanced at the grinning aliens and pointedly added, "For safekeeping, such as it were."

Rice elbowed Zrac and jerked away from his reach, hissing, "Betovan grunge dog." She stalked over to stand by Maymon, her gait a little unsteady, but a fierce fire of defiance burning in her eyes. She touched the small bruises and scrapes on the young pirate's face, clucking and gently removing small bits of debris and sand from his skin. Maymon smiled and encouraged her to continue with a flirtatious wiggle of his eyebrows.

"Enough stalling, Maymon." Seething, Barlow bellowed out his mounting frustration. "Give me what I need."

Maymon stepped around Rice, placing the woman behind him as Barlow took a step in their direction. He could see Barlow's sword hand vibrating, anxious to do battle with anything or anyone.

He purred in a throaty seductive tone, but Maymon's words were filled with a double meaning. "Like to give you what you deserve all right, mate, but a deal's a deal." He lowered his gaze and mockingly looked Barlow over from head to toe. "After all, we're all honest men here."

Barlow advanced on them and Maymon stepped up to intercept the unequal challenge, finally revealing, "You need to go down, mate." He pointed at the sand beneath his feet. "The swag's in a cave, just under the waterline."

Barlow aborted his attack and stood blinking in

confusion.

Maymon subtly moved Rice backward, in the direction of the unattended, open doorway of Barlow's shuttle. "It's true, mate. The cave's only opening is underwater, even at low tide." Maymon shrugged, letting the ocean breeze slide his clinging, wetly transparent, white shirt off one lean shoulder, revealing more of his naked chest. "If no one's ever found it afore this, it's because they've never been stranded here and had to go diving for their supper."

Suspicion turning his unyielding gaze hard, Barlow pulled his eyes from the young pirate's finely muscled chest and lowered his sword a fraction. "How did you find it?"

Pointing to the south end of the tiny island, Maymon took a few more sideways steps toward the shuttle while Barlow's eyes followed his gesturing arm's target. "Followed a giant tortoise down farther than I'd ever gone afore."

He broke off from his tale and offered a side bit of information, enjoying the look of exasperated frustration that fell across Barlow's face as he rambled on. "They make a lovely bit of roasted meat. This one was so grand, I could've bathed in her shell, if I was the sort of gent that had a mind to do that soap and water...thing."

Barlow made a rumbling, hissing sound and stalked a pace closer, forcing Maymon to jump back to the topic the man wanted to hear. "There I was, deep under the surface, following me dinner, dizzy from the lack of air, when a trail of green light caught me eye." He spread his open hands in a wide fanning motion, adding movement and visual interest, painting the picture for his rapt audience. "Since it was either die drowning or starve to death, I decided drowning were quicker. I followed the light and ended up in the inlet of a cave, the walls all slimy green and glowing like."

Barlow raised his sword and advanced on Maymon. "I don't believe in ghost stories, pirate."

This time Rice stepped between the two men. "He's telling the truth. It's called bio-luminescence. It's a very real phenomenon in ocean water organisms, especially in these warm waters. It was probably nudibranches or sea pens on the walls. After seven hundred years, they are probably growing all over the treasure. That would have distorted any attempt to find it by scanning the island. They're slightly radioactive."

Lifting his nose in the air to sniff disdainfully at Barlow's disbelieving glower, Maymon humphed and said triumphantly, "Told you. Perfect spot to hide me treasures, as it were."

A thoughtful expression settled over Maymon's young face, adding years to his looks, eliminating his child-like exuberance in the process. He frowned and looked at Rice, as she was the only person present he cared about whether or not understood his reasoning. "After taking that golden lot from the Spanish, I knew me pirating days were growing short. They'd be looking to hunt me down and every one of me crew for ransacking that ship. This here swag," he pointed at the sand under his new boots again, "was me passage out of the thick of it, you might say."

Although frowning, Barlow relaxed marginally and demanded, "You can find it again?"

Dropping a sly, watch-me look at Rice who was still hovering at his back, Maymon reassured their captor, "'Aye, if the cave's still where I left it seven hundred years ago."

Barlow turned to the tallest of his human guards walking the perimeter of the bonfire. "Syphus, have a laser drill, diving gear and a signal beacon sent down. Make sure you get an extra diving setup for Captain Maymon."

The man wordlessly obeyed, pulling a communication device from his belt and quietly murmuring into it. Within seconds, a mount of equipment materialized off to one side next to Syphus' location through an energy beam.

Opportunist that he was, Maymon used the momentary distraction to quickly pick up the two heavy rocks he had been working his way to for the past ten minutes. He slipped one to Rice and held the other behind his own back. While the Betovans split their attention between watching the laser drill being assembled and the two unarmed captives, the pirate and the doctor made their move. On Maymon's signal they turned and hit the two mercs, rendering them momentarily stunned.

Rice grabbed her man's weapon and began firing at the remaining guards as she tried to find some kind of cover. "Get his gun, Aidan! Don't try to hit anyone, just fire in their direction." Rice fired another round from the energy pulse gun. Maymon noticed she was surprisingly comfortable with the deadly weapon in her slender hands.

Diving behind a small outcropping of rocks and

sparse sea grass just past the bright circle of firelight cast out into the moonless night, Rice pulled Maymon down beside her.

Confused by the alien weapon, Maymon turned it over and around in his hands searching for the proper way to hold it. He glanced at Rice and mimicked something close to her hold on the gun. "Don't see the percentage in keeping them alive, lass." Unable to find anything that looked like a trigger, he fumbled the weapon and had to scrabble to keep from dropping it. "They're trying to bloody well kill us!"

Rice continued to fire, beating off the guards' attempts to rush them. She cast a dark glance and nodded at the only means open to them to get off the island. "Do *you* know how to pilot that shuttle? Through the *air*?"

Looking at the sleek, sail-less vessel, Maymon actually wasted a moment considering it, then frowned and grudgingly agreed. "Good point."

Finding a button that appeared to move, Maymon mimicked Rice's movements and aimed his weapon at the scattered group of men and aliens. Accidentally hitting the correct firing mechanism, the weapon discharged hitting the shuttle to the far left of where the pirate was aiming. The blast struck the shuttle in the forward compartment and the whole interior burst into flames.

The resulting chain reaction of explosions rocked both Rice and Maymon off their feet. Before they could regain their bearings, Barlow's men overtook them.

Without a word, Barlow grabbed a stun gun from one of his men and fired at Rice, dropping her to the sand. None of the guards made an attempt to break her fall and the doctor hit the ground hard.

Maymon lunged for her, but Zrac intercepted his move and backhanded him. Surprised, Maymon staggered, disoriented enough to allow the brawny alien to grab him and shove him down the beach in the direction of the crates.

Barlow eyed Rice's unconscious body, then turned and led the way back to the fire, gesturing to Garn to gather up the fallen doctor. He pulled Maymon from Zrac's grip and brought the young pirate close to his side to murmur, "Come along, Captain. It's time to prove your little fairy tale."

Chapter Seventeen

Marius gripped the armrests of the too large co-pilot's seat and watched the effortless way Talos piloted the small fighter through a dense asteroid field. There were a few close calls, but the Oracan wove a path right down a twisted alleyway of empty space and they emerged on the other side completely unscathed.

Unable to assist in the running of the alien vessel, and with nothing to distract him, Marius fidgeted and tapped his fingertips lightly on the smooth, supple covering of the armrest. He glanced at Talos, then out at the vast empty space outside the front viewer and nonchalantly asked, "You know this Barlow better than I do, do you think he'd hurt them?"

Pausing in the adjustment of altering their course, Talos heard the slight edge in Marius' voice that always signaled the Commander was hiding something. He suppressed a smile, knowing the man refused to talk about the personal connection between the doctor and himself. As fast as the urge to smile came, it disappeared as he thought about the true answer to Marius' question.

Glancing at the Commander's tense expression and the drawn, hard line his lips made, Talos nodded and said, "Hurt them, yeah, he'd hurt them." Turning his head to look Marius directly in the eyes, he coolly added, "He'd hurt them and like doing it." He paused for a moment to let that sink in, watching the Commander's face until the surprise disappeared and a sobering acceptance of the facts registered with Marius. Then he reassured him, "But he wouldn't kill them. He's waited too long and spent too much money on getting the Runt to blow it right at the get go." Partially confident, partially hopeful he added, "He needs them alive."

"Both of them?" Marius looked doubtful and Talos understood his concern. Barlow didn't have a use for a doctor or a woman, that he knew of.

Checking over the multiple weapons strapped to the sash around his chest, Talos tossed a small handgun to Marius. "I can't see a pirate giving up his swag without a fight, but the Runt likes your dame, *despite* what she did to his hair." He nodded once and clapped Marius briefly on his shirt-covered shoulder. "He'd make sure she was safe. For all his thieving and tall tales, he's an ace. In a lot of ways, he's more Oracan than human."

Maneuvering the ship past a small moon on their left, Talos readjusted his ships' settings and kicked it into hyper drive. The stars and the darkness swirled into a bright, twisted mass as the *Dango* rocketed by. Talos sat back and watched the show for a moment before adding, "Which is a good thing for the Runt, since I just claimed him for my mate in front of the entire Planet Council and members of my cache. Being more Oracan than human will definitely help him adjust."

Details of the Hunt

Averting his eyes from the chaotic mess on the viewer, Marius slipped the weapon Talos had given him into his waistband. "He is rather unique."

"Thank the Gods of Delimal for that." Talos snorted and leaned back into the deep cushions of the pilot's chair, a mocking reverence in his voice. "The galaxy isn't ready for more than one like him."

Mimicking his friend, Marius settled back as well, and closed his eyes. "Amen to that, brother."

A comfortable silence descended over the cockpit as they waited for the ship to navigate and cross over the trillions of miles to Earth's orbit. Talos expertly hit and maneuvered through six successive wave portals and the *Dango* skated through each one without breaking hyper drive. Just after passing through the last portal, the view screen cleared and the fighter pulled out of hyper drive to drift into a high orbit around the third planet from this system's sun, Earth.

Taking back manual control of the ship, Talos flipped several control buttons and rapidly reprogrammed the console.

"We're cloaked now. Hold on while I get a fix on the Runt." Talos closed his eyes for mere seconds before they flashed back open. Abruptly standing up, he grabbed a few more bits of equipment from a locker behind his chair and tossed them to Marius, adding some to his own weapon belt.

Strapping on his own weapons and finding pockets for the new ones, Marius asked, "How are we going to get down there without being seen?"

"Easy. It's dark and they'll be concentrating on other things, so we'll have the advantage of surprise

and the fact that we don't need a shuttle to get there."
He stepped in close behind Marius.

"We don't?" Confused, Marius turned around
and bumped into the solid, looming, very near mass of
the Hunter. He jerked his head back so his face didn't
touch Talos' bare chest.

Without explanation, Talos pulled a startled, but
yielding Marius into a tight bear hug and reassured the
man, "We don't." Before Marius could protest or
comment, they both disappeared in the faint energy
shimmer of the Oracan's natural teleport flux.

***

The ocean breeze stiffened and the moon broke
through the drifting layer of dense clouds that hung
over the tiny island. The water sparkled and rippled
under the bright beams of luminous white light,
allowing the white sand and black lava rock that made
up its entire bulk to be seen for an extended distance
under the pale blue water. The air smelled clean and
fresh, tinged with the tang of ocean salt and seaweed.

Under the crystal clear surface, Maymon swam
side by side in the middle of several of Barlow's men.
Barlow had insisted the young pirate use one of the
small oxygen converters his men were using, spending
precious time and patience teaching the pirate how to
use it himself.

Maymon had balked and wheedled at using the
tiny contraption, and Rice had gained a few new bruises
over his resistance, but Barlow won in the end.

Removing his new, black boots, Maymon left
them at the edge of the fire ring. Grudgingly fitting the
small cylinder into his mouth, Maymon had eagerly

jumped into the warm, welcoming water and immediately showed his natural swimming talent in the swirling waves. Unencumbered by the full diving gear, lights and equipment Barlow's men carried, Maymon dove and surfaced, leading the way out of the lagoon to the south edge of the outcropping.

The other men followed and soon surrounded him, hemming him in and forcing the free-spirited young man to adapt to a slower, more cautious pace.

Barefoot, Maymon pushed through the darker waters, diving down deeper, searching for a familiar ledge he had used as a mental marker when he had stored his treasure only a short time ago. Or what had been only a short time to him. Time had altered the island surface, making it smaller and even more inhospitable then when he had last been there, but the rock underneath the waterline had gone practically unchanged over the centuries.

Locating the flat, smooth jutting ledge in the now dark green water, Maymon ignored the men behind him and ducked under the shelf, swimming the final dozen feet in near blackness. Up ahead, the eerie green of water seemed to intensify. Pushing himself up and over a wall of slick green, Maymon broke through the surface of the water into a small, underwater cave.

Barlow's men bobbed to the surface in the water beside him and he hastily pulled himself up onto the floor of the cave. A few feet away at his back sat a small mountain of coins and golden artifacts, all covered with mineral crust and tiny glowing organisms. Although it should be pitch black, thin beams of light filtered down through pinpoint holes in the rock ceiling from the island surface above.

Barlow's lead man, Syphus, roughly grabbed Maymon by the arm and pulled the young man to his feet. Growling in his face, Syphus said, "Stay out of the way and in sight, boy."

Nodding amicably, Maymon moved toward the mound of treasure and stood back against a slimy, green wall. Eyeing his swag, he ran his fingers through a small pile of loose gems and roughly minted gold coins, expertly palming several unnoticed by his busy keepers. Finding just the right moment, Maymon popped the bounty into his mouth and swallowed several of the smooth gems.

Two of Barlow's men began setting up the small beacon they brought down while the other two began filling small sacks with a sampling of the coins and gems. Picking and choosing his items, Syphus tossed several priceless artifacts to one side until he unearthed a golden specter encrusted with huge rubies and thousands of diamonds. He reverently wrapped it in a cloth and placed it in the carrying pack strapped to his own back.

Under the occasional sharp glare from Syphus, Maymon wandered deeper into the cave, looking over pieces of treasure and tossing them aside as he trailed away, pocketing a small dagger he found among the trinkets and gems. Making enough noise and clatter that he knew his captors would be reassured of his continued presence, but too busy to watch him closely, he continued to the back of the cave.

Finally finding what he had been looking for, Maymon bent down and picked up a large ornate vase, using the bulk of the vase to hide his true goal, a green glass bottle sealed with wax. At his feet lay several more bottles, all filled with a sandy gray powder.

Dramatically tossing aside the vase, he blocked the other men's view of the bottle with his body and worked the wax off with the small dagger. Breaking the seven hundred year-old seal, Maymon slipped the bottle upside down into the back of his sash and hid the dagger into the folds of his waist sash just as Syphus took a renewed interest in him.

"Get back over here." The burly guard glared at Maymon and looked him over twice before grunting, "You can help carry some of this."

Gesturing wide with open, empty hands, Maymon grinned and swaggered closer to the treasure mound. "Love to, mate. Nice of you to lend a hand." He walked around the pile, randomly grabbing hands full of coins and gems while keeping his back out of sight of the guards, circling and staggering around and through the treasure. "Had a devil of a time hauling it all down here meself."

Syphus grunted and continued to gather the swag up.

Out the back of Maymon's sash poured a thin trail of gray powder that started at the grouping of unopened bottles and continued up to the main treasure mixing and spilling all over it. Bending down to grab a large red ruby, Maymon popped the empty bottle out of his sash and let it roll across the floor to the back wall covering the sound with the rattle and clatter of the coins running through his busy fingers.

Smiling charmingly at the dark scowl Syphus

shot him, Maymon gathered a large bag of swag and managed to slip one of several ornate, short swords from under the backside of the mound into the long sack.

Jerking his head at the pirate, Syphus gestured at the water and waited for Maymon to drag his sack to the edge. He forced the breathing cylinder into Maymon's mouth then jumped down into the water, pulling the pirate with him. With a tug on Maymon's shirt, Syphus submerged and the other guards followed him.

Last to disappear under the glass-like surface, Maymon gave one final, regret-filled look around, popped a large emerald into his mouth, swallowed it and slipped away into the fluid arms of his beloved ocean.

***

On the far end of the tiny, scrub-dotted beach, a few hundred feet from Barlow's destroyed, smoking shuttle, Talos and Marius teleported into the moonlit shadows. Immediately taking shelter behind the only cover available, they crouched down beside a scraggly rock ledge.

Talos gestured toward the small gathering of figures ahead of them illuminated by the dancing light of bonfire and torches. Both warriors of a sort in nature, both understood what needed to be done without elaborate discussions.

They crept into the sparse foliage that bridged the gap between them and their goal, winding their way towards the group, each intently looking for the ones they came for among the milling figures.

Details of the Hunt

Taking a position behind a large rock close enough to hear the muttered conversations of the men, Talos tapped Marius on the chest and wordlessly pointed to their left where a now conscious Dr. Rice sat in the sand ominously flanked by two armed, and attentive Betovans.

Barlow stood on the opposite side of the fire from the doctor, scanning the beach and occasionally throwing Rice a dismissive smirk. He paced a few steps back and forth in the gritty sand, one hand fingering the hilt of his pirate sword. When the light from the torches reflected the gleam in Barlow's eyes, Talos saw the manic, nearly feverish glint of madness in them.

Scenting the moisture-filled, heavy ocean air, Talos continued scanning the grouping, his senses telling him the young pirate was near. He could smell his body scent and his blood. The latter inflamed his protective nature, making his own blood run hot through his veins.

The surface of the water near the bonfire rippled and the sound of irregular splashing suddenly mixed with the rhythmic pounding of the waves on the tiny strip of sandy beach. Talos focused his inherent night vision on the source of the noise and watched as several men in wet suits floundered out of the dark surf and entered the fire area, Maymon dead center in their midst.

All of the men carried sacks, which Barlow's men poured out onto the sand at Barlow's feet. They were full of gold artifacts, ancient coins and precious and semi-precious gems.

Soaking wet, his thin clothes clinging to his lithe

form and dark hair plastered back from his face, Maymon emptied his sack onto the pile, but made sure he kept a tight hold on it afterward.

Talos softly growled deep in his chest as Barlow's hungry gaze raked over Maymon's body for a moment before turning to the growing mound of gold. Talos watched as Maymon wisely used the moment to back away from the circle of treasure happy men who had eyes only for the vast wealth tumbling down between their boots.

Barlow ran his hands over the precious artifacts and hefted the small glowing red scepter Syphus had placed on top of the pile. Handling it with more reverence and respect than he had shown any live person, Barlow whispered in an awestruck voice while he caressed the jewel-studded line of the royal symbol of powerful and influential Arugalain people.

"It is real. It's *really* real. The Arugalain scepter. I've thought about it, dreamt about it," pausing, Barlow had to wet his dry lips before he could continue speaking, "but I didn't dare hope for it."

Standing on the outer edge of the group, Maymon pouted, loftily asserting with the impudent confidence of a ten year old, "Said it was there."

Syphus was the only one who spared him a glare, yanking the slippery, young pirate back into the bright circle of men, nearly causing Maymon to drop the sack still clutched in his one hand. The guard then turned back to the glinting, glistening heap of riches, saying, "There's a hundred times that down there, maybe more. All just like this. The coin alone makes a small mountain."

Details of the Hunt

Cradling the scepter lovingly in his hands, Barlow pointed it at Syphus and another guard and ordered, "Set up the laser drill directly over the beacon's signal. I want that cave split wide open and every last coin brought up. Now." He looked to the east and the orange colored skyline brightening the horizon signaling that dawn was rapidly approaching. With the light came greater risk of discovery. "We've wasted enough time here."

Working quickly as a precise, experienced team, the men set up the small laser and got to work burning a hole through the pitted lava surface. It only took minutes before the porous substance dissolved and the tiny cave was exposed to the open air. With a sweeping, impatient gesture of his arms, Barlow directed his men to enter the cave. All six of them eagerly responded, leaving the capable Betovan guards behind to watch over the woman and the pirate.

Knowing they only had a short time before the sun rose in the clear blue Caribbean sky and revealed their hiding place, Talos and Marius edged closer. Taking advantage of the noise of the men anchoring cables and climbing down into the cave and the fact that everyone's attention was riveted on the process, they managed to move in very close, hiding among the damaged shuttle pieces.

Syphus' deep voice echoed up from below. "We're all the way through."

Nearly vibrating in place, Barlow yelled back into the hole. "Excellent, excellent work. Now, bring me my treasure." Eyeing Maymon standing by the dying bonfire, Barlow smiled and jerked his head toward Rice.

Zrac and Garn instantly pulled a struggling Rice to her feet and waited for Barlow's next command.

Rice pulled her arm from Zrac's grip and wiped a light sheen of sweat and sand off her face, then straightened her clothes and brushed the grime from the knees of her pants. She shot Barlow a killer glare and held her head up high, ignoring the wisps of matted red hair that the ocean breeze whipped across her bruised face.

Maymon smiled winningly at Barlow. "You've got me treasure, matey. There's no need for the lass and me to be in the way whilst your men work. What say you have us dropped off at the nearest port?" Barlow returned the smile but his didn't reach his eyes. Maymon hesitated, then hopefully ventured, "Or leave us a jolly boat or a gig? Don't need to leave any oars even, just the boat will do."

"It's not quite that simple, my dear Captain." Barlow rested his hand on the hilt of his sword and paced around the rough edges of the fresh hole in the ground he had created. "I dare say your bounty Hunter will be quite displeased to find you missing." He flicked an arrogant, disdainful glance at Rice. "And I'm sure someone will notice the doctor is gone as well." He turned his back on her and sniffed, "Eventually."

"Eh, now." Maymon circled around slowly, walking along the edge of the hole, keeping a fair distance away from Barlow as the man strolled around the opening. In a low, throaty, placating tone, Maymon coaxed, "We're both in one piece, mate. No broken bones, no new holes, so no harm done. What say we just call it a short visit 'tween...acquaintances."

Details of the Hunt

"That does sound more civilized," Barlow amicably agreed, "however, even if you could get the good Doctor to agree to keep silent about this little excursion of ours, which I doubt, I'm afraid your Hunter won't see it the same sensible way you do."

"No one's going to believe we left with these people willingly, Aidan." Rice shook her head, her voice a croaked murmur, dry and brittle sounding. She looked pale and tired, her face full of deep shadows highlighted by the first rays of the early morning sun. She sighed and added, "Marius won't let it go either. He'll be charged with kidnapping, at the very least."

"And I'm afraid I can't let that happen." Barlow walked toward the defenseless doctor, his dark intent clearly written on his face for all to see.

Moving quickly, Maymon jumped to the edge of the pit, grabbed a lit torch from the closest holder and tossed it down into the opening. The flame ignited the aged and extremely potent gunpowder he had poured over the treasure earlier. The first explosion shattered the intact bottles and set off a chain reaction, igniting the multitude of remaining bottles of powder left below.

The resulting explosion was huge. The tiny, unstable rock ledge masquerading as an island shuddered and lurched, knocking everyone to the ground. As he crashed into the ground, Barlow lost his hold on the heavy scepter, and the staff fell from his grip, tumbling back down into the smoking hole into the cave.

An ear-splitting crack snapped in the air, drowning out the few muffled cries from down below in the cave. A large section of the narrow beach broke off and slid into the ocean, forcing a huge surge in the swirling water. A massive wave billowed up and washed up the beach, pulling loose sand and brittle rock back with it as it cascaded over the far side of the tiny island.

Scrambling for dry land, Barlow grabbed hold of Maymon and the Betovans pulled Rice with them to a slightly higher ground. No one emerged from the collapsed hole.

Still hidden behind the shuttle, Talos and Marius could only watch the newest development, their plan to rush the nearby guards suddenly snatched from their grasp by the explosion.

Stunned, Barlow stared at his empty hands, then surveyed the surrounding devastation brought down on his head by the smiling, cock-sure, man beside him. Livid and barely able to breathe, Barlow hissed, "You vile, thieving, deceitful....you sly, dirty...."

Backing away several paces, Maymon grinned and added, "Pirate?" He winked at Barlow and quipped, "Thought you knew that afore, matey. Thought that what was what you liked about me."

Bellowing maniacally, Barlow pulled his sword and advanced rapidly on Maymon. Scrambling inside the long sack still gripped tightly in his hand, Maymon shook off the bag, revealing an ornate steel sword he had taken from the treasure mound in the cave. Comfortable and happy with a blade in his hand, the young pirate's delighted grin widened as he squared off against his attacker.

Barlow hesitated a moment then sneered, continuing his attack.

Details of the Hunt

Using the sudden distraction of the duel to her advantage, Dr. Rice rapidly scanned the area looking for something to use as a weapon. A small move by the abandoned shuttle caught her eye. She hung her head and darted her gaze to one side to watch from the corner of her eye. The movement flashed again and she recognized the two tiny orbs of violet reflecting in the fire's dying flames as the eyes of a Oracan Hunter. Deciding to even the odds a little more in their favor, she dropped to her knees in the sand. When Zrac and Garn turned back to her to drag her to her feet, she bombarded them in the face with handfuls of wet, gritty sand and small rocks.

Jumping up, she ran like hell, heading straight for the disabled shuttle, the two Betovans hot on her heels and heading for more than they had bargained for. At least, she hoped so.

Laura Baumbach

Chapter Eighteen

Dragging up out of the sand, Talos and Marius crouched low and looked over the nose of the battered shuttle, watching the small drama between Barlow and Maymon escalate into a sword fight. The moment Dr. Rice broke free from her Betovan guards and ran like a she-devil at their location, Talos knew that the doctor had spotted them and was bringing her captors to them.

Revising his original estimation of her, Talos grabbed Marius by the shoulder and shoved him toward his medical officer. "Get the dame first. The Runt can hold his own in a sword fight."

"No doubt." Marius nodded at the dueling pair in the fading semi-darkness. "I just wish I had the time to watch."

Breaking cover, they ran from behind the shuttle, taking an intercepting path toward Rice. Drawing nearer to the firelight as the approaching dawn highlighted the horizon in brilliant hues of orange and yellow, Talos' sudden appearance out of nowhere jarred the pursuing Betovans. They stopped dead in their tracks at the first sight of the fierce Hunter and began randomly firing their weapons, retreating backward with each shot.

Talos obligingly returned the fire, while Marius

grabbed hold of the fleeing doctor. Ducking and running, one arm protectively wrapped around Rice's shoulders, Marius dove for cover, shoving the doctor down on the ground behind Talos' substantial bulk as the Hunter continued holding off the sporadic Betovan attack.

Outmatched, and with one last frantic shot at the Hunter, the Betovans turned tail and suddenly teleported away.

One enemy left to go, Talos winked at Marius and headed off down the beach toward his mate.

With a sigh of relief, Marius folded Rice into his arms and gently kissed her brow, his hands rubbing soothing circles over her back and shoulders. "Jaclyn, are you all right? Did they hurt you?"

"Just a little crumpled around the edges." Rice smiled and held tightly onto the Commander. She looked in his eyes and reassured him, "I'm fine, really. Aidan kept most of their attention on himself."

Darting a glance at the battling figures further down the beach, Marius nodded and prompted, "Let's go see if the sly little devil needs any help."

"Don't bet on it," Rice snorted indelicately and grabbed a hold of Marius' hand. They set off at a slight run down the sand strip, picking their way past burning grass mounds and crumbling ash and rock.

Arriving at the smoking embers of the bonfire, the Commander and the doctor halted beside Talos as the Hunter anxiously watched the fierce sword fight between Barlow and Maymon. It was obvious that Maymon was toying with Barlow, who showed a marked lack of practical skill with his treasured sword.

Laura Baumbach

Maymon forced Barlow several feet back in a particularly aggressive and rapid-paced maneuver then taunted the gasping man. "Tiring a bit are you? Sword fighting requires an agile body and mind, mate." He forced Barlow up against an outcropping of rock and pinned him in place with his blade to the man's raised cutlass. "From what I've seen, you possess neither."

Slashing and pivoting in rapid time, Maymon clashed swords again and again with the swiftly fading Barlow. They passed the small mound of swag on the second sweep and the pirate couldn't pass up the opportunity to grab a handful of his hard-earned treasure. He tossed the gold coins in his hand at Barlow, distracting and annoying the man while every gem he fingered was casually popped into his mouth and swallowed down for safe keeping.

Making a full circuit around the smoking, open pit in the ground, Maymon forced Barlow up against the damaged wing of the shuttle.

Barlow retaliated with a sudden unexpected parry, successfully throwing the confident pirate slightly off balance for a brief moment. Taking full advantage of the small opening this created, Barlow charged ahead with several rapid blows.

Maymon stumbled to his knees, his sword slashed from his hand by a well-timed thrust from the other man. Unwilling to let the man who tried to buy his body and soul win the upper hand, Maymon flung a handful of wet, grimy sand into Barlow's face, blinding the man. Maymon didn't hesitate to pull the small dagger from the folds of his sash. Sweeping his arm up and under Barlow's sword, which was jabbing painfully

258

into his neck, he thrust the small dagger into Barlow's unprotected chest.

Startled, Barlow staggered and sagged back against the scorched shuttle. He dropped his sword to press both hands around the golden hilt of the dagger still embedded under his rib cage. He looked up, his face wearing a crushed, disappointed expression and whispered in a stunned tone, "You *cheated*."

Maymon picked up Barlow's discarded weapon, inspecting the blade for any sign of his own blood. "I did the only thing what truly matters in a sword fight, mate. I *won*." He slipped Barlow's prized sword between a loosened fold in his own sash and with a dismissive wave of his hand, walked away from the wounded man.

Turning, Maymon noticed Talos for the first time. Marius and Rice stood quietly watching in the background a few feet away. As Maymon swaggered toward his strict, morally rigid lover, his eyes wandered over the devastation surrounding them. The bright morning sunlight gave him a new perspective on just how much havoc he had rained down on the small island. His gaze trailed over the damaged shuttle, and the scorched, smoking pit in the ground. A jutting ledge of black rock and ocean stood where the tiny strip of sandy beach use to be. His eyes settled on Talos' expectant, unhappy glare. Staying just out of Talos' reach, Maymon opened his arms wide in an innocent gesture and reassured, "I can explain everything, guv."

Smelling the blood of a number of men down in the hole mixed with the acid odor of gunpowder, energy blasts and singed flesh, the big Hunter glanced

Laura Baumbach

at the charred remains of the small rock and said, "It's going to have to be damn good to explain all of this."

Maymon glanced behind them and squinted one eye closed, trying to find a positive angle on the mess. The sun gleamed off the few still unscorched patches of metal on the destroyed shuttle, the bright light making the dark, sooty burn marks look even more terrible than it did in the twilight dawn.

Tapping one insistent finger in the air in the direction of the shuttle, Maymon firmly claimed, "The fire in the ship was *entirely* accidental." He opened his hands in a pleading gesture and gave Talos a wide-eyed, offended look, demanding, "How was I to know how to shoot one of those new gun things?"

Eyes narrowing in a disbelieving glare, Talos bellowed, "Someone gave you a blaster?"

Grimacing, Maymon hesitated then ruefully admitted, "Stole it, actually." His gaze darted to Rice for support, immediately pointing out his altruistic motives. "But it was all for a good cause."

Stepping forward, Rice touched Talos' weapon's belt, pulling his attention to her earnest face. "He saved my life."

Maymon grinned and winked at the doctor, eager to have her support in his campaign to wiggle out of some of the blame for the rampant destruction on the island.

"And the explosion?" Talos looked from his lover to Rice and back again to the suddenly pouting pirate. "Half the beach is missing. *How* did you do that?"

Taking the stunned accusation as a compliment,

Details of the Hunt

Maymon smiled and swaggered at bit in place, proud of his resourcefulness. "Cannon powder." He pointed a the open pit and swept one arm around to indicate the entire surface of the now nonexistent hidden cave that had been under their feet. "Had bottles and bottles of it down there." He kicked at a large piece of burnt rock by his bare feet and it crumbled into a pile of ashen rubble. "The whole island is made out of honeycombed rock." He wrinkled his nose and leaned in close as if he was imparting some great secret. "Not very stable, that."

Taking his eyes off the wounded Barlow, leaning heavily against the shuttle, Marius looked over the edge of the pit and incredulously asked, "Why would you take the trouble to hide gun powder with gold?" Rice came to his side and they both peered into the hole.

"Are you daft, man?" Just as incredulous, Maymon huffed, "Good powder's bloody hard to come by. Near as valuable as the gold."

Nodding in sudden understanding, Talos chuckled and added, "And you never know when you'll need to blow a cannon hole in something."

"Exactly! You'd make a right fine buccaneer, me luv." Maymon smiled up at the bounty Hunter and moved closer to his lover.

Talos' expression softened and he made a soft, faint clicking 'ta-ti' sound in the back of his throat that brought a gleam of pleasure to the pirate's weary, dirt-smeared face. Talos ran a concerned glance over the wet, disheveled young man and gently asked, "You jake?"

"That I am, mate. He never touched ‒‒."

A tiny sizzling crackle registered with everyone

Laura Baumbach

a moment too late and Maymon's cocky reassurance
was cut short by the sudden unexpected blast from an
energy gun. Eyes wide in uncomprehending shock,
Maymon pitched forward, falling directly into Talos'
arms. He was unconscious before he hit the strong
supporting arms of his mate. Smoke and the smell of
burnt flesh wafted up from a large, blackened circle on
his back.

As the young pirate fell, Barlow came into Talos'
sight over Maymon's shoulder. Hands pressed to his
wound, Barlow was still leaning against the shuttle. But
now the dagger was missing, and on either side of him
stood one of the Betovan mercenaries, weapons drawn
and aimed at the group.

A spent energy blaster dangled from one of
Barlow's hands, slowly dropping to the sandy patch of
ground at his feet as he proudly proclaimed, "The pirate
was right. Cheating *is* the best way to win." Before
anyone could react, the three disappeared in a shimmer
of teleporting energy.

Left holding an unconscious, critically wounded
Maymon, Talos immediately scooped the pirate up into
his arms. Without looking anywhere except at his
injured young lover, he yelled, "Marius, you and the
dame, get the hell over here. Now."

Rice hesitated but Marius pulled her over to
Talos and grabbed hold of the Hunter's belt.

Rice panicked at the closeness of the tight hug,
but calmed down after a comforting murmur from the
Commander. She hugged Marius close and hid her face
in his shirt, muttering, "Why do I feel like I'm so going
to regret this."

Details of the Hunt

Not sparing a moment to reassure anyone, Talos grabbed a hold of both Rice's and Marius' clothing with his fingertips and closed his eyes to concentrate. Without even the shimmer of an energy flux, the island was suddenly empty of humanoid life.

Chapter Nineteen

Disoriented by the journey, Webb and Rice barely obtained their bearings before The Hunter thrust Maymon's unconscious body into Marius' arms and took his seat in the pilot's chair.

Marius stumbled a little under the sudden weight and asked, "What are you doing?"

Talos didn't even glance at him. "Something forbidden. I'm going to time warp back to the Pathos Six. Only by a couple of minutes, but fast enough to get Aidan to the sick bay before we lose him. Hold on."

No waiting for anyone else to strap into position, Talos grabbed the arms of his chair and closed his eyes again. The entire ship and its contents blinked out of time and then rematerialized. The outside view screen show them in orbit around the space station.

Demanding emergency clearance with Marius' codes, Talos docked the fighter and grabbed the three others in a huge bear hug, interrupting Rice's attempts to apply pressure bandages and burn sealant to the pirate's wound. With the exception of the Hunter, they swayed and staggered when Talos released them in the bright, sterile surroundings of the sick bay.

Staff present in the room blinked and stared at their sudden appearance, then came running as Rice began shouting commands for equipment and supplies. Rice bent over Maymon, examining him while some of the staff began cutting off his wet clothing. Rice listened to the pirate's chest and announced to her staff, "He's got a pulse but he's stopped breathing. Get the intubation set-up."

Talos caressed the visible side of Maymon's pale face and commanded, "You god damn, brainless, little shit, listen to me and just breathe, Runt, just keep *breathing*."

More medical people converged on them and Rice issued more orders. Tubes and wires appeared and were connected to the young man. Marius and Talos were pushed further away from the bed with the arrival of each new staff member and pieces of equipment as they tried to save Maymon's young life.

"Greedy, honorless, morons." Talos ranted at the foot of the bed, a statue made of stone but for the angry words pouring loudly from his mouth. "The Runt escapes a whole shit load of blood-thirsty pirates, a whirlpool of hungry sharks and the entire god damn ocean that tries to drown him and then an asshole like Barlow blows him in the back. Stupid little... idiot... brainless... *pirate!*"

Rice turned to Webb. "Get him out of here." She spared a glance for the distraught Hunter and reassured him, "I'll take over from here. He'll get the best of care, but you're in the way right now." She looked at Marius and then back to Talos. "Both of you." Rice jerked her head toward the exit. "Take a walk." Dismissing the men with one final look, the doctor turned back to her patient and began to intubate him, watching the rapid heart rhythm on the monitor as she worked.

Webb nodded and pulled Talos from the bedside, guiding the reluctant Hunter away from his lover and out into the corridor. The sick bay doors closed on the new and frightening sound of equipment alarms chiming urgently.

Feeling the Hunter tense, Marius increased the strength of his grip and said, "She's an outstanding doctor. He's got a good chance."

"Chance?" Talos shook his head and numbly murmured, "I took away any chance he had the minute I brought him here. Just like Bakus. One more life ruined because I brought them into my world."

"Bakus knew the risks," Marius scoffed. "Your brother wanted to be a Hunter, just like you. You're not responsible for his death, no matter what you think." He pointed at the closed sick bay door. "And you're not responsible for Aidan's either. You didn't shoot him."

"It doesn't matter." Talos turned his back to his friend and leaned one meaty fist on the wall to support his weight as he hung his head to study the scuff patterns on the corridor flooring. "I should never had brought him here. He walked right into that attack." He heaved back slightly and punched the wall under his fist. "He didn't even know that Barlow still had a weapon on him. It was just a little metal box to him, with bright shiny lights." He the wall again, this time leaving a small divot in the metal surface. "He'll die here, if not this time, then the next time he's faced with a situation he can't recognize as deadly because he's seven hundred years behind the times." Talos slammed his hand against the wall so hard it crushed the surface leaving a crumpled crater in the shape of his fisted knuckles behind.

Talos turned around and looked at the silent, patiently waiting Commander and friend. He sighed and said, "Council voided Barlow's Hunt today. I claimed Aidan, as my own, as my mate, but now," he walked over and stood in front of the closed entrance to the sick bay where people were fighting to save his lover's young life and rested his open palm on the smooth, cold surface of the door. "Now, I don't know if I had the right. Am I being selfish to force him to live in this world, this here and now, with me?" He slowly pulled his hand off the door and turned to look at Marius, arms gesturing at the world around them. "Danger is a part of my everyday life, Marius, that won't change. And he'll be as unprepared for the next set of dangers as he was this time."

"Then let the Council handle this," Unable to answer such a personal question, Marius tried to console his friend. "Is relocation so bad?"

Talos closed his eyes, remaining silent.

Marius frowned at the Hunter's reaction and pressed, "Where do they send him? A frozen tundra? A lava colony?"

Opening his eyes, Talos released the breath he had been holding. He looked around the empty corridor and scented the air to make sure no one was near enough to overhear them and whispered. "A stasis chamber." He dropped his arms uselessly to his sides and turned back to stare at the closed door again.

Stunned, Marius moved nearer to the Hunter and leaned in close to him to whisper back. *"What?"*

Resting his forehead against he metal, Talos tried unsuccessfully to hear through the thick, bulkhead type doors. "A stasis chamber!" It was still a whisper, but a growled one. He rushed through an explanation, spitting out the words like they were dirt in his mouth. "Relocation means they drug him and they pack him into a stasis tube and they seal him in a chamber room under the Council Hall. Forever."

Leaning his back against the sick bay wall so he could see Talos' face, Marius countered, "You're not serious."

"I am." Talos raised his head and his deep violet eyes pinned Marius in place for a moment before drifting back to stare at the door. "It's considered painless and humane." He gave a mirthless grunt. "After all, they're not really dead." He shook his head. "Except that over time, the neural pathways degenerate and brain activity stops, even in stasis."

"Then what?" Marius demanded.

Giving the curious Commander a frustrated glare, Talos explained, "When no neural energy is detected, the bodies are reduced to ash and disposed of. Nice and tidy. They're relocated all right." He lightly punched the door, making a dull thud echo through the corridor. "Right into the land of the dead."

Talos snorted in frustration and pounded the wall again, harder, leaving a second dent. "Those are the two choices I can give him if he lives, certain death or life-threatening danger from places he'll never suspect on a daily basis for the rest of his life as my mate." He pushed away from the wall and Marius, mockingly adding, "Ain't love grand?"

Details of the Hunt

He stalked off to a shadowed corner of the hallway where he pushed his back against a wall and silently faced the world, waiting to hear the fate of his beloved pirate.

***

An hour passed when the door to the sick bay opened and a nurse motioned for Talos and Marius to come back in. Talos charged past the woman and moved to his lover's side, taking the pirate's small fingers into his own massive paw, gripping the fingers tightly, careful not to dislodge any of the wires and tubes.

Now on his injured back, the wound protected by a gelatinous pad full of nutrients and antibiotics for absorption through the skin, Maymon lay still and silent for the first time in days. Numerous machines were connected to the young man, one trying to assist his breathing, one monitoring his heart and vital signs, while others analyzed his blood and pumped him full of medications to heal and sedate him.

Rice and Marius stood on the opposite side of the bed. Rice looked tired and worried. Rice adjusted and reset a small dark machine strapped over the pirate's abdomen, her face more and more unhappy with each new adjustment.

Rubbing gently at an open patch of skin on Maymon's lean chest Talos made a faint clicking sound in the back of his throat and Maymon's rapid heart rate slowed on the monitor to a more normal level. Startled Rice frowned at the Hunter, but he ignored her and continued to make the faint 'ta-ti' noise over and over again.

Marius watched the Hunter, then looked around him at the rushed staff and Rice's increasingly drawn expression. "How is he?"

"Better since I took these out of his stomach..." Sighing, Rice rattled a clear container full of gems on the bedside stand. She gave him a weak smile then looked back at Maymon and frowned. "But still not good."

Hefting the gem container, Marius shook his head, obviously impressed. "Can't stop being a thief, even when he's kidnapped. Amazing. There must be a fortune in here."

"It won't do him any good." Rice watched as the Hunter tenderly ran a soothing hand through the pirate's hair, still occasionally making the 'ta-ti' clicking noise, ignoring everyone else in the room. She took a deep breath and spoke louder, aware that Talos was listening even if he didn't look like it. "The blast seared both of his lungs. He can't breathe." She swallowed and added, "And... he's not responding to the tissue regeneration."

The Hunter's head shot up and he fierce stare held Rice motionless as he demanded, "Why not?"

"The same reason he's unaffected by your skin." Rice pointed at the device strapped to Maymon's abdomen. "The seven hundred years of evolution between his time and ours has produced a difference in our DNA patterns."

Rice pulled a hand held computer out of her lab coat pocket and offered it to Talos, who ignored it. Marius took it instead and glanced at it, saying, "I thought evolution took millions of years to produce changes in cellular structure?"

"It does. This is infinitesimal, barely traceable, but it's there. Add in the factors of exposure to solar activity and added chemicals in our food he's never been in contact with, and you have a change." Rice closed her eyes for a moment before admitting, "And there's something else."

Marius and Talos both turned to her, their attention grabbed by the ominous, confused tone in her normally confident voice. "Something about his body chemistry is different then the last time he was a patient." She looked helpless and frustrated. "He's changed and that change is affecting the machine's abilities to heal him and I have no idea why."

Talos riveted his attention back on his critically injured lover.

Marius handed Rice back the computer and she put it on a tray table. "What do we do?"

"My medical equipment can't match up his DNA patterns to repair the damage quickly enough." Rice looked at a readout a nurse handed her and shook her head. The nurse silently left. "I'm working on it, but I'm sorry, but until I can figure out the needed changes for the recalibration, there's nothing I can do." Her voice dropped to a low, sympathetic tone and tears brimmed at the corners of her green eyes. "He's on his own."

Talos didn't take his eyes off of Maymon's lax body. "It's my fault. All of it."

"Talos..." Marius admonished his friend.

"No. It's the truth. I did this to him."

"You had nothing to do with his injuries."

"I'm not talking about that. It's the changes in his body. I did that."

271

Laura Baumbach

"What? How?"

"When Oracans take a mate we do it for life. And when we mate, our body fluids are absorbed by their partner's body. Their chemistries blend and the partner is marked for life as belonging to the other by their scent, their taste,.... Their blood is joined. But that's between two Oracans. I didn't know it would happen to him. No Oracan has ever mated with a human before. No human has been able to tolerate the touch of a Oracan before, let alone mate with them. I did this to him." He stared at Maymon and a realization hit him in the gut. "My loving him is going to be what kills him."

An alarm sounded and Rice moved to silence it, adjusting a medication pump.

Face turning expressionless, Talos claimed, "I should never have cut the Runt loose from that barrel."

"Don't be ridiculous," Rice harshly chided him. "You saved his life."

Marius and Talos both looked at her, surprise written on both their faces. She looked hurt then elaborated, "He told me all about it. He thought you were his own personal Cemi Sea God come to save his drowning spirit." She sighed and gently smoothed a strand of hair off the young man's face. "He idolizes you...loves you. He said so."

The blank, stoic expression melted off the Hunter's face and he grimaced, fighting to keep his raging emotions under control. "And I left him alone to get plugged." He paced in the small confines of the cubicle. "I'm not going to let him die. I might not be able to be with him after this is all over, but I'm not going to sacrifice his life, either."

Details of the Hunt

Talos grabbed Marius by the shoulders and frantically demanded, "If I don't come back, will you look after Aidan for me? Find him some place safe? Make sure he understands I did this for him?"

"I don't understand --," Marius stammered.

The Hunter shook him harder and shouted, "Will you?"

Relenting, the Commander darted a glance at Rice and at her nod of cooperation, he agreed. "Yeah, okay, sure, but what are you going to do? How are you going to do it?"

His voice dropped to an ominous tone and Talos straightened his shoulders, one hand resting on Maymon's sweaty gray forehead. He rubbed his thumb over the smooth, feverish skin, staring at his unconscious mate and firmly announced, "I'm going to do the most forbidden thing a Hunter can do."

He looked up at Marius' and Rice's confused, frightened faces and explained, "I'm going to time travel for my own personal gain." He took a deep breath and glanced down at Maymon's handsome face. "I'll be a rogue after this. My family will shun me and my own people will hunt me down. But if I can't have Aidan beside me, it won't matter. Life won't be worth living without him."

Rice moved closer to Marius and he wrapped his arm comfortingly around her shoulders. They shared a look that said they understood the Hunter's pain only too well.

Talos glanced at the two of them and moved away from the bed, with one last lingering gaze over his fallen lover. "I have to use it." Voice resigned, the

Hunter quickly checked over his weapons. "It's the only way to fix everything at once by myself."

Alarms began to beep in their sign-song chime that signaled a serious problem. Rice and two nurses raced to shut off the alarms, adjusting equipment and working on Maymon. Pushed aside, Talos and Marius moved back to stand at the edge of the room.

A faint commotion drew Marius' attention and he walked to the doorway to see what it was all about. Surprised, Marius jumped back from the opening just as Talos closed his eyes in preparation to dematerialize, declaring, "Take care of him if I don't make it back."

Zeban and another Oracan Hunter, Kawa, suddenly appeared in the doorway. The medical staff scrambled to get out of their way as the Hunters strode forcefully into Maymon's room. Zeban immediately blocked Talos in a corner.

Talos' eyes strung open and he prepared to fight his way free when his brother soothingly insisted, "I think you can spare a moment just yet, little brother."

Several machines began to alarm and panic raced across Talos face.

Rice rushed to give Maymon medication through an IV port. "He's weakening." She looked imploringly at the group of aliens that had invaded her patient's room. "It won't be long. He just can't survive on the amount of lung tissue he has left."

Talos looked to his older brother for understanding. "I have to do this. He's my *mate*, Zeban. Our people will have to understand. We give everything, including our lives and our honor for our chosen mates." He remembered his brother's own loss

274

of his mate three years ago and softly added, "You of all people know this."

Zeban's expression softened. He quietly said, "But you don't have to destroy your honor to save your mate, Talos. Council has been informed of Barlow's plans. His weak-minded aide, Sherman, decided he wanted to live longer than the next sunrise and informed us of the man's insane plans."

Smiling, Zeban hissed, "Barlow and his mercenaries have been made the bounty in a group Hunt." He winked at Talos and stepped back, motioning for his brother to follow him. "Come. Council has approved a plan, little brother."

Another alarm joined the others. Talos instantly lowered the lights, and plunged the room into darkness. The alarms stopped as time shifted and turned back on itself.

Chapter Twenty

Time bent and shifted....

Smiling at Rice, Maymon snorted and casually tossed the apple core into the corner of the room. "You find a sense of humor in him, save it for me." He picked at the remaining fruit on the tray, popping a few grapes into his mouth, outwardly pleased with their strange new flavor. He threw the grape stems after the apple core. "I'll be needing it more than the likes of you will."

Rice laughed. "I'm sure you will." Shaking her head, she reseated herself at the table and popped a grape into her own mouth sharing a grin with Maymon.

A light crackling sound filled the air and a segment of the room erupted in a shower of bright sparkles and a shimmering field of energy. Zrac and Garn stepped through the energy field. Heavily armed, with weapons drawn and aimed directly at Maymon and Rice, they advanced on the startled pair.

Surprised but used to thinking fast on his feet, Maymon instantly reacted by grabbing the silverware off the table and then flipping the small piece of furniture in the air, showering the Mercs with dishes and uneaten food. Throwing a dinner knife with the practiced eye of the keenest of assassins, Maymon was able to stagger Zrac for a moment.

Details of the Hunt

Another silent flux of energy bent the air of the suite directly behind the two intruders. Zeban and Kawa suddenly appeared, and after a few moments of rough and tumble fighting that left the suite a shambles, but left all life intact, they overpowered the startled mercenaries.

Awestruck, Rice backed away from the center of the brutal fight, wisely huddling behind the overturned table.

More curious then frightened, and not one to back away from a good bar fight, especially if he was on the side that looked to be the stronger team, Maymon offered encouraging curses and waded into the thick of the battle.

After Zrac and Garn were properly beaten, Zeban turned the two chained and subdued Mercs over to Kawa. He pulled Maymon off the prisoners and held him at arms-length, studying him. Maymon returned the intense stare, flinching only when Zeban pointedly sniffed him.

Setting Maymon back on his feet, Zeban towered over the pirate, glaring down at him, but Maymon didn't blink. The young pirate reached out and jabbed at Zeban's bare chest, testing to see if he was real or another fantasy sea monster created from his own mind. When the massive Hunter didn't budge, Maymon shoved harder, rocking himself back on his feet instead of the Oracan, who merely grinned at him in response to the attempt at manhandling.

Maymon made a satisfied humphing noise and declared, "Got one just like you meself around here somewheres. Off visiting the folks right now or some such."

He looked Zeban over very closely, getting right up into the Oracan's personal space. "You may be just a wee bit bigger than me own great sea monster." He nodded to himself, tapped his index finger against his lips, and then thoughtfully added, "but you all really need to be green, mate. It'd bring out the color of your eyes."

The Oracan Hunter's eyes grew wider in surprise and his lips parted in an amused smirk.

Dismissing the huge alien continuing to tower over him, Maymon stepped around Zeban and cast an exasperated and angry look at the total destruction in the room. Turning on his heel, he smartly stalked up to Zrac and jabbed a finger in the Merc's ugly face. "And don't be thinking I'll be paying for all this." He threw his hands in the air in frustration. "Tals never lets me keep any pretties I...," He darted a guilty look at Rice, knowing she knew the true source of his 'pretties' and amended his words, "find. Amends'll be coming out your purses, to be sure, gents."

Still smirking, Zeban came up behind the pirate and lifted Maymon up and out of his way, depositing the small human on a high side table, one of the few pieces of furniture left intact. He looked Maymon in the eyes and rumbled authoritatively, "Stay there, boy."

Scowling, Maymon frowned and complained, "You're related, aren't you? You and my great beast? I can tell, ya know. Got the same imperial tone to your voice, ya do."

Zeban ignored the question. "Talos is securing the vessel these festering boils of flesh came in. He

278

wanted to be here, but I wanted the chance to meet you myself."

His eyes roamed over Maymon again and he sniffed the pirate's neck. "My brother has chosen well, if oddly." He ignored the affronted pout the pirate gave him and demanded, "You never saw us come or leave." He glanced menacingly at Rice and she quickly nodded her head in agreement.

Maymon watched the doctor's instantly compliant reaction. He pondered the alien staring at him from only a few inches away and gave in, shrugging amicably. "No problem, mate." He leaned down and plucked a still half full-mug of juice off the floor and took a swig, then declared, "Have hallucinations all the time, if the drink's worth the coin."

Zeban blinked when Maymon winked conspiratorially at him then moved back to rejoin Kawa. Closing their eyes, the Hunters and their prey instantly disappeared from the room.

Jumping down from the table Zeban had perched him on, Maymon walked over to the place where the aliens had vanished. He paced around in a circle looking for clues to how they had disappeared. "Right useful skill." He turned thoughtful and wondered out loud, "Wonder if they can teach me that." He looked hopefully at Rice.

Staring, Rice came out of the corner of the room and asked, "Who *was* that?"

Maymon sighed, shook his head and offered, "Relatives, I'm guessing." His gaze darted around the room looking for something out of place. He frowned, cocked his head and suspiciously asked the doctor, "Do ya feel like we've done this afore, lass? The same, but not?"

Rice rubbed the short hairs on the back of her neck and shrugged, a slightly uncomfortable expression on her face.

***

Inside the sleek, but small Merc fighter, Zrac sat stiffly in the trim, functional pilot's chair. He hit the commlink and Barlow appeared on the communication systems' view screen. Outside of the fighter, open space could be seen through the front view panel, a scattering of stars off in the distance sparkling brightly against the dark field of black. As Barlow appeared on screen, Zrac glanced uncomfortably to his left before he began talking.

Obviously agitatedly and excited, Barlow rapidly asked, "Have you got him? Is he alive?"

Zrac quickly reassured, "He's fine." He glanced down a moment then added, "Couldn't be better."

"Excellent!" Barlow puffed out his chest triumphantly. "You've earned something extra for this."

Giving a mirthless chuckle, Zrac sarcastically scoffed, "Yeah, right." He glanced to his left again, and then back at the screen, his expression resigned. "There needs to be a little change in our exchange site. We can't make it all the way to you. We've got a leak in one of the energy chambers in the forward thrusters. Garn's working on it now, but I can't guarantee it'll hold. We need to meet someplace closer to our present coordinates."

Barlow's face clouded over but his anticipation

overrode his usual suspicious nature. "Where are you?"

"Just outside the Matrix Column, coming up on Dolph."

Barlow paused for a moment, apparently thinking over the situation. His eyes narrowed, but he said, "Dolph is fairly barren. It will do nicely." He leaned a little closer to the viewer, his voice turning hard and said, "Remember, nothing more will be deposited into your accounts until I am safely home with my prize."

Zrac nodded. "I don't think that's going to be a problem."

Barlow bristled, demanding, "Make sure it's not."

Ignoring the implied threat in Barlow's tone, Zrac informed him, "We should be there in twenty-eight point six croms. I'm sending you the landing coordinates where we'll be, now."

"Fine. I'll join you as soon as I can." Mellowing his harsh attitude slightly, Barlow added, "We'll celebrate."

Zrac glanced off to his left again and then glanced at Barlow and sneered, "It'll be a regular party." He tapped a button, instantly breaking the link.

Pulling a long, thin, blood-smeared knife out of the back of the pilot's chair, Talos emerged from behind Zrac. He transferred the knife to the Merc's exposed neck. Zrac stiffened and tried to pull back from the pressure. Blood trickled down his skin.

"Your last act has been an honorable one." Talos whispered in Zrac's ear. "You have earned compassion."

***

Dolph was a truly inhospitable planet, barren of any resident humanoid life and inhabited by only a few creatures low on the evolutionary scales. The light from its three moons illuminated the sparse landscape, highlighting the few boulders and outcroppings of beige, nondescript rocks. A large fire blazed in the center of a small clearing, fueled by chemical pods and dry grasses.

The air was filled with an oddly thrilling, yet ominous primal chanting, made by three deep, guttural voices that trilled and chirped in a singsong harmony.

Blood-splattered and adrenaline-hyped, Talos, Zeban and Kawa were each hunched over a desecrated, eviscerated body on the ground. Talos paused in his song to hold up a fat, dark red organ in one massive hand.

Speaking to his companions, he proclaimed, "For the honor of my mate." Talos glanced down at the bloody, open carcass beside him. "Compassion will have to wait for another day." He swallowed the organ, a human heart, whole without difficulty, then wiped a trickle of blood from his chin with the end of a distinctive, blood-stained, yellow sash.

Chapter Twenty-one

Unaware that time had shifted back on itself, Marius met up with the returning Talos outside the docking bay shortly after Rice reported on the visiting Mercs and Oracans. Curious, Marius accompanied his friend on the Hunter's way to his and Maymon's suite.

"Welcome back." Marius gave his usual friendly nod, and then hesitated for a moment before cautiously asking, "I know I shouldn't ask for details, but how did the...'things' go?"

"Sweet as candy." Talos grinned and increased his pace, anxious to see his lover and reaffirm for himself that the young pirate was safe. "Barlow should have paid closer attention to the Details of the Hunt." He thought about both the Mercs and Sherman betraying the scheming, weaselly buyer and added, "And who he hires for help." Turning serious he reassured the Commander in a grave tone of voice, "He's *permanently* out of the mix."

They continued to walk down the long corridors, taking a short tube ride up several levels to the one where Talos' suite was located while Marius contemplated the gravity of what the Hunter's emphasis on 'permanently' meant and decided it was best if he didn't know. So he did what any good friend did when faced with a subject that couldn't be discussed, he changed the subject. "Then I assume you know all about what happened here with Aidan?" He accepted Talos' silent nod as if he knew it was all the answer he was going to get.

Raising an eyebrow, Marius gave a faint whistle and said, "That must have been *some* meeting."

Weaving their way past any oncoming pedestrians in the corridor, they stopped right outside Talos' door. They turned to face each other as Talos checked his weapons sash for bloodstains and mockingly quipped, "Sang a few chants, ended a few lives, nothing special."

Marius' expression froze, and then he let out a slow breath and said, "Almost sorry to have missed it." He raised his eyebrows and whispered, "Almost."

Talos shrugged, and then nodded toward the closed door of his home. "How's the Runt? Did he behave himself?"

"Didn't have a choice. The only person in or out of there, besides the earlier visitors, has been Jaclyn."

Grinning, Talos asked, "Making up?"

"Kind of." Marius rolled his eyes. "She brought him breakfast and an apology for yesterday."

"So there *is* a heart underneath those big brown eyes." Talos arched the ridge of nubs above his eyes and smirked. "I was beginning to wonder."

The door to Talos' suite silently slipped open without any prompting from either man. Standing in front of the keypad lock on the inside of the room, Maymon stared at the two men with wide, startled eyes, caught red-handed with two pieces of silverware in his hand. The metal plate covering the locking mechanism hung from the wall, circuits exposed and still blinking. Maymon's eyes darted from Talos' frowning face to the mangled knife and fork in his hands. He instantly tossed them over his shoulder further into the room behind him.

"Tals!" Maymon ran out of the suite and threw himself at Talos, wrapping his arms around the alien's neck and his legs around the Hunter's waist. The pirate grabbed Talos' face, and planted a huge kiss on the Hunter's willing lips. Voice deep and throaty, Maymon murmured, "Missed you." He winked at his lover. "Welcome back to port, luv."

Talos disentangled himself from the snake-like grip and set Maymon's feet on the floor. "Stop that shit." Talos growled, but his eyes remained playful.

Maymon ignored the growl, giving the Hunter a huge, suggestive smile and a swagger of his hips.

Talos eyed the broken lock for a moment, and then transferred his concerned gaze to the pirate. "How are you, Runt?"

Maymon moved to block Talos' line of vision, swaying seductively to hide the damaged lock from his lover's suspicious stare. "Must have caught a fever." He cocked his head and leaned forward slightly as if he was going to impart a secret. His voice dropped low to a falsetto whisper as he darted a half-lidded glance at Marius. "Been seeing you, I have. In twos." He opened his eyes wide and nodded knowingly at the Hunter. "All right pushy they were too." He pouted slightly and added, "Must be a family trait."

Smiling at the imagined meeting between the

cocky pirate and his older brother, Talos nodded and suggested, "We'll have to get you something for that fever then."

Maymon's eyes lit up and he eagerly said, "Brandy. It's the decided lack of brandy in me day, luv. Causes hallucinations. I've seen it happen lots of time. To other blokes. Always careful not to let it happen to me afore this voyage."

Talos gave Maymon an affectionate pat on the head, and then lifted him bodily out of the way. "We'll see." He gave the dangling, broken lock a sharp glare then looked at his lover. "What happened?"

Maymon cast an innocent look at both men and backed a few steps down the hall away from the damaged wall. "With what?"

One glance at the mildly disbelieving expression on the big Hunter's face and he quickly turned a wide-eyed innocent look on his audience. "Oh. That. Well, now." He took a deep breath, shrugged, and then emphatically claimed, "Door were jammed." He put one hand on his hip and shook a finger at the broken mechanism. "Had a right hard time of it, too, getting it to close properly after the doctor left." He slipped a few more paces away. "I was... fixin' it...for you."

Talos edged closer to the pirate, matching each of Maymon's backward steps with one of his own. "I'll bet. Probably went bad right after you tore it out of the wall trying to break out."

Maymon yelped and made a break for it, but Talos easily captured him. He spun the lithe pirate around by the waist and shoved him through the still open door into their home, landing a hard swat on

Maymon's backside as he crossed the threshold.

A pained, "Gotta stop *doing* that, for bloody sakes!" came from the swiftly retreating pirate.

Talos slammed the dangling unit back into the wall with one hand and the door closed on Maymon's frustrated sputtering. The massive Hunter shook his head and turned back to Marius. "Lucky the little shit didn't fry himself. He doesn't even know what electricity is."

Marius grinned in agreement, tipped his head toward the closed door and the cursing man behind it and asked, "So what happens now?"

Talos' expression softened, but his voice was full of deadly determination. "I'm keeping him."

"Good thing you've got broad shoulders and a peacekeeper's patience." Marius teasingly shuddered. "You're going to need them both for a lifetime with that one, brother."

Chuckling, Talos agreed. "The past few days put me wise to that." He raised the corner of his mouth in a self-satisfied smirk and added, "I just wonder what you're going to use."

"Me?" Marius stopped grinning and gave Talos a confused frown. "Why me?"

Talos' smirk grew wider. "We'll be flopping here for awhile." He winked at the startled Commander and taunted, "A long while."

"May the gods give me strength." Marius closed his eyes and put his hand dramatically over his heart, playing his part in the charade. He sighed, opened his eyes and went to walk away, but turned around. A shy, embarrassed look of curiosity dominated his expression and he hesitantly asked the Hunter, "By the way, how did you know to call me in Jaclyn's room earlier?"

Laughing out loud, Talos slapped the Commander on the back, muttering, "Hell, Marius her scent is all over you. You couldn't hide the fact you two are hitting the sheets if you tried."

The neat and formal Commander fought a losing battle with a blush that spread up his neck, past his high-collared uniform, all the way to his hair line. "You have such a romantic way of putting it."

His friend patted Marius' back again in sympathy. "I call 'em as I smell 'em."

Suddenly intrigued, Marius stepped closer to Talos and haltingly asked, "What exactly does she smell like to you? Cinnamon, sandalwood, fruit?" There was an underlying note of sexual tension in his voice.

Talos motioned the Commander closer and dropped his voice to a confidential whisper to reveal, "Way more exotic than that."

Latching onto the thrill of potentially learning an intimate secret about his lover, Marius whispered back, "Really? What?"

Checking to make sure no one was close enough to overhear in the hallway, Talos dropped his voice to a low, sexy growl and said, "Disinfectant." He slapped Marius hard on the back and added, "But top shelf, antibacterial disinfectant, the expensive stuff," before he pulled back, grinning like a wild man.

Eyes closed in humiliation, Marius simply shook his head, saying in a low defeated tone, "I don't know why I even asked." He moved away from the triumphant Talos, ignoring the muffled chuckles and delighted stare of the alien.

Glancing meaningfully at the door of the suite, Marius sighed and asked, "What are you two going to do now?"

"Ever been on a treasure Hunt for pirate swag?"

At Marius' surprised, speechless stare, Talos grinned, then spun on his heel to activate his door. As it silently slipped opened, a small square pillow landed squarely in his face. He caught the cushion before it fell to the floor.

Looking first at the pillow, then at Marius, and then into the destroyed room, Talos bellowed, "You should have kept this pillow, Runt. Because your crazy, little, pirate ass is going to need it to sit on for the next week."

A defiant, challenging voice carried all the way out into the corridor claiming, "Gotta catch me first, luv. And if you paid as much attention to me bow as you do me stern, I'd be a happier man."

Growling deep in his chest, Talos stormed into the room, the door sliding shut to the sound of breaking furniture and sharp cursing in two different languages.

Marius stood staring at the door for a moment until something hard thudded against it from the inside. "We'll be under a full military quarantine inside of a month." He heaved a sigh, woefully shook his head and walked away.

Chapter Twenty-two

Stalking through the door to his home, Talos expected to have to capture Maymon before he could greet him properly. He was surprised when the lean, young pirate came running at him and leaped into his arms as soon as he crossed the threshold of their suite and the door slide closed. Tossing the small pillow in his hand to one side, the huge Hunter grabbed onto his naked pirate, tightly embracing Maymon.

Talos had hungered for this moment, agonized about never having the chance to see or hold the young human again, worried about Maymon's future if Talos had been unable to return to him, and ached over the very real possibility that they could never be together as mated partners again. But danger had been overcome and dishonor had been averted with the help of his brother and the Council. Talos had taken part in his first Group Hunt and claimed his place in his society as a newly mated Hunter. Both events had moved his already high status within his culture to more prestigious level. And with change came more responsibilities, like the one clinging to his neck, devouring his mouth with insistent, ravenous kisses and raining demanding caresses over his shoulders and sensitive breastplates.

Details of the Hunt

Grabbing onto Maymon's firm ass and tightly muscled thighs, Talos kneaded the smooth flesh as he carried the slender human into the bedroom. He returned the voracious attention, stroking Maymon's tongue with his own and skating the coarse tip of the agile muscle over the soft palate at the roof of the pirate's mouth, drawing a low moan of pleasure from his lover.

Maymon's fully erect cock jabbed against his upper abdomen and chest as the pirate squirmed in his arms, trying to get closer. Talos felt as if Maymon was trying to crawl down his throat. Knowing that passionately kissing another male was a new, exciting adventure for the young man, he opened his mouth wider and allowed his lover to explore and to dominate the kiss, returning the fervor of the embrace, but letting Maymon keep control.

As he walked into the bedroom, Talos released the lock that held his weapon's sash together. As it dropped from his shoulder, he shrugged it off, pulled it from between their bodies. He slapped it onto a wall hook as he moved toward the bed. Once he reached the foot of the bed, Talos turned his back to it and dropped supine, arms and lips still attached to the pirate.

Maymon's lips suddenly disappear from his and the pirate moved up Talos' broad torso to straddle the Hunter's chest. Knees tucked into both of the Oracan's underarms, Maymon planted his bare ass on Talos' sternum and sat up straight, his eager cock bobbing in the air between them.

Maymon jabbed an accusing finger against Talos' soft breast plate nubs, declaring, "Afore we lose our reason and bury our knobs, there's a few details what need clearing up betwixt us first, Tals."

The stern, disapproving expression on the young human's face made Talos curious, but he chose to ignore Maymon's dark glower. Arching his body to lift his torso off the bed, Maymon included, he released and kicked his pants off to fall to the floor. Finally as naked as his lover, Talos slid them both up the bed to rest his head on the pillows. Maymon merely hung on by pressing his legs together and grabbing onto Talos' shoulders until the bronco ride was over.

Giving Maymon an innocent smile, Talos pulled Maymon's hips farther up his chest to bring the human's straining cock closer. He kissed the purple head, then swirled his wet, hot tongue around it once before asking, "You want to talk?" Pulling the foreskin back with one hand he lavished another long lick over the crown and around the sensitive underside.

Maymon shuddered, his hips involuntarily jutting forward, seeking out more of the deliciously forbidden stimulation. He groaned and closed his eyes then covered his cock with one shaky hand, demanding, "Here now, none of that. You'll not be distracting me before I get an explanation."

"I did it all because I love you. Is that explanation enough?"

"Not that! Of course I know you love me, you addle brained sea monster!" Maymon let go of his cock, relinquishing it to Talos' caressing hold, to jab both his fists onto his bruised hips, outrage and determination in his eyes. "I want to know what you did to me that makes me love ya back!"

"Did to you?"

"Aye, did to me. Never afore have I been weak in the knees at the sight of lover. Never got the shakes when they came near and never had me innards roll and ache at the thought of losing them. So it stands to reason," he jabbed Talos in the chest with each word, "you've done something to me. Charmed me, drugged me, put an ancient sea god's curse on me, but I'm different inside now. I know it in me head and I feel it in me gut, so you might as well own up to the facts and lay them on the deck so as we're clear on what be happening betwixt the two of us."

Before Talos could comment, Maymon frowned, adding, "The waters ahead look rough enough for the two of us as it is. And not that I be believing it's the wisest choice all the time, but for a change, I be thinking the truth is the best course to sail."

Talos rested his large hands on Maymon's knees and soothingly slid them up the man's bent legs to the pirate's widespread thighs still molded around his chest. He'd been trying to come up with a way to tell his mate about the chemical changes he would be going through, he just hadn't anticipated the wily young man figuring it out on his own and confronting him with it so soon. He'd have to remember not to underestimate the pirate again. But for now, he wanted to make love to his mate.

Maymon cupped his cock and balls with his hands, preventing Talos' searching ones from creeping into his lap to distract him and return to more pleasant things. Thwarted, the Hunter sighed, stopped advancing his caresses and contented himself with stroking Maymon's soft inner thighs with his thumbs.

"Okay, you're right. You are experiencing a few changes." Talos took a deep breathe and burrowed the back of head deeper into the pillow. This could end up being a long discussion.

Pulling away, Maymon's frown deepened and he crowed, "Aha! Knew it! You put a siren's love spell on me!"

"There is no such thing as a love spell!" Scoffing, Talos grabbed Maymon around the hips and pulled the pirate back into place to sit high on his chest. "They're real changes in your body, but," he added softly, "I didn't know they would happen to you."

Studying Maymon's suspicious expression, Talos slowly let out another deep breath before explaining. "Whenever two Oracans mate, they do it for life. There is no one else ever, for the rest of their days together. They are called together by a genetic snare that we call the 'ritual'. It's primarily based on scent, but there are other factors involved, as well." Talos cocked his head to one side and gave Maymon a pleased smile. "Your scent called to me the moment we left the water that day I grabbed you."

Maymon's frown weakened and he admitted, "Snatched me right from the bloody jaws of death, you did."

Drawing Maymon's lower half a few inches closer, Talos wiggled his hands under the pirate's and dislodged them from the man's still hard cock and tight sac. He stroked the length of the shaft as he continued, causing the pirate's eyelids to flutter occasionally in unspoken delight. "After they mate for the first time, their body fluids are absorbed into each other's blood system and they both under go a change that creates a special bond between them. That's what you're feeling."

"So you did do it to me! Knew it!" Maymon slapped Talos' chest with both hands and leaned over the Hunter's face to assert, "Some kind of sea serpent, voodoo mischief, was it?"

"No, it wasn't." Talos stared intently into Maymon's dark eyes. "It was just me, loving you. And now we both have to pay the price for it."

Unable to resist the scent and sight of his lover so near, Talos grabbed the pirate's neck with one hand while keeping the other lightly caressing the man's stiff cock, and yanked Maymon down for a mind-bending kiss.

"What price be that, luv? Me sanity?" Struggling up from the Hunter's tight hold, Maymon gasped, heaving and bucking into the fist milking his eager shaft. Fluid leaked from the tip and Talos used the cream to wet the sensitive tip, passing his thumb over and over the red-rimmed slit.

Half-serious, Talos said, "That's been missing for years, from what I can tell." He wrapped an arm tightly around Maymon's slender hips and kneaded the curve of his firm ass. "I meant our hearts. We're a bonded pair now, and nothing will be allowed to separate us short of death."

"Sounds a might extreme to me, luv," Maymon grunted as Talos slid the pirate's hips forward and began nuzzling and licking his sac, ignoring his own eagerly dancing, thick cock. "Jesus, man, you shouldn't ought to be doing that with your mouth."

He teasing at the soft strip of flesh between the man's thigh and groin, watching Maymon's reactions with lust-filled violet eyes.

Maymon shuddered and gasped, "Then again, could have been wrong."

Talos shifted on the bed and pulled Maymon forward, swallowing his cock down to the root.

Maymon hissed and threw back his head, whispering between pursed lips, "Until death is a long time, but then again, could be I could tolerate a few decades of this."

Growling his response deep in his full throat, Talos worked his agile tongue down the shaft and flicked the tip of his tongue along the underside of Maymon's cock.

Maymon snapped forward, grabbing a fist full of sheet and pillow in either hand, panting heavily.

Talos swallowed convulsively around the shaft while sucking and stroking Maymon's cock with his lips until the pirate began to tense, his slender hips rapidly bucking in time to the Hunter's movements.

Slipping one hand behind Maymon, Talos groped his own writhing cock. He gathered a sampling of his copious, leaking fluids from its crown on one long, thick finger and then deftly inserted it between Maymon's spread cheeks. Sliding into the tight, fluttering opening to the pirate's body, Talos worked his finger in and forward, nudging the pea-sized gland of pleasure he knew was hidden inside the human male's body. When Maymon yelped and moaned, he rubbed over it again.

"Bloody, fucking, amazing, accursed, sea *beast*!"

Details of the Hunt

Maymon cried out, his body going rigid, every muscle frozen, limbs locked in place for a split second. He bucked against Talos' face, fists white-knuckled and body seemingly torn between burrowing deeper down the willing throat sucking him dry and plunging harder onto the stout finger impaling him from behind.

With a groaned shout that turned into a throaty grunt of satisfaction, Maymon heaved and gasped, as his climax peaked and began to fade.

Talos slowly moved the pirate's hips down his chest and allowed the man's fading cock to fall from his mouth. He rotated his finger at the loosening ring of muscle at the entrance to Maymon's ass, enjoying the hiss of surprise from his lover. He slowly withdrew his finger, taking pleasure from the way Maymon's ass tried to grip onto his hand and keep him inside.

Moving Maymon's pliant, still straddling body down to rest against his own groin, Talos enfolded his lover in a warm embrace, holding Maymon to his chest and running his face over the pirate's loose, dark hair. The scent of his lover after climax was dizzyingly seductive for the Oracan. He yearned to fill his mate with his own fluid so he could smell and taste the product of their combined bonding. Nothing was sweeter or richer than that distinctive musk of their lovemaking.

Talos realized that nothing would ever be the same in his life again if he were parted from this small, exasperating, unruly, clever, tender human. He silently made a vow that nothing and no one in the entire galaxy would separate them. Even if he had to eat the heart and liver of every race that might dare to interfere with them. Taking Barlow's soul and honor had shown him that revenge did have its sweeter side. He licked his lips a the memory and looked down at the only person in existence whom he would willingly kill for to protect again, his lover, his heart, his mate for all time.

Talos made a rich, deep clicking 'ta-ti' sound at the back of his throat and pinned his young lover with a look of pure, white-hot desire.

Maymon returned his heated gaze with his own passionate, sultry stare that fanned the inferno of their desires.

***

Pushing up from Talos' body where he lay cradled in the Hunter's arms, Maymon sat back and stroked his open palms over his lover's softly-yielding breast plates. Smiling, he watched the huge beast between his legs close his eyes, enjoying the sound of pleasure that rumbled from the Hunter's throat and vibrated deep in his chest.

The pirate's ass clenched at his lover's seductive response and his ass spasmed, anxious to be filled properly this time. A blunt poke from behind reminded Maymon that there was more delightful differences in Talos' body then just his valuable and appreciated ability to swallow things without gagging. Maymon scooted back on the Hunter's torso until his ass rested directly above Talos' impatient cock.

Maymon hissed, and then panted as the suction cup-tipped tubulars surrounding the Oracan's long, stout cock tapped the sensitive flesh of his spread and presented opening, each tip grabbing and nipping at the surface of his body until it found a suitable spot to latch onto. The sensation was thrilling to the young pirate, full of tiny pangs of needle-like jabs and soft, teasing sucks that felt like small, nipping kisses to his skin. Several questing tubes burrowed under his body, seeking out and finding the delicate flesh of his scrotum and the bulging root of his shaft where it attached to the floor of his perineum.

Maymon moaned, rolling his head on his shoulders, absorbing all the sensations his lover's exotic body gave to him. He had never felt the way this hulking beast made him feel, never knew he *could* feel the things Talos made him feel. The sultry pleasure, the intense desire, the wild abandon that came with giving himself to a person with no fear of reprisal, and with no shame in returning the pleasure, was too much to ever think about giving up.

A surge of primal possessiveness boiled up from a place inside of him Maymon didn't know existed. He knew then with a certainty he rarely experienced in life that he was never giving up his place by this Hunter's side, his own mythical sea serpent mate and lover.

Wanting to retain his dominant position as long as he could, Maymon raised up as far as the attached tubulars would allow him, swiftly reached behind, and guided Talos' eager cock to his opening. With a sultry glance at Talos' half-lidded, violet eyes watching him from below, Maymon slowly sank down onto the long, smooth shaft, gasping and grunting as it undulated into the deepest reaches of his body.

Grinding his ass against Talos' active groin, Maymon tried to remain still and concentrate of the unbelievably thrilling sensations moving through his

Laura Baumbach

body. The opening to his ass fluttered and clenched around Talos' cock as it thickened and moved inside of him. His own shaft, now fully revived, bobbed and strained between his wide-spread thighs, leaking pearls of milky white. His swollen, hot nipples ached to be touched and suckled like the last time he and his lover had enjoyed each other. Sitting still only lasted a moment before the urge to rock and slide on the velvety, stiff rod became too overwhelming to ignore.

Steadying himself with one hand on his lover's pressure sensitive, heaving chest, Maymon began to raise and lower his hips, delighting in the delicious rippling effect that the combination of his movement and his cock's own wiggling produced. Maymon's eyes had drifted shut, but they popped back open as Talos' warm, tight fist engulfed his cock and began a slow, leisurely caress up and down the length of his shaft in time to his own rhythmic hip movements.

The Hunter shifted under Maymon's weight, bending his legs so that they supported the pirate's back. Maymon leaned into the warm, muscular thighs of his larger lover, relaxing into the seductive tempo of their private dance.

Watching as Talos slowly moistened his lips, Maymon moaned with need, falling forward to grab the Hunter's face. Maymon gasped as the change in position shifted the shaft inside of him to rub directly over his prostate. He shuddered at the ripple of sizzling sparks that shot up from his groin to explode along his nerve endings with each new touch of this hidden jewel of delight.

He pulled Talos' face to him and rubbed his own

300

wet, hot lips over the Hunter's willing mouth. He rained
a volley of quick, wet kisses over his lover's parted lips,
murmuring in between each one, "Kiss me, kiss me, kiss
me, you arse-slapping, heart-stopping, bloody
marvelous beast!"

Talos eagerly complied and Maymon lost
himself in the glorious passion of a kiss so deep and
ravenous that the pirate thought his very soul had been
devoured. When his breathing grew shallow and
labored, Maymon tried to draw back, but Talos held
him pinned to his broad chest and continued the kiss
until the pirate was limp and compliant in his powerful
arms.

When they finally broke off the embrace,
Maymon panted as if he had just climbed to the top of
his ship's crow's nest and back down again.

"Bloody well trying to kill me, luv." Cheek to
cheek, Maymon hissed and wiggled his ass against
Talos' clutching, sucking groin. "Saved me scarred hide
just to do me in yourself, did ya?"

Talos wove a hand through Maymon's hair and
turned the pirate's face so he could purr in his ear,
proclaiming, "Never going to let you die, Aidan. I'll
never leave you. You're at my side forever." He ended
the husky declaration of love with his 'I love you'
clicking sound of "ta-ti" and another deep, blistering
kiss.

Afterward, Maymon rested his forehead on
Talos' shoulder until he was able to breathe easier, mind
battling with the variety of stimulus still assaulting his
body and soul. Brief, rough buggering in a dark bunk or
a dank alleyway had never been like this. Not even

nights spent with the tavern whores had come close to the pleasure this rough and domineering, gray-skinned beast gave him.

""Bloody hell!" A sudden sense of fullness blossomed in Maymon's lower abdomen and the massaging motion of Talos' cock became barely tolerable. The alien's nub-studded hood that surrounded the crown of his shaft had engorged. Each undulation now raked soft, ridges over Maymon's nerve-filled lining, and grazed his prostate with a renewed vigor.

Maymon arched up and pounded his as firmly into Talos' groin, impaling himself deeply onto the Hunter's shaft. The next pass of the nubbed hood knocked hard against the tiny pea of ecstasy and Maymon cried out, "Tals!"

Without warning, the young pirate climaxed, shooting thin, milky strands of white from his cock, coating Talos' hand and chest.

His ass clenched and shuddered at the action inside of him continued, pushing his climax's peak even higher. He could feel Talos' shaft grow thicker, stretching the ring of muscle at his opening to a red-hot burn that sent a flush of pain/pleasure racing along every nerve to his passion-addled brain. A seeping blast of warm fluid filled his inner passageway, hot and slightly burning. The sudden intensity brought a bright flush to his tanned skin and stole his breath away.

Gasping Maymon gritted out a strained, "Lord have mercy on me blasphemous soul, but I love you, you great, gray beast."

Maymon's orgasm began to recede and

exhaustion replaced urgent need. Slumping down onto his lover's chest, ass still locked to Talos' groin, Maymon moaned and shuddered as the shaft within him seemed to grow larger, locking itself tightly inside of him. He shimmied his ass experimentally then lay still as fresh burst of fires erupted along his nervous system, making his entire body tremble and his vision blur.

Laying his cheek to rest on Talos' chest, Maymon played with the silver band still around his wrist. He blinked bleary at his lover and scowled. "When you said you'd never leave me, I didn't think you were talking about now, luv." He pointedly clenched and unclenched his ass around the part of Talos that was refusing to leave his body.

Talos soothed a hand down Maymon's sweaty back and cupped one firm, small ass cheek. "You didn't object last time."

"Last time, I didn't notice. You made me pass out." Maymon lifted his eyebrows, mock suspicion in his tone as he coyly added, "This time, I'm still awake. Are you losing the ability to satisfy a younger lover so soon, luv? Should I be looking for a replacement then? Do you think his Lordship the Commander is happy with that fine lass of a doctor?"

A sharp crack of flesh slapping bare flesh sounded and Maymon's outraged hiss of surprise broke the air. "Gotta stop *doing* that!"

Laura Baumbach

Printed in the United States
104075LV00003B/79/A